Dreadful
Stories

*A treasury of awful folk
tales from the British Isles
and a bit of one from
Nigeria*

KITTY BROWNBELT

Dreadful Stories: A Treasury of Awful Folk Tales from the British Isles and a Bit of One from Nigeria copyright © Kitty Brownbelt 2014

All rights reserved. This book or any portion thereof may not be reproduced, stored in or introduced into a retrieval system, or transmitted, in any form or by any means (electronic, mechanical, photocopying, recording or otherwise) or used in any manner whatsoever without the express written permission of the publisher except for the use of brief quotations in a critical article or review.

Cover image and woodcut restorations copyright © Nick Skerten 2014

Published by Chimney Books

Names, characters, places and incidents are either the product of the author's imagination or are used fictitiously, and any resemblance to any persons, living or dead, business establishments, events or locales is entirely coincidental.

The White Glove copyright © Margaret Stamen 2014

@kittybrownbelt

ISBN-13: 978-1500509255

ISBN-10: 1500509256

For

Charmain Beacom

───────●○●───────

And in loving memory of

Richard Skerten

(1952 – 2013)

CONTENTS

The Clough Urchin ... 1
Lundy's Flock ... 7
The Devil's Hill ... 12
The Bellock Stones ... 20
The Poisoning of Lady Ethel Brewgham ... 30
The Giant's Cave ... 30
Mrs Munnion's Kitchen ... 33
Esmund's Beard ... 39
The Red Handkerchief ... 50
The Gonderfish ... 57
The Sand Martins ... 64
The Red Hare ... 71
The Bishop's Diary ... 74
The Crows of Whitesaddle Woods ... 81
Black Har ... 86
The Travelling Man's Barrel ... 96
Twenty-Noses ... 101
The Brilby Marriage Stone ... 105
The Pineapple ... 108
The Sunday Nail-Cutter ... 121
Captain Pickerel's Companions ... 128
The Worm Garden ... 135
Joan and Thomas ... 140
Bad-Mouth Peppermere ... 146
The Ivory Comb ... 151
Crossing the Stobley ... 159
The Weather Vane ... 163

Hole-in-the-Head	*179*
Two Lace-Makers	*184*
Boastful Master Kelly	*188*
The Wolves of Wodlesham	*195*
Uncle Darwyn	*200*
Mr Willow	*208*
The Poacher and the Devil	*215*
Daddy Coppernut	*221*
The Lady Who Lived in a Pinecone	*225*
The Singing Bastard of Cobley Penn	*229*
Brownie Blackbonnet	*234*
The Frenchman's Ghost	*240*
Father Bloodwick and the Cobbler's Cat	*245*
Nurse Cottishole's Surprise	*253*
The Toby Jug	*259*
The Flea-Catcher of Kipplenead	*266*
The Gossley Boggart	*275*
Tomkin Teadwig's Toothache	*281*
Vicar Pearnet's Yew Tree	*285*
Anne and the Shug Monkey	*293*
Cup o' Salt & Bedderkin	*299*
Miss Mummisfere's Curse	*306*
Chukwuma's Bag	*320*
Afterword	327
Appendix I: *The White Glove*	329
Thanks	337

About the Author

Kitty Brownbelt lives alone in Shadwell in East London. She is the author of the novel *Venus Amen*, which is no longer in print. She appears regularly in the Watney supermarkets and can be found on the Twitter (@kittybrownbelt) and the Facebook when she can work the buttons and hasn't misplaced her magnifying glass. She was born in 1930.

Explanatory Note About the Title

I made a very conscious decision to use the words 'dreadful' and 'awful' in my book title and subtitle, as I am sick almost to doomsday with how words keep changing. I'm afraid to say that I'm very much of the thirteenth-century mind when it comes to vocabulary: 'dreadful' means something that causes intense dread; 'awful' means something that inspires great reverence or fear. How apt for these *pathetic* stories. I'm quite well aware of the huge risk I'm taking when it comes to selling my book and some of my friends have begged me to rethink the title. But I've put my foot down now and that is that.

— K.B.

Introduction

I was very fortunate to have had two masterful storytellers in my family when I was growing up – my great grandmother, Joyce Berrial (1862–1966) and my great aunt, Vulna Vankov (1829–1973). In case you think that Aunt Vulna's dates are typographical errors, I'd best tell you now that they are quite correct; her Bulgarian birth documentation was mislaid in a terrible filing accident, so we had to take her word for it. She certainly looked very old.

The folk stories these marvellous women told me and my sisters form the basis of the book that you are about to read; these are tales of monstrousness and grace, jealousy and revenge, cruelty and love. Because the themes are so powerful, and because the stories on their own can be so disturbing, I present each narrative with a warming introduction, followed by a thorough, almost forensic analysis. This book's format is very important, as it will allow you to be guided sensitively through the horrors that lie within, as well as offering a strong 'moral compass' to orientate yourself by.

Folk stories themselves are chiefly part of what has been termed 'the oral tradition' of storytelling – and by that I do not mean to imply they are about the history of dentistry. They are stories that are best told aloud, in the company of friends or relatives. If you are friendless or orphaned, it might be a good idea to put an advert in the classified column in your local newspaper appealing for a companion, so that you are not alone when reading these stories.

One of the pleasures of putting this collection together has been to use the original accompanying woodcut illustrations that I discovered in Grandma Berrial's carpetbag shortly after she died. It might have been nice to say that this book was 'lavishly illustrated', but unfortunately it isn't. Rather, I would say that it is 'modestly illustrated', largely because I simply do not have the time to sit down and watercolour all the blasted pictures. You may wish to do this yourself; although I'll tell you now that the value of the book will depreciate quite sharply the moment you start daubing the pages with your amateurish dabs and smears.

It's hard to describe how much toil has gone into compiling this volume – I've had to root through old diaries (never very pleasant, chiefly because of the suppressed memories that are unleashed), pull cases of transcripts from the loft (uncomfortable because my attic has become the domain of a species of moth that is overly fond of flying into the apertures of one's head), transfer files from floppy disk (at some considerable personal expense), as well as having to operate the local library's microfiche reader during a series of very irritating intermittent power cuts. I do hope my travails have been worth the bother.

There's a good range of stories in this book – I've made sure that there's a mixture so that the respective fans of the animal, vegetable and mineral kingdoms won't be disappointed. Unfortunately, I struggled to recall or uncover any folk tales about radiation, so those of you who are fond of atomic explosions and isotopes will be dreadfully disappointed. However, this omission should not fool you into believing that these folk narratives are hopelessly old-fashioned; they still have a good deal to teach us about relationships between people, and relationships between people and animals – I don't think you could say the same for your average Hollywood romantic comedy blockbuster.

I have absolutely nothing else to say now – so please pick a story and start reading.

Kitty Brownbelt,
Shadwell, London
July 2014

The Clough Urchin

If you're anything like me, you will occasionally wake in the night, convinced that a burglar is sneaking about the garden, and arm yourself with a maul hammer before edging down stairs, ready to bludgeon the intruder. More often than not, the culprit is not a robber at all, but a hedgehog nosing around the patio for food. The following yarn magnifies those midnight fears to such an extent, that I recommend you skip this story if you have recently undergone major heart surgery. It also features a very loud explosion, so the more imaginative amongst you may wish to ready yourself for the shock. When I first heard this story, Aunt Vulna and I were in the middle of an air raid and an actual bomb went off. I have tried my best to use the most exciting words to convey the might of that bellowing detonation when the moment comes for this tale's big bang.

Clough Hulme was a small mill town that was kept in good prosperity because of the large number of travellers who passed through on their way to Pollard Dramley. It was remarkable for having twenty inns of varying sizes, all of them offering hospitality to the weary traveller. Clough Hulme's problems started one year when the town's cows kept being sapped of their milk overnight by a mysterious suckler.

The next difficulty the town had was one that threatened its very livelihood: they were afflicted with a dreadful highwayman who quickly became known as the Clough Urchin (he was named this because of his astonishing resemblance to a hedgepig). The monster was as tall as a man and covered from tip-to-toe in enormous needle-like spines; his appearance was so frightful that any unfortunate who was pounced upon handed over all their money and jewellery in their haste to be as far away from the snaffling nuisance as quickly as possible.

A soldier called William Bedwick was garrisoned in Clough Hulme during this disturbance and took great pity on the inn-owners whose trade had been suffering because of the reputation that the town had begun to earn. One particular inn-owner – a spirited woman by the name of Sally Muzzleclasp – told Bedwick that not only was trade drying up, but so too was the cows' milk, for a single hedgepig is quite capable of withering the dugs of a whole herd of cattle with its insatiable nocturnal sucking.

Well, Bedwick was a brave soul but even he was so terrified of the ghastly creature that he would not dare to confront the Clough Urchin during night or day. This was in spite of the fact even the most dunderheaded clot knows that hedgepigs were always fast asleep during daylight hours anyway.

One afternoon, Bedwick was talking to Sally Muzzleclasp in the Gangley Inn when the most brilliant idea befell her.

'This here urchin horrifies the whole town don't it?' she said.

'So much is true. Come, Sally, we ken this already', Bedwick replied rather sharply.

'Nay, you must listen. I have a plan. *We* must scare the hedgepig, rather than *it* scare us.'

Bedwick was puzzled at this and asked her why.

'I'll show, ye', she said with a canny grin. 'You must have some gunpowder in your billet. Fetch me a barrel, and two stout pikes.'

'Sally,' replied the soldier, 'many men have tried already to shoot it, an' the shot cannot penetrate the thorns o' the urchin. 'Tis a numbskull's fancy.'

'Do as I say. Meet me at the hollow oak on the Shepley Road in a half hour; we must prepare this before the sun is down.' Sally pinched his ear and pushed him on his way, before hurrying to her closet to fetch her black cape.

A short while later, Bedwick met Sally in the agreed spot, just as the sun was sinking behind the treetops. She opened the barrel that the soldier had lugged up the hill and stuck a fine taper into the dark saltpetre, before drawing its cord into the hollow of the oak tree. She beckoned William within and pointed at the shaded oil lamp that flickered dimly in the gloom. She reassured the man that the Clough Urchin would soon be about his business as this was the main road out of the town.

'But,' she whispered, 'be most careful to utter not a thing from this moment, for we will be in great peril.' She put a finger to his lips before he could say anything, and they waited in the deepening murk of dusk.

Luck was on their side that night, for the full moon was soon up and the bridleway was lit well. Before long a loathsome hissing was heard along with the scuttling of clawed feet in the stones and soil of the road. Sally peered out through the narrow opening of the oak tree and spied the wretched hedgepig standing in the road. The moonlight showed it to be just as abominable as the stories had described – its wet nose glistened and twitched to-and-fro, as if scenting something. Before it could leap upon them, Sally lighted the taper and watched as the flame raced up the wick before disappearing into the keg. Suddenly, there was a terrific explosion that shook the tree so hard that it rained down acorns on their heads and sent their ears a-singing.

'Take your pike, William!' shouted Sally, as she pulled him from their hiding place.

'Alas, it lives!' cried a despondent Bedwick, perceiving the huddle to be breathing rapidly as it lay next to the shattered barrel. But Sally, who knew much of animals, was most pleased, for the Clough Urchin had done just what she had expected:

'Look, William! It has rolled itself into a ball! Quick! Use your pike to help me push it into the Beggar's Well.'

Stunned by the blast, the pair was able to roll the hideous mass of quills off the road and pushed it down a mossy slope that led to the old well. The spiny menace, still wound into a bristling orb, teetered for a moment on the brink of the well, before plummeting into its shadowy depths and hitting the foul water below with a great echoing slosh. The hedgepig's howls of protest caused great amusement and the pair had some sport in dropping pebbles down onto its thrashing head; Sally and William, beaming victorious, dashed back into town to tell everyone how they had finally vanquished the Clough Urchin and ended its pernicious reign for good.

They were soon wedded and often visited the hedgepig in the well to feed it slugs and worms.

Most hedgehogs do not grow to such gross proportions as the fellow in the above narrative; I'm sure this will come as a relief to the more credulous amongst you. Walk into any pet shop these days and you'll be harassed by dozens upon dozens of animal foods that claim they can make one's pet bigger and more muscular with so-called fortified biscuits (it's an old trick, and they used to do the same with digestives in the past). If anything, what with there being over six billion people on this tiny planet, we should be urgently exploring ways of making animals smaller, so that there's more room for human beings. The above story also raises the uncomfortable question about what the Clough Urchin did with all the money and jewels that it pilfered. Whilst the prospect of meeting this beast on the road in the dark is an unpleasant one, the image of it walking into a public house and spending a shilling for a pint of stout is nothing short of comical. I would ask Grandma Berrial about this conundrum, but unfortunately she is dead.

Lundy's Flock

It's easy for us to laugh at stupid people and criticise them for their mistakes, without recognising our own follies too. Often, your average nincompoop fails because of a fatal lack of preparedness. I do not wish to join the worldwide roster of cretins, so I always carry about a pocket calculator in case I am ever asked to do a difficult sum in my head. It's also worth having a stock response to a tricky question someone may ask you. My favourite reply to a taxing enquiry is always 'Why do you ask that question?' Usually one's interrogator is so busy trying to justify their original query that you can be out of the shop and halfway home before they realise you've gone. You can then have a cup of tea in your own living room whilst you ponder the question before arranging to meet your interlocutor later that day to make your reply.

There was a nit-witted farmer called Benjamin Lundy who was the subject of many cruel jokes in the village of Little Goddsting, though all of these jests were at least partly based on fact. Lundy was a sheep farmer, and very poor he was too at this noble job of animal husbandry.

One May morn, Lundy was much concerned, for there was not one sheep left grazing on his pasture. He called on some of the neighbouring farmsteads, but each time he asked if anyone had seen his sheep he would be met with a slap on the back and told to be on his way. On leaving the last grange, he heard the farmer's wife shouting over to her husband 'O! John – Lundy's lost his sheep again!' before laughter boomed from their lungs.

Despondent, Lundy returned to his empty field and kicked the gate post in frustration. Well, the next day all of the sheep were back, but unfortunately, the day after that presented the daft farmer with another empty field. This pattern repeated itself for the next fortnight and it was always the same: one day the sheep would be there, the next they would not. Lundy even tried waiting in the field after dark to see where the sheep went, but because he was so dull-witted, he always fell asleep and woke to an empty field once more.

The first day of June was particularly irksome, for it was time for the flock to be sheared, but not a single ewe or lamb was in sight. In a great rage, Lundy threw his shears into the water trough and cursed loudly.

Now, it just so happened that a passing wise-woman, known locally as Nunny Bess, heard this commotion and walked over to the purple-faced farmer and asked him what his trouble was. Lundy explained the miserable mystery before thumping his own head twelve times, for he was much aggrieved.

'May I take a walk in your field?' asked Nunny Bess.

Lundy assented, but he could not see how it would do any good. The woman entered the field and walked its border all the way around to the far wall where she stopped abruptly and beckoned him over. Lundy trudged over to the short lady and asked her what she had found.

'You are a fool, Benjamin Lundy!' laughed the wise-woman. 'You should keep your field more carefully weeded. This here herb is a chicory bush.'

'I don't have no chickens!' cried the numbskull farmer.

'Tsh!' said Nunny Bess, 'I did not say 'chicken'. I did say 'chicory'.

'What be chicony?' said the farmer, still not understanding.

'Chicory is a magic herb you muddled pillock. Any sheep that eats that is sure to vanish for a day. If chewed, this here herb makes the muncher invisible. Can you not hear your flock's bleating? They never left your field!'

Nunny Bess helped Lundy uproot all of the chicory from his pasture and she stowed it most tenderly in her basket – for she would have much use of it later. The noodle-brained farmer, whilst never free of mishaps again, made sure he kept chicory out of his field from that day forward and his sheep were always clear to see, except on foggy days.

This story rather simplifies the lore surrounding the chicory plant, as I always understood that it only gave the gatherer invisibility if cut on St. James's Day at noon or midnight, and only if the collector cut the stalks with a gold blade in total silence, otherwise death would surely follow. I'm tempted to risk gathering some chicory one day, as death surely follows everything we do, and even Auntie Vulna had to admit that there was no strict timeframe to one's demise after some chicory-cutting undertaken in the incorrect manner. What's always prevented me from doing this in the past is that St. James's Day is a very special one, as he was the patron saint of rheumatoid arthritis sufferers. As I am myself tormented by this crippling condition, I always spend the whole day in church, praying for an end to my suffering.

As these entreaties have never actually worked and, if anything my pain has worsened over the last decade, I fully intend to acquire some chicory this summer and enjoy the furtive delights of entering friends' houses unseen and looking through their drawers and cupboards. I have done this many times in the past whilst not being invisible, but only when my host has gone to the lavatory, which means that my prying searches are often very time-pressured and stressful.

The Devil's Hill

Some people are so fearful of Beelzebub that they will go to astonishing lengths to ensure he doesn't come near them. I once knew a woman called Jane Lane who was so apprehensive that her next door neighbour's vacant house would be sold to the Devil, that she erected an eleven-foot cross outside her front door. Of course local misfits used to turn the thing upside down overnight, and eventually she succumbed to a heart attack with the stress of it all. It's better to have a good, solid, practical plan in place, lest the Devil move in next door, because loud rock music and dog excrement will be the least of your worries.

I have several plans, as does the clever gentleman in the following narrative, should this horror ever come to pass. Unfortunately I cannot tell you what mine are as you might be Satan, and I'm not willing to reveal my trump cards just for the sake of creating a genuinely useful introduction to a folk tale.

For some unknown reason the Devil had decided to torment the quiet village of Belbriar. On the last day of September 1692 he was first seen squatting on Hushleigh Hill as a retinue of his odious servants, all streaked with matted hair and loathsome swellings, dug a shaft down into the centre of the once beautiful mound. Whilst his fiendish menials scooped out the heart of Hushleigh Hill, the Devil would delight in taunting any villager who got too close – peppering the air with appalling insults and curses that would have made a coalminer wince.

By early October the reason for the Devil's travails on Hushleigh Hill had become all too apparent. For the Devil, along with his misshapen simian henchmen, began a series of raids on sweet Belbriar. Not a man, woman or child was safe from these plunderings, nor were their livestock. Be it pot or pan, boot or shovel, all were taken in the relentless attacks. By the third day, even the sconces in the church had been stolen along with the vicar himself and, as with the rest of the hoard, tipped down into the centre of the hill. The village was now a truly ghastly place to behold: the humble cottages were shredded and splintered and all about were pools of blood spilt from those valiant folk's veins who had fought against the Devil and his marauding imps.

That night the Devil, dancing in rings on the top of Hushleigh Hill cried out:

'Look at all the dust I've raised! What a store of treasure is mine!' The moans and sobs of the poor people of Belbriar issued from the pit at the centre of the hill, fearing all was lost. Already the survivors within could hear the sounds of burrowing and rocks cracking from beneath them – it would not be long before their miserable cave would open up from below, sending them hurtling into the sulphurous caverns of Hell itself. To add to the suffering of the trapped villagers and their mewing animals, the Devil and his dreadful brood emptied their stinking bowels onto the wretches below.

'Prithee quiet in my privy!' laughed the Devil as he showered them with another sortie of putrid coils from his diabolical breech. The Devil's imps – who are very easy to please – found this tremendously funny and giggled with mirth at their master's foul games.

However, the Devil, despite all of his cunning and wiles, is apt to make mistakes. He had supposed that all the folk of Belbriar were trapped in his abominable flue-hole, but he was wrong. One man was still at liberty. Daniel

Yeadley, a cunning old man most adept in the art of hiding, had watched the Devil's ransacking of Belbriar from his many and diverse hidey-holes and dark refuges. With a growing horror, Yeadley suspected he was the last villager left uncaptured and he swore that he would use all his guile to save his beloved friends from the clutches of the Wicked One.

The Devil's dancing was halted the moment he heard a commanding voice imploring him to cease his revels and come down to the foot of the hill.

'What have we here?' laughed the Devil most imperiously. 'Restrain the rascal,' he bellowed to his sniggering familiars. They tumbled and cartwheeled down the hillside and held Yeadley as the Devil sat down at the top of Hushleigh's peak.

'You are a fool to have wandered into Belbriar, you withered old scamp. I shall add you to my pot.' The greasy imps began to drag Yeadley towards the hill when he shouted:

'Stop! Stop! I am no stranger to these parts. I hid from you. I am most artful. In fact, I am so sure I can defeat you, that I wish to make a wager with you!' shouted Yeadley as he struggled against his filthy captors. The Devil, who is always supremely confident, was amused by this little man's attempt at a bargain - so much so that he trotted down the hill and loomed over him as the imps pushed Yeadley to his knees in the bristling old holly-leaves that carpeted the hill's foot.

'Facetious worm!' said the Devil. 'I would make a pudding of your kidneys. You cannot beat me! And yet something about your droll manner delights me. What is your gamble?'

'I bet you that I can get to the top of that hill and you and your…children will not be able to stop me,' said Yeadley, defiantly.

'Ho ho ho!' laughed the Devil. 'You are most impudent! And, how do you intend to do this?'

'Why,' said Yeadley, 'with these.' The old man held up six lengths of brown string. The Devil laughed so heartily at the man's nerve that the trees around them shook with his derisive gales of mirth.

'You believe that my fellows and I can be held back with a few old strings! You are a blethering ninny! Ha ha! What do you ask for in return, nincompoop?' said the chuckling fiend.

'I ask for the release of all my fellow villagers, their animals and their property that you have pinched,' said Yeadley steadily, showing not an ounce of fear.

'Very well! You have a bargain, little idiot, on the condition that if you fail to climb the hill, you will be mine and I keep everything in the shaft too – from the burliest man to the smallest bristle brush!' said the Devil, still cackling with glee.

'Agreed,' said Yeadley. 'Let us shake hands to seal the deal.' They shook hands. Yeadley tried not to recoil from the Devil's scorching shake, for he had to remain firm.

'Now,' said the Devil, 'begin!'

At that, Yeadley took two paces to the nearest holly tree and broke off six small branches. He tied one length to each of his legs and the same for his arms. He wound the longest branch around his midriff and secured that with the fifth string. Lastly, he wound the smallest stem around the crown of his head before fixing that to his pate with the final length of string. The holly leaves cut into his papery old skin, and blood, as bright as the berries on the holly-sticks issued in gouts all over his body. He strode towards the hill, laughing.

Yeadley laughed because he knew that he had outwitted the Devil; for as any wise-man knows, holly is a strong protection against all forms of Evil – from the basest witch's curse to the most malevolent demon. With every step he took up Hushleigh Hill, the Devil and his minions' attempts to stop him were quite futile – they could not touch the lucky man. As Yeadley neared the peak, the Devil let out a cry of anguish. Every boulder he threw at the old man simply bounced off him and rolled to the bottom of the hill.

Yeadley at last reached the hilltop and spread his bleeding arms in jubilation. 'I have done it!' he yelled. The Devil roared before exploding into a cloud of yellow smoke along with his squealing familiars. The hill shook violently and split in two; dozens upon dozens of villagers spilled forth - sheep and cows bolting in all directions.

Daniel Yeadley had succeeded in defeating the Devil and the villagers of Belbriar made sure that their saviour lived in great luxury for the rest of his days on earth. Any rambler who cares to visit Belbriar today will notice its two beautiful hills, the Hushleigh Twins, formed when the original split asunder after the Devil was tricked by a canny old man with six lengths of string.

Wasn't Daniel Yeadley heroic? I have to say that when Aunt Vulna first told me this story, I fell completely in love with him. I'm sure that if I'd had the misfortune of being born in 1692, I'd have made the most of it by marrying Mr Yeadley. I do realise that this would have meant being captured by the Devil and deposited in his hill-hole and bespattered by his expulsions, but there's no limit to what we would do for a true love. By means of a comparison, I would have done almost anything for my late husband Desmond, but there were limits. One day I found him splashing about with a strange woman in the local municipal swimming pool. I had just popped down there myself to acquire some sachets of mustard from the cafeteria (we had run out and I couldn't afford to buy condiments from the market that month); I thought I'd stop and have a rest on the viewing gallery (my handbag had become quite heavy as I had indulged in a bit a free-for-all while the waitress's back was turned – tomato sauce, mayonnaise etc.), when I was shocked to see my husband doing breaststrokes with a mystery blonde. I confronted Desmond about this when he returned home. He insisted that he had just finished a business deal with the woman and she had suggested a swim to seal the agreement. I was minded of the story that you've just read, and I said to Desmond that a handshake will suffice even for the Devil, and I'd never heard of anything so ridiculous as to take a swim to finalise a contract. Everything he said subsequently to justify his odd behaviour was littered with double entendres – he had had to 'release her assets', how he'd 'bent over backwards to complete the merger'. Needless to say he slept in the greenhouse that night and ate a raw marrow for his supper. I rather regret telling him the next day that in the event of a house fire I would not brave the flames to rescue him, but I would go back into the inferno for my Royal Doulton service. Sadly, this declaration acted like a curse upon our marriage and a series of misfortunes followed that began with one of my precious ceramics being shattered and ended with Desmond's death thirty-two years later. Please, never go to bed on a quarrel.

The Bellock Stones

The following story relates how the famous Bellock Stones came to be and why there are twelve of them. A recent archaeological survey has discovered that there may have been over forty stones at one time. Mark my words: there are a dozen stones – I even went to Bellock to count them. I can only assume the archaeologists must have been studying the site at night and had erroneously included some of the various scattered beer cans and cigarette packets in their stone count.

Twelve sisters (this was during those days when such a large family was not rare) from the village of Bellock went out one night to pick henbane so that they could each attract a lover, for they all had monstrously excessive noses and were still woefully unwed. The sisters had been told by a wise-woman that this magical charm would undoubtedly work, but that the picking of these rather unlovely flowers must take place after dusk and strictly no later than midnight, lest they be visited by some dreadful misfortune.

Being young girls they had dallied in the lane before reaching the meadow in which the sought-after blossoms flourished. Too busy picking prettier flowers, the twelve sisters came upon the henbane ruefully late – they only became aware of this when the mournful toll from St. Earnest's was heard. On the instant the bell struck twelve, the maidens were affrighted to see a huge white bee, the size of a cat, fly down from the deep, dark sky and land on the plant they had been picking. This was a dying queen bee, quite pale from all her life inside the hive, and, as a dying queen is wont to do, she was crying most lamentably for she was fatally fatigued from all her egg-laying.

Alas, any who hear the sound of a dying queen bee are fated to petrify into stone, as the song is so melancholy. The sisters dropped their posies and were quite turned to gritty rock with the sad ululating melody. The bee herself, upon decease, scattered to form the daisies that now pepper the site with their blooms.

I remember very clearly when I first heard this story as my aunt and I were stuck in a snowdrift and I was very anxious for it to be summer again. Aunt Vulna pulled me under her blanket and whispered this one into my ear. She pinched me hard on the thigh at the climax, but I suppose that sometimes the oral tradition needs enlivening and, at any rate, it lent a certain shock to the fable. As I mentioned in my introduction, I've visited the Bellock Stones, and all of them appear to have very distinct noses, though I suppose you could say that of any rock. I can also confirm that a prodigious quantity of henbane also grows in the location. Unfortunately, as I was camping there, I set up a small bonfire to keep warm in the evening chill. Unknowingly, I placed a large amount of henbane stalks on the conflagration without knowing that the fumes from the blaze would cause temporary insanity. I shan't declare much more than that, but needless to say when I came out of the hallucination I was in a nearby oak tree, quite unclothed, and with a very intimate understanding of how fallow deer socialise after dark.

The Poisoning of
Lady Ethel Brewgham

Dear old Katherine Hepburn once said 'I wonder if men and women really suit each other. Perhaps they should live next door and just visit now and then.' This would have been good advice for the characters in the story below. However, it's unlikely, even if this story were true, that Ms Hepburn would have been alive at the time of the events occurring in this narrative, so she wouldn't have been much help. On the other hand, it is possible she was about three hundred years old when she died, as many women in Hollywood lie about their age. Officially, she died aged ninety-six, but, I suppose, in reality she could have been much, much older. It's an interesting thought. Please contact me if you are interested in negotiating the film rights for this potentially fascinating story.

Sir Joseph and Lady Ethel Brewgham had been married for twenty years, and not a single day in those two decades had brought either of them happiness. Their marriage had simply served to continue the Brewgham line; all that could be said of the union was that it had secured Sir Joseph's father's dynastic ambitions and twelve unhappy children had been raised, all of whom had now left their mother and father to their bickering.

In her late middle age, Lady Ethel began to sicken quite rapidly and was confined to her bed. It was around this time that Sir Joseph sold the family house and had himself and his ailing wife installed in a new home, which he named Glaze Hall. And a very remarkable place this new home was too; Sir Joseph had built a new mansion, in the latest fashion, with as many windows as could be fitted.

The servants believed that this was a rare kindness on Sir Joseph's part to allow his dying wife more light, perhaps in the hope that she might recover.

However, the truth was that Lady Ethel had accused her husband of poisoning her and that he was simply abiding by the old superstition that opening windows in the house of a dying person eases their departure and prevents phantoms from haunting the building that they died in. Sadly, on both counts, Lady Ethel was quite correct, although her husband did not admit this to her. Instead, he patted her sweat-dampened head and told her that she was feverish and foolish.

By late autumn Lady Ethel was so sick she had fallen into a permanent swoon and lay quite insensible on her bed. The moment of her passing was drawing ever nearer so Sir Joseph told his servants that all the windows in Glaze Hall should be opened, from the smallest to the largest, to allow his 'dear' wife's departure.

On the last day of November, Lady Ethel finally succumbed to her husband's slow murder and she took her last breath. The family physician, a good friend of Sir Joseph's, was called and he confirmed the good lady was extinct. Over the course of the next week, the windows of the house were left wide open, in spite of the terrible cold airs howling through Glaze Hall, and preparations were made for Lady Ethel's funeral.

By mid-December, Sir Joseph's wife was buried in a remarkably deep grave; the mourners came and the mourners departed, and by Christmas Sir Joseph was alone in his marvellous hall of windows, relieved to be rid of his nattering and interfering wife.

However, it was not long before the murderer was troubled by a number of strange occurrences. Several clocks, all of which had glass windows that had not been opened at Lady Ethel's death, began to chime thirteen throughout the night. This was easily dealt with, reasoned Sir Joseph – the clocks were smashed and burnt.

This did not bring an end to the man's growing misery, for next all the pictures that hung on the wall behind glass began to show lurid, hellish scenes instead of images of pastoral beauty. Glazed portraits no longer comforted with kindly eyes – instead they began to leer and grimace. Sir Joseph was angered that he would have to tear up the pictures that had been in his family for so many generations, but he did this anyway. The pictures were unhooked, the glass shattered and the paintings were burnt.

Thinking that his wife's malevolent spirit was defeated at last, Sir Joseph began to enjoy his solitude once more. But it was not long before trouble started again. Sir Joseph particularly enjoyed spending time in his orangery in the gardens of Glaze Hall, picking fruits and reading his history books, but this was soon spoilt when Lady Ethel's spirit turned most of the fruit in the orangery black, or when the man bit into a peach, the stone within would seem to bear the resemblance of his dead wife's face.

As much as he loathed the idea, Sir Joseph knew that he would have to have the orangery dismantled as it had been quite ruined on account of Lady Ethel's malicious trespasses. The orangery was taken down and the glass was ground into dust and carted away.

Servants began to remark as to how ill their master was looking – he had grown thin and careworn; some of them started to worry that he too was dying of the same distemper as his wife.

One night in January, Sir Joseph had taken himself into the ancient chapel that he had had his house built next to. Of course, this holy place had a good many stained glass windows, none of which were built to be opened, so Lady Ethel's wraith had focused her attentions on this place for her final assault on her deceitful husband. Whilst he was not full of remorse about killing his wife, Sir Joseph was resentful of her continuing presence, and so he prayed to God to be released of this tormenting demon. He gazed up at the great window behind the altar and was sickened to see that the scene of an angel telling Joseph to accept Mary as his wife had transformed into a hideous circus of cackling demons, and the Lord's angel was now the devil, made of black glass.

Sir Joseph took a prayer book and hurled it at the window, which dashed it to pieces.

A servant of Glaze Hall, so affrighted by the sound of the chapel's glass being broken ran into the town to fetch a constable. It was not long before Sir Joseph was seized and hauled in front of the magistrate. He was found guilty of what the judge described as 'an atrocious and most ungodly act of wicked vandalism' before being thrown into a filthy underground cell.

The dungeon he found himself in was not without some natural light, for high up, well out of reach of the diabolical Sir Joseph, was a small, barred window, which by chance was well-glazed with a grimy lattice of glass to prevent members of the public from passing food down to the prisoners below. As the man lay sobbing to himself on the cold cell floor, he heard the unmistakable laughter of Lady Ethel, and the growing sound of rattling chains, begin to echo about the chamber.

There was a one hundred and fifty year period in British history when properties were taxed according to how many windows they had. I like to imagine that the story you've just read is set around that time (1696-1851) as the expense of fitting so many windows would make Sir Joseph Brewgham even more evil than he seems to be in this story alone. Amateur historians and conspiracy theorists may like to note that the window tax appears to have been repealed in the very year that the Crystal Palace was constructed for the Great Exhibition, which needed almost 300,000 panes of glass. I'll leave that with you to ponder. Someone on the local council recently gave the go ahead to erect an enormous block of flats near my house, for what is now termed 'contemporary living'. Unfortunately the new residents' modern lifestyles are on show to all and sundry as the entire block seems to have been built from just glass and steel – absolutely everything is on show. The consequence of this town planning is that a number of my neighbours appear to have developed a sudden and somewhat obsessive bird watching hobby – you can't buy a pair of field glasses for love nor money in a five mile radius of these 'spacious new apartments'. I am still using the same binoculars that I acquired from Desmond after the war – but I keep them focused on the near distance (my garden). My favourite birds to watch are chiff-chaffs (so named because of their distinctive cry of 'chiff-chaff').

The Giant's Cave

Those fond of giants and mermaids are in for a rare treat here. I recognise that this may very well spoil the revelation at the heart of the story below, but this is an academic study of folk-tradition, and it is certainly not about passively absorbing the tale. If you want to enjoy a story then I suggest you go back to nursery. Such a folly would most likely see you arrested for trespass and impersonation anyway. As you will soon see, the village in the story no longer exists; I am keen however to see if its remains are to be found. I have a small dinghy, so I am looking for someone with a sonar device and the qualifications to operate it. The mission will be dangerous, so only people over the age of sixty-five should apply, as you will not be missed as much as younger people, should we drown.

A giant once inhabited the caves under the coastal village of Guyvor Badhale in Cornwall. He spent his whole life holding up the mighty rocks for the many cottage-dwellers whose houses tottered by the cliff edge. The giant had pledged to undertake this colossal task after the townsfolk had saved his life from marauding giant-slayers back in the days of the barbarians.

One day, the giant was holding up the many tonnes of stone when he saw a woman struggling in the water. He reached his arm out to her, but it did not stretch far enough.

He straightened his crooked leg instead and his toe was close enough for the drowning maiden to cling to it.

The giant was surprised by the strength of the female, who, instead of clutching him for her life, drew the giant out of his cave and pulled him into the water when he finally lost his tenacious grip on the slick black rocks. For the drowning lady was not a normal woman at all; she was a mermaid, and she most ardently desired a mortal to give her a soul. She dashed him over the head with her looking-glass before drawing her comb through his knotted hair and dragging him down head-first into the boiling sea. Shortly afterwards, the village of Guyvor Badhale foundered and tumbled into the thrashing waters of the ocean below.

My grandmother was very fond of Cornwall, but she told me that the locals were always rather reticent when it came to sharing their folk-tales. This one was extracted from a man who was very near death, lying on a camp bed in a half-abandoned croft. She worked on him very hard and said the sole possession this man owned, a very bright battery-powered torch, came in handy when coaxing the tale from him. He was doubtless some kind of itinerant derelict, as not even the bed beneath him was his, fashioned as it was with rather effeminate curlicues and had the words 'Maureen's Bed' scratched on to the footboard. Grandma Berrial hinted that the pillow was instrumental in persuading him to speak. Alas, as she tried the same technique on me when wresting a confession from my lips, I'm sure she used the 'muffle-gasp' method to finally convince him to talk. As a way of explaining away a natural disaster to simple-minded people, it's quite effective, but it does rather perpetuate the myth that women always seem to want to do men harm. Women and mermaids are simply not interested in trapping and tormenting men. Grandma Berrial would be the first to testify to that.

Mrs Munnion's Kitchen

Kitchens are such convenient and efficient places these days that it's sometimes hard to believe that there was a time when they meant hard work and thankless toil. If you're particularly slovenly, all you need today is a fork to pierce the film lid of a ready-meal, a microwave to heat up the unctuous mess and a spoon to scoop it into your slobbering mouth. If you're especially lazy, you won't even need the spoon. The following story features a cookhouse with a very surprising complication. I'll not spoil the story by saying too much more, but I will say that the resolution involves a pie. There are very few difficulties in this world that can't be resolved by the baking of a pie.

The uncompromising and punctilious cook Mrs Munnion ruled over the kitchen of Gorble House for many years. When absolutely necessary, she would exercise fairness, but most of the time she was greatly feared by all who worked under her and by a good number of those who worked above her too. Like all who are born into this unforgiving world, one day Mrs Munnion died. However, her death was most singular and the cause of some merriment amongst the scullery maids, for she choked to death on an artichoke.

A new cook by the name of Ira Nabbs was employed to take over Gorble House's kitchen and she proved to be popular amongst the staff in that great pile. Ira Nabbs was as round as a balloon and just as playful and jolly, but it was not long into her new position before something rather serious happened. One day, when Mrs Nabbs was cutting steak for that evening's supper of beef collops, the knife she was using spoke to her:

'There's too much fat on that strip!' it said.

Mrs Nabbs threw the blade down onto the table-top in a fright. The kitchen maid, Emily, looked at the cook and said, 'Why, Mrs Nabbs! How come ye to make such fine mimicry of Mrs Munnion?'

'Hush, child! It was not me!' said the cook, somewhat disturbed by the voice.

Emily chuckled to herself and continued to chop her carrots. But when Mrs Nabbs returned to her fillet, the same voice issued from the knife and continued its uncanny scolding: 'That strip's too thick,' squealed the knife.

It wasn't long before every utensil in the kitchen was complaining when it was picked up. Every pot, every pan — from the smallest pastry nippers to the largest meat saw — all squealed and muttered with admonishments. Before long, even straining the gravy became a terrifying task, and soon the master of the house, Sir Henry Panby, heard of the disturbances and made a rare appearance in the kitchen to hear for himself what was ailing the staff. He picked up an egg whisk and a loud voice emanated from the implement: 'Dah! What good's the whisk when ye ain't yet even cracked open an egg?'

This was enough for Sir Henry so he held up a biscuit pricker (which was whistling an Irish air next to the stove) and spoke to it with an admirable deficit of embarrassment: 'Mrs Munnion! You are dead. You must leave my cook to her work. You have no business haunting my spoons. Be gone!'

The only effect this had was to heighten the unholy clamour; a larding needle flew up from an open draw and poked Sir Henry most balefully in the rump with an obscene shriek of 'Not much meat there!'

'Please, Sir Henry,' said Mrs Nabbs, 'might I make a suggestion?'

'By all means, Mrs Nabbs,' said the man, rubbing his tweedy buttocks.

'If I might use the pastry intended for tomorrow's game pie, I think I should like to fill it with these 'orrible tranclements and have the 'ole lot buried with Mrs Munnion. Maybe that'll shut 'er up!'

'A very good idea. I'll get Friggs to open up the grave this instant,' said Sir Henry.

The Master hurried back upstairs and Mrs Nabbs and Emily set about rolling the pastry and making the biggest pie Lancashire had ever seen. In it was deposited every last kitchen implement and the whole thing was slammed into the oven and baked for the next two hours. It was a job to keep the oven door closed because the pie was rattling most restlessly within, but eventually the crust was brown and the great pastry was removed.

The butler and two footmen lugged the pie down to the churchyard and Sir Henry, along with Mrs Nabbs and Emily, watched as it was thrown into the pit of Mrs Munnion's plot. The pie made several remarkable attempts to leap from its hole, but Friggs the gardener was quick with his spade and the earth was shovelled back into the old cook's grave.

The kitchen was restocked, at considerable expense, with new utensils and the only discord ever heard again in that room was when the Sir Henry's cat stole into the larder and lapped up the cream. Mrs Munnion's haunting was over, though for many years after, it was said that her grave smelt of newly baked pastry.

I think everyone in Gorble House missed a trick with the hasty vanquishing of Mrs Munnion from the building. With a little effort they might have succeeded in harnessing the old cook's formidable powers and got her ghost to run the kitchen. That way Mrs Nabbs and Emily could have put their feet up and trusted in the supernatural to cook the meals and do all the washing up as well. Granted, most poltergeist cases only last for relatively short periods of time, but what a treat that would have been in their hard-working lives to have had just a month or two of rest. I have a poltergeist that makes inconsistent manifestations in my home and it has always tried to help with the clothes washing. Admittedly the spook is an irksome presence on the whole as it tends to wring out blouses by twisting them into ropes which is a real nuisance when I have to iron out all the creases, but, I suppose, I'm as negligent in training my ghost as the women of Gorble House seem to have been. The poltergeist did prove useful for a brief period in the 1970s when I became enthused by the idea of tie-dying and it helped make some absolutely super prints on a number of cheap cotton skirts I bought at the market. Sadly, I had to throw all of these garments away as I became aware that they were haunted. I won't go into too much detail, but I will say that a cold, ectoplasmic hand is quite unwelcome when attempting an unannounced how-do-you-do below the waist.

Esmund's Beard

Initiation ceremonies are often inexplicably odd to the outsider, but once accepted into the institution you so desperately want to be a part of, all the rites-of-passage you endured no longer seem odd at all. I, however, experienced a reversal of this process upon joining my local library back in the late 1930s. As a young girl it seemed completely reasonable to me that in order to be able to withdraw a book I had to attend an after-hours ceremony where I had to drink a finger of goat's blood from a silver goblet at midnight whilst a tall man in a red velvet robe watched me. After I'd drunk the liquid the man removed the crown of antlers he'd been wearing and stamped the day's date on my left hand. Only years afterwards when I was filling out a form at my new library did I realise that this rite is not standard amongst all libraries. The woman at the desk seemed very puzzled at my asking whether I had to bring my own goblet that evening. I spoke to some friends of mine about this and they confirmed that when joining a library all you tend to need is your passport and a council tax bill. I sometimes wonder what I was inaugurated into in 1938. I don't suppose I will ever know. The story you're about to read has a number of twists and turns as a boy goes through his rites-of-passage. The ending is quite complex and traumatic, so you may need to take a few days off work on sick leave after reading it. Therefore, it would be unwise to tackle this story if you have an important deadline looming in your professional life. Just stick a little strip of coloured paper on this page and come back to it when you're less busy.

In the middle of the little village of Pulverdell lived an old blind man called Stanley Thumpet and his nervous young son, Esmund. A long-standing tradition in Pulverdell was for all the young boys to prove their manhood by catching and killing a buck rabbit from the woods on the hills.

On Esmund's thirteenth birthday Stanley sat his son on his lap and searched his child's soft face with his old, withered hands.

'Tsh!' hissed Stanley, 'There's still no beard, son. Nothing. Not even a wisp! Did your damned mother give me a useless girl? Did she die whilst birthing you just to give me a weak little bitch?'

Esmund said nothing, which enraged his father all the more. Stanley had always been a bully but he seemed only to be getting nastier as he grew ever older.

'It's time for you to become a man – you're thirteen for G—'s sake,' said Esmund's father, spitting as he did so. 'You must do what my father made me do.'

Esmund knew very well what this was because his father would tell him almost every day. He knew his progenitor was anxiously waiting for him to grow his first beard because then and only then would he be ordered down into the rabbit hole to catch the King Rabbit.

Unfortunately, Esmund was a meek lad and the idea of going up to the woods at night, sneaking into the rabbit hole, catching and then killing a screeching buck rabbit was too much for him to bear. At night-time he would secretly pluck at the wiry blonde hairs that had begun to burst through his chin, hoping vainly to delay the inevitable journey into the woe-begotten nightmare of the rabbit's lair. Every evening and every morning he would have to pull painfully at his hairy chops because this was preferable to undergoing his initiation into manhood.

Stanley Thumpet's favourite supper was rabbit pie, and if possible, he would eat rabbit at breakfast and lunch too. He was growing tired of having to catch them himself and earnestly desired that his son take on the responsibility instead. For any man who loves his tender rabbit flesh their sworn nemesis is the fox, and Stanley hated those sly creatures more than anything in the world. When his son was of age, he wanted nothing more than to teach him the ways of snaring the foxes that forever snatched his beloved rabbits. In spite of his blindness and growing infirmity, Mr Thumpet was still an expert catcher of these ginger menaces and this was very useful for the maintenance of their farm. Not only did the slaughter of foxes mean that the supply of rabbits was plentiful and that their chickens and geese were safer from attack, but it also meant that there was always a good stock of foxes' tongues. As any countryman will tell you, the fox's tongue is a very effective talisman to ward off the Evil Eye as well as being an excellent means to instil courage when worn on a chain about the neck. Indeed, Stanley would often make young Esmund eat a broth of boiled fox tongues in a seemingly futile attempt to embolden his effete son.

One warm summer's day, when Esmund had been tending to his horse, he met with a horrid accident. The young boy had laid down his dusty curry comb and was upon the point of retrieving the hoof pick from the ground when the mare took fright at a scurrying mouse and kicked the boy hard on his forehead. The farrier's son, John, heard the commotion and raised the alarm when he found his friend lying on the cobbles, bleeding profusely from a ghastly wound. Stanley was called over to tend to his injured son, cursing with exasperation at Esmund's ineptitude.

John helped Stanley carry Esmund back to Thumpet Cottage, where he was laid on the bed. John dressed the wounds, for, of course, Stanley could not see to do this. The poor child lay insensible for almost a fortnight until eventually he awoke and had the power to speak once more.

'Father,' said Esmund, 'the horse – it kicked me!'

'Yes, I know,' replied Stanley. 'But you're on the mend.' Esmund noticed a strange note of glee in his father's reedy voice and mistook it for affection.

'We'll soon have you down that rabbit hole!' announced Stanley.

'But, Father, I do not yet have a beard and –' but the boy did not finish his sentence, for as he said this, he brushed his hand over his chin as if to vainly prove his unreadiness to his sightless father, and felt the coarse prickle of hair all about his chin and top lip.

'That knock on the head must've woken up your manhood!' said his father who was now at his bedside and running his rough hands over the boy's face.

'At last! My son is almost a man. You will go up to the rabbit hole tonight. You'll kill the King Rabbit, bring him back here and we'll eat him. Then, tomorrow I'll teach you how to catch 'em proper. The day after, I'll show you 'ow to snare the d—d foxes!'

'But how do I know how to catch my first rabbit without your help?' asked Esmund.

'Tsh! Every lad has to do it by his-self first,' said Stanley. 'You only learn by makin' mistakes. 'Ow d'you know what's right when you don't know what's wrong?'

Esmund turned his sore head away from his father. He knew there was nothing to be gained by remonstrating with him.

Later that day, when the sun had sunk below the hills, Stanley helped his son to put on his stockings and fixed a thick black cape around his shoulders. His father's agile fingers fixed the clasp before he laid both of his strong hands on his son's slight shoulders.

'Now,' said Stanley, 'the hour has come. You have your knife and you be dark as the night in that cape.'

'My head aches awful bad, father,' said Esmund.

'Stop your mithering, boy or I'll give thee another clout. Don't you cut me such a caper! Tonight is the night you stop being a boy. When you come back here you'll certainly be a man,' said Stanley. With that he pushed him out through the entrance to the cottage and slammed the door shut.

Trembling with anxiety, Esmund made his way to the farm gate and began to climb the forbidding black hill that led to Pulverdell forest. He staggered through the whipping branches and snagging brambles growing ever more fearful. He had made this journey many times before, but always in daylight; now everything seemed unfamiliar and strange. His head throbbed and his eyes watered as he continued to stumble through the woods, the wind howling mournfully as it swirled through the black branches of the gigantic trees.

After another half hour of scrambling and tumbling, the mist had thickened and Esmund was on the point of giving up altogether, fearing he was hopelessly lost. The threats and taunts of his father echoed about his aching head, and this drove him on. He must find the buck rabbit or his father would surely disown him.

Eventually, he came upon the peak of a hill that looked familiar. Relief washed over him as he saw several burrows on the mound. He set down the sack he had been carrying and dropped to his knees. The oil lamp he held illuminated a tunnel that he was sure would lead to the King Rabbit, because it was so large. As he crawled into the tunnel it became noticeably warmer and his breath no longer turned to mist in front of him. A growing desire to prove himself to his father overtook him – the dried fox tongue that hung around his neck seemed to reassure him as it turned and tapped on his ribcage underneath his cloak.

Before long he found himself in a large chamber. The smell of soil was overpowering, but not enough to conceal another smell - a musky odour that permeated everything. He was wondering which tunnel to turn into next when he heard a deep growling. He froze in terror. He knew very little about rabbits, but he was sure that they did not growl.

'What draws thee into my home this night?' snarled a deep, wicked voice.

'Who is there?' cried Esmund as he dropped his lantern.

'Why, it is I – the Dog Fox!'

'I am so sorry, Dog Fox. So sorry. I meant to find a buck rabbit. I came here by mistake. Please forgive me,' said Esmund. 'If you'll let me pass I shall go and never return.'

'I think not. No, I think not.' The Dog Fox padded over to the trembling boy and for the first time was lighted by the flickering glow of the lamp. The beast was as big as Esmund but had considerably sharper teeth than he. His fur glistened like rust and amber aflame. The Dog Fox's tail switched in flashes of white and his black eyes stayed fixed on the terrified boy.

'Thou cannot leave. Thou hast my wife's tongue hanging about thy neck. I can smell her. Remove it along with thy cape and place them by thy lamp,' said the Dog Fox.

Esmund did as he was told. The fox tenderly placed his paw on his dead wife's shrivelled tongue and said this:

'Good. Now, I shall eat you.'

The Dog Fox tore Esmund into shreds and ate half of him. The rest he dragged into the next chamber and fed to his squeaking cubs; when this was done, he put on Esmund's cape, left his burrow and darted off down the hill towards Thumpet Farm.

Stanley was sitting at the fireside smoking his pipe when there was a knocking at the door. His heart leapt for joy because he knew his son had returned a man. He strode over to the door, his heart brimming with pride and love for the first time in his life.

'My son!' cried Stanley 'You are finally a man!'

The Dog Fox stepped into the room, disguised in Esmund's cape and standing on his hind legs. His father embraced the Dog Fox.

'Oh, your beard is so fine and thick! See what a man this has made of you, son. Such a rich, full beard – better than mine!'

'Let me stroke you beard, Father,' said the Dog Fox.

'Your voice is so deep. My son truly is a man!' said Stanley.

The Dog Fox tugged at the old man's beard so forcefully that he tore it off completely.

'My son!' was the last thing Stanley said because the Dog Fox bit off his head and ate it in one great slavering crunch. The King of the Foxes howled with vengeful delight before taking the rest of Stanley Thumpet's body back to his den at the top of the hill, just as the sun began to rise again.

That was quite a long one, wasn't it? I think the trouble with some folk stories is that people will forever keep adding their own bits to them. It's like that Heathrow Airport – they keep putting new runways here and new terminals there – it just gets bigger and bigger. I honestly believe that by the 22nd century the UK will just be one giant airport. Still, we should remember that the joy of the oral tradition of storytelling is that it is forever in motion and always changing. I don't like change, so that is why I have chosen to write this book. Now these stories can be saved from the fiddling additions of others and petrified in one small volume written by me. I will be keeping a close eye on this book after it's published and I will be merciless with you should you start trying to add bits without my permission. I have employed a solicitor to continue this surveillance in the event of my death and I have secured enough funding to maintain this instruction *for seventy-three years post-mortem. After this time, I'm sure no one will be interested in reading folklore — everybody will be far too busy listening to disco music instead.*

The Red Handkerchief

The following story features magic and justice. Now that the United Kingdom is under the yoke of European Union dictates, justice is a funny thing, and I've certainly not yet seen any magic made by the mandarins of Brussels. The Maastricht Treaty didn't even come close. If, after reading this story, you feel like rushing off to find your handkerchief to see if it makes magic, then I would caution you. Your dreams, like most people's now days, are far too big, and you'll probably end up doing yourself an injury. If you insist on doing this, I recommend thirty years of hermitage on an Orkney island and a strict diet of boiled kelp before attempting this folly. Hopefully by the end of your self-imposed exile you will have died and learnt some lessons about life that are more important than acquiring some tricks to amuse your friends at dinner parties.

An exceedingly kind and genteel man called Godfrey Watts lived in the village of Skurstead. He was universally loved (in his small village) as he had the extraordinary ability of giving the residents of Skurstead what they needed when they were most desperate. Should an important key have been mislaid, Godfrey would be able to generate another. Should a ring have been lost in the mud whilst digging, Godfrey would surely provide a replacement.

When he was a child, poor Godfrey had often been accused of stealing because he was always able to produce the lost item that was so earnestly sought by his hapless neighbours. However, it soon became clear that the young man was no thief. Occasionally, the lost items would turn up after they had disappeared and the unfortunate man or woman who had lost the thing would now have two of the same.

Godfrey's method of fabricating the lost item was most strange. He would take a red handkerchief from his pocket, wave it in the air, pass it over his lips, and then open his mouth. There, resting on his pink tongue would be the missing item. Once, Godfrey had even opened his mouth and a lamb clambered out, though this was so painful for the young man that the villagers vowed never again to ask him to recover anything larger than his open maws could easily release.

One pleasant spring morning Godfrey was walking across Skurstead Common when he was struck on the neck by an odious footpad by the name of Nathaniel Hagbarth. As Godfrey fell into the heather, Hagbarth clutched his victim's thin neck with one hand and searched in the kind man's pockets with the other. In a moment the robber had found what he had come for – Godfrey's magical handkerchief. News of the miraculous red cloth had spread to other, less gentle, places and was greatly desired by the greedy and cruel men who lived there.

'Sir! Please! I beg you, do not take my handkerchief!' said Godfrey as he lay bruised on the ground.

'Gah!' sneered Hagbarth, 'A pox on thee, weakling runt!' he replied before running off with the handkerchief into the pine trees.

When the footpad had disappeared, Godfrey picked himself up from the ground, dusted down his jacket, wiped a tear from his eye and walked home.

Later that day, in the grimy neighbouring town of Bitchard, Nathaniel Hagbarth met with his bibulous, dwarfish accomplice Nicholas Wynster in The Slaughtered Cock Inn. Wynster was most adept at thieving when drunk, so he was rarely sober. In a corner of the inn the pimple-faced robber showed Hagbarth his day's snatchings: a glass bowl, two doorknockers and a crumpled pair of velvet curtains stolen from a nearby church. Hagbarth was, in every way, a contrast to this. Not only was he distressingly handsome, but he also had just one pilfered item with him: a red handkerchief.

Wynster laughed mockingly upon spying this:

'What is this, Nathaniel? A scrap of cloth? Thou art growing feeble!'

'Be not quick to judge, cock-mug. There art powers and properties in this square o' cloth that thou dost not ken,' replied Hagbarth.

'Fie! What be so d—d special about that? 'Tis but a lady's hanky!'

'No, Short Nicky, no. I shall prove it. Put your ale down! Answer me this – what have you lost recently?' asked Hagbarth.

'My honour from consorting with a clot-head like thee, for sure!' replied Wynster sardonically.

'Shush,' said Hagbarth, 'what hast thou lost *in truth*?'

Wynster took a sip from his cup and then pursed his thick, wet lips:

'I cannot find my black stockings.'

Hagbarth picked up the handkerchief, waved it in the air, passed it over his lips and opened his mouth. And there, filling the cavity, were a pair of black stockings.

'Ha! So you stole them! Never mind, never mind. Another. I have recently misplaced a pheasant's egg I poached,' said Wynster.

Hagbarth picked up the handkerchief, waved it in the air, passed it over his lips and opened his mouth. And there, filling the cavity, was a cream-coloured pheasant's egg sitting atop Hagbarth's tongue.

'Quite the magician!' exclaimed Wynster. 'One more. My iron file. I dropped that in the gutter outside the debtor's gaol. I wish to see that again.'

Hagbarth picked up the handkerchief, waved it in the air, passed it over his lips and opened his mouth. And there, filling the cavity, was a gleaming metal file.

"Sblood I think you have something here,' said Wynster as he put his bag of loot on the floor. 'Give it me; I shall see if this trickery works on thee!'

Hagbarth handed his villainous mate the handkerchief, who examined it closely. 'Whose name is this embroidered in the corner? Godfrey Watts? Was he not the fellow thou spokest of yesterday?'

"Twas indeed. Now,' said Hagbarth, 'ask me what I have lost, and thy mouth shall receive it.'

With a smirk Wynster picked up the 'kerchief and asked his friend what he had lost.

Hagbarth took another gulp from his flagon of ale: 'Why,' he said, 'when I was a child, I lost my father's pearl-handled dagger.'

Wynster took another sip from his brew, lifted the red handkerchief and waved it in the air as he had seen his accomplice do. He then swiped the cloth along his fat lips.

As Wynster opened his mouth, his body jerked forward and his plump hands began to claw desperately at his hairy throat.

'My friend! My friend! What ails thee?' cried Hagbarth.

Words did not issue from Nicholas Wynster's mouth. Blood did. Blood by the pint and then by the gallon. The whole of The Slaughtered Cock went deathly quiet as Wynster's chair fell backwards, fountains of blood spraying from his gaping mouth. Hagbarth was so drunk, he leapt up to help his friend, but fell over and hit his head on the corner of the table, as Wynster lay dying in an abominable lake of gory red spew.

A justice of the peace was summoned who dispatched the unconscious Nathaniel Hagbarth to the town gaol. He was swiftly tried for the murder of Nicholas Wynster; evidence at his brief trial was shown to the jury – a bloodied pearl-hilted poniard that had been found lodged in the dead man's throat. Hagbarth was hanged for murder one month later.

Godfrey Watts was given back his handkerchief, somewhat redder than it was originally, and he continued to put it to good use for the rest of his days.

A life of criminality can be very enticing for the weaker ones amongst us. Great Grandma Berrial was keen to make this clear to me, and I vividly recall her telling me this story after some of my father's brothers had been over for the evening and were freely telling stories of robbing and murder. They were from the East End, and there was a certain lop-sided glamour about killing a rival fruiterer. Bananas were scarce in the 1940s and some men would stop at nothing to have a bunch on their stall. I was once in a supermarket and watched as someone stood eating monkey nuts from the shelf like she was an anteater loose on a termite mound. I made a citizen's arrest and attracted the attention of the security officer who promptly tackled the miscreant to the ground (this was during an especially fascist period in retail whilst Margaret Thatcher was Prime Minister) and the seven year-old girl was bundled home in the back of a Ford Transit. Theft begets murder, and murder begets murder; I'm sure I was doing God's work when I apprehended her. Even if it was the God from the Old Testament who can be rather harsh. Maybe He turned the supermarket thief into a pillar of salt. I don't know, but whatever He did, I'm sure it was just.

The Gonderfish

What lengths would you go to, to pick a flower you really wanted? I was once given a fine by a very officious little constable for picking a few bunches of daffodils from the grass verge on a motorway. Yes, it was raining quite heavily, and yes, my car could potentially have caused an accident, parked as it was diagonally across the hard shoulder, but I'd put my hazard lights on, so it wouldn't have been my fault if some idiot had ploughed into the boot of my Austin Allegro. I came out of the whole exchange as the winner anyway, as I was only fined two bob, and that was a great deal cheaper than what the florists would've charged for the same quantity of daffodils. The story that follows features a rather lovely flower, but really it's a tale of friendship. Grandma Berrial first told me it after I'd let down my good friend Margaret Stamen rather badly, so unfortunately it dredges up feelings of shame and embarrassment. Why not invite your best friend over right now, fry them something nice, then read this story together with some mood music on the stereo or laptop (however you choose to live your life), whilst holding hands? I think you'll both appreciate the effect.

Deep in Gonderly Woods was a huge lake, as still as a mirror, at the centre of which was a small island. It was said that if a passing maiden were to stop there she would immediately see a most beautiful, lonely pink flower blooming in solitude on the island. The flower was so pretty and the perfume so sweet, that many a young woman had tried to pick it, and all had come to their death in the attempt.

It was a mightily strange place, Gonderly Woods, for a married woman or any man, whatever age, could never see the flower. Once in a generation, a local girl would steal into the wood, perhaps because of a whispered rumour as to what lay there, or maybe because she desired some solitude in the peace of the forest; each maiden unlucky enough to happen upon the pool would surely meet the same fate, and was never seen again.

One day, two friends, Inga and Helena, were talking upon the hearsay of the flower that grew in the forest in the middle of Gonderly Lake, and Helena announced that she was determined to pick the flower, and show it to her friend on return.

Inga begged Helena not to be so foolish, as she had heard that young girls never returned from the woods and she could not bear to lose her friend for such a fancy.

'Hush,' said Helena, 'do not worry so! I shall go tomorrow morning, and when I return in the afternoon, I shall put the flower in your hair, and it shall make you twice as lovely as you are!'

The next day, Helena was true to her word. She walked into Gonderly Woods and, after some trying, came upon Gonderly Lake. To her delight, she saw the pink flower, caught in a ray of sunshine, glowing like a thousand gemstones, and at that moment she decided she had to have it for her friend.

She was just pulling off her stockings so that she could wade into the water, when a queer green light started to form in front of her. Before long the strange glow had formed itself into the shape of a woman, not unlike her, and the figure seemed to be crying great sparkling teardrops, like emeralds.

'Who are you, poor soul? Why do you cry so?' asked Helena.

'I am the one who came before you, and I desired the flower too. I paid for it with my life. Beware the Gonderfish! Beware the Gonderfish!' said the sobbing ghost. 'Quick, my dear,' said the ghost, 'you can ask me but two questions, before I pass; be quick!'

Helena thought about this for a moment then said:

'What will the Gonderfish do if I walk into the water?'

'Eat you! You will be eaten!' cried the spirit.

'How do I kill the Gonderfish?' asked Helena.

'Draw the Gonderfish from the water, my love!' said the sad phantom.

The apparition began to fade, but not before the shade had pointed repeatedly at a fishing rod that lay by the bank. In a few moments, all that remained of the ghost was its fading sobs.

Helena, who was a spirited young woman, was more curious than scared. She considered what the ghost had said and supposed that she was lucky, as all she had to do was catch the Gonderfish on the line, pull it free from the water, and then she would be safe to walk into the pool and pick the flower (which grew more and more beautiful by the moment).

Helena found an earthworm, hooked it on the end of the rod and cast out the line. A few moments later there was a great tugging, and she cried for joy at having caught the Gonderfish so quickly.

She reeled the great slimy beast in and bashed it over the head with a stick. She looked at the fish – it certainly was very large and could easily have eaten her, as it had a very big mouth indeed.

She made sure that the Gonderfish was dead, looked at the glorious pink flower on the island once more (which by now was even more lovely than before), and waded into the lake.

Helena did not return that afternoon, nor was she back by midnight. Inga was inconsolable at the loss of her friend, and was determined to go to Gonderly Woods as soon as dawn had come.

The sun had barely risen before Inga had made her way into the dark forest; she was surprised at how easy it was to find the lake at its centre, almost as if it was calling her. She knew she had found the right spot because there, in the middle of the lake was the island and growing on it was the most radiantly beautiful flower she had ever seen. She cried out her friend's name once, twice, thrice, and then suddenly a green glow appeared before her, which resolved itself into the translucent shape of her dear friend.

'Oh, Helena, can that be you?' asked Inga.

'I am the one who came before you, and I desired the flower too. I paid for it with my life. Beware the Gonderfish! Beware the Gonderfish!' said Helena's sobbing ghost. 'Quick, my dear, you can ask me but two questions, before I pass, be quick!'

Inga thought about what her friend had said, but she was a clever girl, and she asked the question that every maiden before her had failed to ask, and they had paid for it with their lives. She asked this question:

'Helena, you say beware the Gonderfish. Is that one or many fish?'

'Many, my dear, many, many!' said the shade of Helena.

'How many Gonderfish are there in the pool, sweet friend?' asked Inga.

'Five score, no more! Five score, to be sure!' said the phantom of Helena.

Before Helena's ghost faded, she pointed repeatedly at an old fishing rod by the bank of the lake, and then she was gone altogether.

Having asked the right questions, Inga set about fishing out every Gonderfish from the lake. It took her two days and two nights, and by the end of that time, she had pulled one hundred of those ghastly fish out of the water and thrown them on a great belching bonfire she had made.

Trusting her poor dead friend's words, Inga walked into the water and pulled herself safely onto the island. The pink flower was larger and more glorious than ever before – she plucked it.

At that instant, as she held the bloom, the petals of the flower fell from the stem and whirled about in the air before her; the petals grew larger, until they had transformed into the shapes of all the missing girls from over the many centuries – hundreds of them. The last petal to transform was the brightest and rosiest of them all – it was Helena, returned.

This has to be the only folk tale I've heard of whose resolution depends entirely upon an understanding of the trickiness of English grammar. I suppose it's only fair that after many centuries of fish breeding and human illiteracy, someone was bound to come along with an awareness of the singular and plural nouns. Good grief, it was all my English teacher ever talked about, so I take comfort knowing I would have asked the same questions and been just as successful as Inga. I can only speculate as to the field day the men in the nearest village would have had, after three hundred unattached, fragrant maidens came wandering into their midst. Personally, I rather hope that Helena and Inga lived together afterwards, as it would be nice to think that just for once in a folk tale that there was a lesbian love story. I imagine the libraries on the isle of Lesbos must be groaning with such literature; I would go there and find it out for myself, but, alas, I cannot bear the Greek heat.

The Sand Martins

Whether you prefer real-life murder, or the extinction of human life in fictional form, you'll enjoy the following narrative. Personally, I am uncomfortable with all forms of homicide and prefer a torture story with a happy ending. Sadly there's no agonising torment in this tale and if you are a birdwatcher fond of prolonged suffering and punishment, you'll be doubly disappointed because there are no birds in this story either, in spite of the title. Feel free to annotate the text with some evocative adjectives that describe gulls and sandwich terns screeching if you wish. I elected not to add these descriptions into the narrative myself, as I couldn't be bothered — I've got a hundred and one better things to be doing with my time.

Three brothers, who had once been great fishermen, had fallen on hard times and had taken to a life of begging. After their ancient boat had been dashed against rocks in a terrible storm, they had no money left to replace it so they decided to dig nests into the sandy cliff-face, from where they used to set sail, and beg for scraps from passing beach-walkers. This turned out to be a fine arrangement because Frypole Beach was so beautiful that it attracted many people from far and wide, and very generous they were too with the three poor men.

The brothers were all called 'Martin' because they had very unimaginative parents; this earned them the nick-name of the 'Sand Martins' amongst the locals, and even on woeful days when the beach was whipped by lightning and hail, the young girls of the nearby village would bring the Sand Martins stews to help them through the dire weather.

One warm summer's afternoon, the brothers were each sitting inside their sand-holes waiting for another stroller to pass their way. There had already been many visitors to Frypole Beach that day but all the Sand Martins had received were a few strips of salted meat and a handful lard cake each. One of the Sand Martins started piping with excitement when he peered from his hole and spied the approach of a very handsome couple that were perambulating along the flats. The brothers jumped from their hollows and started ambling towards the pair of walkers.

At the sight of the ragged Sand Martins, the woman dropped her parasol and clung to her husband's girth, whimpering in fright. The man, whose name was Colonel Proudport, drew his sword (for he was a military man) and bounded over to the beggars, his face as red as his fine jacket, and despatched a ferocious reprimand:

'How dare you, filthy vagabonds! What is the meaning of this vulgar intrusion?' he cried, 'I should cut you down for spoiling our constitutional!'

'Please, kind sir, called the first Sand Martin, 'we are but humble folk who ask only for a little charity.'

'Yes,' beseeched the second Sand Martin, 'we beg only for alms!'

'I shall show thee *arms*, wretch!' shouted Proudport, and he pulled a pistol from his britches and shot the second Sand Martin through the heart.

Yelling in terror, the two surviving brothers scurried into their holes, whereupon the colonel's wife let out a winsome giggle, for she now found the whole thing very amusing.

'We shall put an end to your scrounging ways!' said Proudport as he brandished his gun. The infuriated colonel pounded up the steep sandbank and blasted the darkened interior of each cavity until he was satisfied the beggars were dead. He descended the bank, smoothed his great drooping moustache, and put an arm around his comely wife.

'Those cadgers shall terrorise us no more, my dear,' he said.

'And the fish shall have a fine supper in him!' laughed the colonel's wife as she pointed at the bloody corpse of the dead Sand Martin with the end of her recovered parasol.

'Indeed,' said the colonel, 'now we must continue our walk; I tire of this dismal spot. I grow hungry for my beef – let us proceed.'

Unfortunately for the terrible Proudport, he had underestimated the Sand Martin's resourcefulness; the brothers had created a honeycomb of tunnels that ran for several miles along the seafront, and they had many a peephole along the couple's intended path up the beach. Trembling with rage, the two brothers scampered and crawled through their tunnels until they were some way ahead of the awful couple that dawdled and pottered about the sands.

The Sand Martins knew that below one great cliff of tottering sand it was only their timber-strutted tunnels that kept it up at all. They tied all the ropes they had to the wooden frames under this portion of cliff and retreated back down the main underground burrow, peering out of a hollow in the cliff further down the beach.

At last, the dallying couple walked past them, so close that they could hear the arrogant colonel's boastful tales and his wife's simpering returns. The brothers said nothing to one another as they waited for the Proudports to walk into their trap.

The instant they were next to the giant sand bank, the brothers gave a mighty heave, and then another, and yet another before the sticks gave way and the mighty scarp subsided in one giant and explosive cascade. The Proudports did not have time to scream, for the sand was on top of them before they could utter a syllable of surprise.

Jubilant, the last two Sand Martins scrambled from their hole and gloried at the new golden tide of sand that had spilt onto the beach. All that was left of the couple was the lady's snapped parasol and the colonel's leather satchel. Inside the bag were two hundred gold coins. The brothers used this money to give their poor younger brother a beautiful funeral; the rest gave the Sand Martins enough money to buy a new boat and a little cottage, overlooking the sea. They fished until they were old men and, if plied with enough rum, they used to delight in telling the story of how a murdering colonel and his cruel wife were defeated by two simple beggars.

There's nothing quite like seeing a toff getting their comeuppance, and Colonel Proudport certainly got his here. Times have changed though, and it's often difficult to make distinctions between the wealthy and the poor in 21st century Britain. I once saw a very haughty fellow in a cashmere polo neck being incredibly abusive to a cashier about her shop not stocking those Sobranie *cocktail cigarettes. After he gave her a very eloquent tongue-lashing and impressing me most distinctly with his pedigree, he spun on his Cuban heel and attempted to leave the corner shop bristling with righteous indignation. Unfortunately, he lost his footing and fell onto the pavement outside, completely shattering his enormous regal chin. A small quantity of unsympathetic Sri Lankan ladies broke into applause at seeing the loquacious complainer topple over. As I walked home, having absent-mindedly shoplifted my week's groceries in the confusion, I got to thinking about the well-heeled man. If he was so wealthy, surely a servant ought to have been buying his cigarettes for him? You just can't tell who's rich and who isn't these days. Even the Queen wears headscarves that look like they've been picked up off a trestle table in a village hall jumble sale. If you might allow me some space to shift this commentary and return to our avian friends, I would say that Auntie Vulna told me that the burrowing bird species riparia riparia (commonly known as the 'sand martin') acquired* *its name from these ingenious digging brothers in the above story. Sadly, old age brings with it many tedious friendships, and I recently became acquainted with an ornithologist called Everett Blesson who told me that my aunt's story was preposterous. I told him that his name was preposterous too, making a mental note never to engage someone in conversation again if they are holding binoculars.*

The Red Hare

Every man, woman and child holding a British passport loves nothing better than to spend the afternoon in the pub with a strong drink, perhaps sharing a jocund anecdote or two, before conversation turns to darker subjects (such as murder, kidnap and rape). I was with my dear Aunt Vulna in a pub on Cable Street when she told me this story. She actually set this tale to music (she was quite adept at the piano) and entertained the saloon with this superbly. Unfortunately I am not at all musical, and present this tale in leaden prose.

There is a public house (The Red Hare) in the small town of Disslenorth in Yorkshire that plays host to a most singular event on St. Lucy's Day every winter. The spectres of each man, woman and child who are to die that year are to be seen walking solemnly to the pub, before enjoying an evening of carousing and merriment within. Before the sun rises, all the people vanish. It is believed to bring bad luck on any soul who peers at the wraiths from without (such as through a window or a carelessly unclosed door) for they too will surely die before twelve months have elapsed. It is believed that the titular Red Hare herself makes an appearance amongst the roistering melee serving pork scratchings and other sundry snacks. The Red Hare is always last to leave, if indeed she makes an appearance, and worse woe befalls any man who meets her in the shadowy lanes of Disslenorth that night. For her name was not gained through any mistake. She is drenched with the blood of late-night passers-by whom she chomps at most terribly with her giant incisors.

This folk-legend is almost impossible not to deconstruct. It is transparently a story put about to stop the police from spoiling a lock-in at the local. It's quite clear to me that all of the merry-makers within disappear because they all go to bed totally pole-axed, including the children, which is a complete disgrace. Aunt Vulna liked a drink or two, and said she had visited the town in the hope of finding the pub. Alas, she found that it had been demolished and, as far as my enquiries could confirm, it is now a Spar supermarket. The Red Hare herself is a more troubling presence and resists an easy explanation such as the one I have forwarded for the revellers. It's not so much the gory nature of the beast, but its implied size that makes me anxious. I once had a rabbit that grew too big for its hutch, so Grandma Berrial removed the mammal from its ill-fitting home and wrung its neck. Needless to say, Susan was served for supper that evening – the flesh was quite odious but at least we ate it *before* it *ate us.*

The Bishop's Diary

Diary writing is a funny pursuit. I have kept a diary since I was a teenager, and on occasion, when the television has broken down and I don't fancy reading another Daphne Du Maurier, I will dip into my archive and surprise myself with how uneventful my life has been. For example, the entry for Friday 17th March 1972 reads like this: 'Woke from more nightmares. Had an egg then went to Woolworths to buy a dustpan and brush. Desmond was cleaning the windows when I got back. Skirt smelled of mothballs, so took it to Sketchley's. Gammon for dinner. Bed.' I'm left wishing

I'd described the nightmares, as that was surely the only interesting thing that happened that day. The narrative below features a much more intriguing diary. I have no idea whether any of the story is based on fact or not — although the main male character had the same name as an ex-lover of Auntie Vulna's, so the whole tale may have been a convoluted way of reproaching him for some heartache she blamed him for. She could be very spiteful, so it's entirely likely that she made this story up.

In the diocese of Bradford there used to live a squat little man called Bishop Richard Widegate. He was well known to be an excessively lazy man who rarely left his palace, only ever doing so if official duties were completely inescapable.

The Bishop was secretive in his ways and indulged in all manner of carnal sins at every opportunity. However, he was foolish enough to keep a very detailed diary of his varied saucy escapades and this he carried with him in a large leather portmanteau wherever he went. The key to the leather case always hung on a fine golden neck-chain that swung about his befatted breasts.

Many an over-curious young servant had tried to free the key from the bishop's neck as he slept, in the hope of reading the diary, but on each and every occasion the holy man would be roused from sleep in a terrible temper and would thrash the youths with his crosier before ravishing them in dozens of improbable ways, and several impossible ones too.

Widegate's pleasure-seeking continued thusly for many decades until one baking summer when he decided that he would have the palace grounds extended so that he could enjoy riding his ponies undisturbed by the peering peasants of the neighbouring village of Brenkham. Unfortunately, to effect this expansion, it meant that the copse by the palace walls would have to be uprooted, along with the stout little cottage that minded its own business in the centre of this idyll. An old crone by the name of Fanny Meades dwelt quietly in the cottage, and she was most horrified one morning when a retinue of palace guards hammered on her door and began to rudely shift her from her beloved home. The old woman begged to be left alone, but the guards listened not: she was manhandled over the threshold and kicked into a ditch before being pelted with sundry items from her property.

Now quite homeless, Fanny spent the night sweating with rage in a disused kiln, plotting her revenge on the heartless Bishop Widegate who had demolished her home without a single qualm. Like all the villagers of Brenkham, Fanny Meades was well aware of the bishop's lewd diary, having heard tales from fleeing servants who had caught a glimpse of the sordid journal. It was said to be illustrated with the most extraordinarily lewd sketches that betrayed a precocious talent in the depiction of human anatomy, alongside dozens of inventive designs for mechanical devices whose purposes were most ungodly.

Fanny's sole desire was to confiscate the diary and humiliate the foul bishop for all of the torment and misery he had caused her. She was well acquainted with the Old Ways of witchcraft and she still kept her familiar, a narrow little ferret with an enormous head called Dunkpot, close by her.

That night, Fanny instructed Dunkpot to slither into the Bishop's Palace and steal the wicked diary from the sleeping primate. The ferret duly obeyed and pattered and scuttled down many corridors before reaching Widegate's bedchamber. With supernatural celerity, the little ferret darted over to the recumbent man and chewed off the key from its neck-chain, before scampering off with both book and key in his vice-like jaws.

Fanny Meades was delighted with her familiar's return and patted him most tenderly for his endeavours.

The old woman wasted no time in the commencement of her revenge.

With Dunkpot in her apron pocket, she strode over to the palace walls, opened the loathsome book and began, at great volume, to read aloud its outrageous contents.

Moments later, as she boomed a description of the bishop's youthful encounter with a sea-lion, a window in the palace's upper storey blazed with light, and Widegate's dewlapped head poked out, shouting most furiously at this indignity, vowing swift death on the thief. Fanny laughed heartily and dashed off into the nearby wood, warmed by her successful night of insults and the public disgrace she had heaped onto her enemy.

Well, old Miss Meades spent the next twelve nights repeating the humiliation, and she began to draw some very appreciative crowds from Brenkham village who revelled in her lurid theatrical readings of Widegate's squalid adventures. On the twelfth night, during her latest oration, the bishop had been wily enough to conceal himself in some bushes by the palace wall, and he leapt onto the woman as she read. A fierce struggle ensued, both throttling one another in a protracted battle. Fanny's audience had left swiftly, for they desired not to suffer the bishop's wrath should they be caught and subjected to his odious degradations. Gradually, the couple's struggles – the bishop clawing at Fanny's back as she continued to free his seamy prose into the night air – led them to the edge of a great lily pond; soon the pair fell in, and were drowned in their grappling battle.

For some unknown reason (though it is likely as a result of witchcraft), the Church had both

Widegate and Meades's remains interred in the same crypt at the nearby abbey. Embarrassed by the wretched diary, church officials demanded that the execrable tome was entombed with him, to rot and wither with his body. However, any visitor to this underground vault, even to this day, will see that whenever the gate is opened to inspect the room, the bishop's coffin lid is always upended, his skeletal hands seemingly clutching at the wholly absent diary. Should such a visitor care to wonder where the diary got to, he or she need only prise open the lid of the neighbouring coffin to find the smiling corpse – remarkably incorrupt – of Fanny Meades, her hands fastened to a mouldering book, filled with fading obscenities.

Richard Widegate wasn't the first man fuelled by decadent lusts and he certainly won't be the last. I often access the Internet at the Watney Market Library and the whole thing seems to be full of men describing their lascivious adventures to the whole world. At least Widegate kept his philandering tales under lock and key. After I've tired of reading these men's blogs, I tend to use the library photocopier to run off some 5p duplicates of a birthday card I bought back in the late 1990s. I would really encourage you to do the same as card shops really do charge far too much for something that only gets thrown in the bin. Last week I only spent 35p on photocopying; you may suppose that this means that I have a lot of friends, what with having seven acquaintances with birthdays in just one week. Sadly, this is a result of me losing my address book about ten years ago, so I had to try and draw all of my pals' names and addresses from memory. I was not very successful in recalling this information, and as a result, I think I have generated almost four hundred imaginary friends who may or may not have ever existed in the first place. I also stopped putting stamps on the envelopes years ago because you can buy a whole tin of spaghetti for the price of a second-class stamp. I really have no idea whether any of my photocopied birthday cards ever get to anyone.

The Crows of
Whitesaddle Woods

Last year, I spotted my tedious neighbour Lillian Bynster whilst I was out walking in Regents Park, and I felt obliged to sit with her a while after she waved me down. During a very dreary story about a refund she was pursuing for a rubber shower mat, I was thrilled by the sudden appearance of squirrel who very boldly jumped up onto the armrest of the bench we were sitting on, before taking my offering of half a ginger biscuit I had been nibbling. Impressed by this, Lillian threw her sandwich on the ground, declaring that she had grown bored of the egg mayonnaise and that the squirrel was welcome to it. The rodent ignored this benefaction, jumped off the bench and scurried up into a nearby sycamore tree. Humiliated by the rejection, Lillian shouted at the squirrel: 'You stupid animal, I've just given you half a sandwich,' before tutting crossly. This got me thinking about how idiotic it is to cast judgements on the beasts of this world; I felt fine about judging Lillian as stupid, but to call an animal stupid seemed absurd. We haven't the first idea about what is really going on in their furry, feathery, scaly or sticky heads. Please bear this in mind as you read the story below.

One warm spring day in Whitesaddle Woods, two crows were sitting side-by-side on their great messy tangle of a nest when Cock Crow heard a splitting sound. He flapped his great wings and perched himself on a higher branch before peering down at the knot of twigs where his wife, Hen Crow, was still sleeping in the pleasant dappled sunshine.

'Hen Crow!' he squawked, 'Hen Crow! Wake Up! Our egg is hatching!'

'Hush, hush, Cock Crow!' replied his feathery wife. 'You'll wake all the owls in the woodland with your cries! 'Tis our twenty-second chick! We know what to expect!' she replied.

Then Hen Crow ruffled her beautiful black plumes and flew up to join her husband on the branch. She tilted her head sideways and looked into the bowl of the nest.

'Aye,' she said, 'it fair be comin'. Now you rush off and fetch a mouse for Chick Crow. I'd best be about warmin' 'im as he breaks out.'

Cock Crow did as he was told and flew off to the field to catch a mouse.

When he came back two minutes later, the chick had splintered its shell and sat chirruping beneath its mother's feathers. Cock Crow had found the biggest mouse in the field, but Chick Crow wouldn't take it. Both parents were quite surprised with this.

'Silly Chick!' chided Hen Crow softly, 'Why eat you not this lovely mouse?'

'May I have a worm, mother?' asked their featherless son. Hen Crow and Cock Crow looked at each other with concern.

'Or a grasshopper? I fancy a slug. Are there any slugs?' said the infant bird.

'I…suppose there be some round 'ere', said Cock Crow.

'Your father be most skilled at catching voles. What say you to a vole, my dear?' said Hen Crow, quite discomfited by their chick's less than wholesome appetite.

However, no matter what manner of furry creature they brought to the nest, their babe would not eat it. Eventually Cock Crow gave up catching them and had to fetch caterpillars and beetles instead. He was most ashamed to be doing this for all the other woodland birds laughed at his new catches, as they were so small and puny that they certainly didn't befit the diet of a crow. A nuthatch fell off its tree trunk with mirth when he caught sight of Cock Crow plucking ladybirds from the old lime tree.

Day in, day out, both parents took it in turns to prey on the smallest of the forest's beasties. After a month of doing this, the crows were getting quite tired and grouchy, and they often used to fly off from the nest and discuss their queer chick.

Well, that evening, they caught a couple of farm rats and ate them with relish before returning to the nest. Hen Crow leant over her chick, who was by now quite large, and said:

'Now, Chick Crow, thou is grown mighty big. I think ye shall have a shrew for supper.'

'Yes,' said Cock Crow, 'a shrew. A juicy fat shrew. Now what say you?'

'Cuckoo' said Chick Crow.

Cock Crow's feathers shuddered. 'What did ye say?' he asked nervously.

'Cuckoo!' echoed Chick Crow. 'Cuckoo! Cuckoo! Cuckoo!'

And with that, Chick Crow fledged the nest, spreading his thick, grey wings, which seemed to glow gold at the tips, as he flew off toward the rising moon.

Make of the above story what you will. Is it a criticism of short-sighted parents? Is it a document that censures the greed of children? Is it a reproof for the perceived silliness of nuthatches? I think I'll let you decide. For me, it plays on my deep-seated fears of the invasion of the domestic space, and I've a story of my own about that. To cut a long story moderately short, an unemployed Korean tree surgeon had exploited the fact that I'd left my front door unlocked and he had moved into my spare bedroom. He was fond of playing very fast music rather loudly on his cassette player and he wouldn't accept my argument that there are only lazy tree surgeons or employed ones, what with there being so many trees in this world of ours. Rather than getting cross with him when he slammed the door shut on me and continued listening to his pop music, I decided the clever way to eject him would be to befriend him. I made him a welcome cake, whose mixture contained enough crushed codeine tablets to lay out a Swiss ox for a fortnight. I leant against the doorjamb as he scoffed the offering, and he even accepted a glass of Desmond's old scotch, which I had also laced with codeine. In a matter of moments he was slurring his words; a minute later he was asleep. The rest of the story is less pleasant; I received an upbraiding from a circuit judge at the local Magistrates' Court for this 'misdemeanour', but I did have my house back to myself, and I have my own resourcefulness and eloquence in the dock to thank for that. Whilst the libellous news report that followed was quite embarrassing for me, I was amused to discover that the squatter's name was Ken Khoo, which does sound a bit like 'cuckoo.'

Black Har

As a keen amateur psychoanalyst, I'm well aware that Sigmund Freud believed that the horror associated with the loss of body parts like the eyes or fingers is in fact just a substitute for a much more troubling fear: the dread of the loss of some part off of our toilet area(s). I make the disclaimer now that I am in no way responsible for drawing to the surface any of your darkest anxieties that you have complacently buried in the sewage-strewn chambers of your unconscious mind. As I detail in the analysis after the story, I am still greatly troubled by the symbols and images of this folk tale. Unfortunately, I cannot afford the airfare to New York to find a reputable psychotherapist. The sweats I suffer nightly as a result of this story, and the never-ending laundering of fresh sheets, are, I suppose, a small price to pay in comparison to Virgin Atlantic's fees.

Drearslow was a small village in the Wystan Valley, perpetually troubled by fog. Even in summer the villagers worked outdoors swaddled in layers of linen and wrapped in woollen coats and cloaks. It was, in every other way, an unremarkable place, except for one very strange and fearsome inhabitant. His name was Black Har and he lived in the marsh on the edge of Drearslow. For as long as any villager could remember, the marsh was a place to avoid, for Black Har would use every trick he had to lure unsuspecting fools into his domain, whereupon he would bite off their fingers and toes.

Sometimes Black Har would imitate the voice of a female, crying to unwary passers-by that she was stuck; sometimes he would send sweet smells of baking bread and meat wafting over the marsh to tempt the hungry into his miasma. The villagers had grown wise to this perfidious trickery, but it didn't stop the occasional travelling stranger from having his or her digits chomped off by the creature.

Perhaps the reason why Black Har was regarded with such terror was because no one had ever properly seen him. For sure, survivors of his dread nibblings reported that he was indeed very large and very black, but quite what he was was still something of a mystery to all in Drearslow. Some said he was like a great growling cat; others claimed he was more like a hellhound with a dozen slavering heads; some insisted he was a dragon, and there were those who declared that he was more like a great dark jelly or slug, the size of a horse.

Whatever Black Har was, he was best avoided – the villagers knew that.

Well, one day there was a terrible storm in Wystan Valley. It was so severe that many great and ancient trees were torn from the soil and tossed hundreds of yards from whence they were rooted. Even the stout and sturdy cottages and barns and stables had been given a terrible lashing, and the whole village was littered with the shredded and splintered detritus of buildings and trees and dead or dying farm animals.

Black Har had not escaped the wicked winds either; in fact, his marsh had been at the very centre of a mighty whirlwind. Most of the smashed and ruined rubble of Drearslow village had been swept into his marsh; the wicked vortex had swept Black Har up into the sky, cocooned him in the dross and debris, before hurling him back into the ruined marsh.

It took the Drearslow folk a long time to repair their village, but eventually this task was complete. One benefit that appeared to have come from the storm was that Black Har seemed to have been killed, for he was no longer heard, smelt or seen to be tempting anyone into his marsh. No one really checked to see if the storm had been Black Har's demise because the bog was dangerous enough with its choking gases and swamps.

Time passed, although in the decades that followed Black Har was not forgotten about entirely. He passed into legend and bedtime stories to frighten intrepid youngsters from leaving their mother's watchful gaze and wandering into dangerous places.

But Black Har had not died. Tangled as he was in ropes and branches and nets and six dozen other knotted things, he was tied fast in a great bundle of litter and lumber and was barely able to move. He was so muffled by the rubbish that his cries and impersonations could not be heard; he spent his wretched days inching painfully through the mud, and if he was lucky he might suck a minnow through a tiny hole in his imprisoning faggot. Thusly did Black Har eke out his days in the marsh, slowly starving and cussing.

One cool day in early autumn, many years after the storm, a pair of travellers was walking through Drearslow on their way to Canterbury.

The older of the two had gone to the inn for supper, but the other, a lad by the name of Dick Bulburton, had taken a stroll over to the marsh, to enjoy some much-needed solitude. The weather was pleasantly chilling after the day's hot walk, and the boy found the puddles and ponds of Drearslow marsh quite appealing, in spite of the addled stench. The chirruping bluethroats and trills of the water pipits lulled him into a pleasant stupor; he eased his back onto a great mossy rock he had found some way into the marsh, and fell into a doze.

When Dick awoke, he instantly realised he must have been asleep for many hours because the last rays of sunshine were just disappearing behind the Wystan hills. The marsh had become quite unfamiliar in the gloaming light and the mists had risen all about him. Dick Bulburton was a bold lad, and he was not afraid; indeed, even as he began to hear a soft, heavy slithering sound he was sure this was rescue of some sort.

'Hulloo there!' Dick shouted.

There was no reply, but the sliding, writhing sound of moving mud seemed to be growing more distinct.

'I say again, hulloo there!' repeated Dick.

All of a sudden the mist cleared slightly and he saw amongst the thickening gloom what appeared to be a great damp bonfire mound within arm's reach of his stone. For perhaps the first time in his life Dick shuddered with alarm when he noticed that the great heap of sticks and leaves moved with an unsteady lurch towards him.

'What game is this? Who's trying to frighten Dick Bulburton?' demanded the boy, trying to sound as valorous as possible.

'Why don't you answer me, villain?' said Dick.

The clod of branches seemed to tremble a little, before heaving itself even closer.

'Come out of your heap or I'll pull you out!' said Dick.

From deep within the mound of litter Dick was sure he heard a feint rasping sound.

At his wit's end, Dick leapt from his rock and began to tear at the strange tumulus of sticks.

'I'll soon have you out of there! Why, perhaps you're a poor child all caught up,' he said as he tore at the slimy mass. Soon, young Dick had ripped a hole in the bundle big enough to peer inside – he did so, but all was black within.

'Well, something must be in there!' said Dick, 'Here, take my hand and let me see if I cannot pull you out,' he said.

Dick should not have put his hand inside, for, of course, Black Har was within and had been waiting for many a year to chew on a finger or two again. Dick screamed as his little finger was bitten clean off, and almost fainted with shock upon withdrawing his hand from the hummock of rubbish to see but four fingers only on his hand. He kicked Black Har's cocoon savagely before tearing off his stocking and binding his bleeding hand.

'By God's name I shall kill you, monster!' he shouted as he began to splash and stumble across the marsh towards the dim lights of the village, and away from the awful heap.

The good folk of Drearslow were most appalled and sickened by young Dick's injury when he ran into the inn and told his story. Limping Edward, the oldest man in Drearslow, clacked his tongue and announced that Black Har had returned, as his grandfather had prophesied many years ago. The villagers chattered nervously and drew the sign of the cross; if anything Black Har's absence had magnified his fearsome status and no one alive could recall the days when the village had lived knowingly but grudgingly side-by-side with the beast.

However, Dick was a canny fellow and he asked three questions at that moment that should have been asked many, many years ago.

'Did any of your grandparents ever mention seeing this 'Black Har' outside of the marsh?' asked Dick. The villagers shook their heads and Limping Edward declared that such a thing had never been mentioned.

'Very well,' said Dick. 'What feeds the marsh?'

Limping Edward said: 'Why, that's Placket Stream, what runs off the Wystan River, young Dick.'

'Good,' said Dick as another stab of pain pulsed where his finger had been. 'My last question is this: does anyone need the marsh?'

The villagers all quickly agreed that the marsh was a blight and not a soul amongst them had any use for it.

'I have an idea,' said Dick. 'As soon as it is light to-morrow will a few of you come and meet me by Placket Stream?'

Limping Edward spoke for all the assembled drinkers in the inn when he said 'By Gad, we will! I have a fair idea what you're saying, lad. We'll see Black Har off for good! Ho-ho!'

He emptied his pot of ale and ordered another for himself and one for Dick Bulburton too.

Well, the very next day, Dick and fifteen others gathered by the stream and set to work digging a great, deep trench that looped around the back of the village and re-joined the thundering Wystan River by a bank of swaying hazel trees. Though in great pain, Dick was the one to dig the last shovel of soil that sent the Placket rolling down its new route. He set his spade down and gazed satisfyingly into the murky Drearslow marsh. Now all he had to do was wait.

During all of this work, Black Har had managed to free himself from his abominable burden of tangled branches and had set to work on trying to entice others back into his bogs. However, the villagers knew his game, and waited patiently for nature to take its course.

Before long, the marsh began to dry out. Black Har could scarcely find even a midge to eat, and his cries became more desperate than ever. He was defeated because he could not leave his marsh or he would surely perish. In desperation, he began to tunnel underground to find more stagnant water as everything on the surface had all but dried up. Down, down, down he dug, muttering and swearing as he did so. Eventually the earth closed in on him and he was forced to continue digging, snapping and gnawing at worms as he dug ever deeper in search of water.

After many years he emerged on the other side of the Earth, in Australia, where he found a pleasantly stinking billabong to live in. Many curious folk sought out this new beast living in their creek, and for their troubles had their fingers confiscated. Ask any Australian about him, and they'll tell you a tale or two, though he's not known as Black Har anymore. For now he is known only as the Bunyip, though he would never deign to mention how he was once defeated on the other side of the world by a young pilgrim called Dick Bulburton.

Many years ago I became interested in my family tree before becoming very disinterested in it, as they're all effectively strangers who didn't bother to put any cash away in a bank account for needy descendants. I did discover that two of my cousins were exiled to Australia after stealing six sausages between them. Whilst this punishment might seem harsh to some of you, I can't help supposing that they were being sent on the holiday of a lifetime for the tempting price of minus six sausages. If this retribution was still statutory, I imagine every Tom, Dick and Harry would be looting all the butcher's shops in the kingdom, so it's no wonder that they repealed it. Part of me feels rather pleased that the Antipodes also got Black Har, though the logical side of my nature tells me he might have encountered some trouble tunnelling through the rather tough silicate mantle of planet Earth, let alone burrowing through the molten core at the centre of this blue-green orb we call home.

The Travelling Man's Barrel

It's not only authority figures that we need to listen to carefully — sometimes the humble street vendor has something important to say. Most Big Issue *salesmen and women have interesting stories to tell, though I've never once stopped to ask any of them what they are. Anyway, I'm completely cash-free these days because of my Visa debit card, and I don't see why I should have to weigh my purse down with twenty-pence pieces to buy a lifestyle magazine. I acquired my lifestyle many years ago, and I won't have anyone tell me how to live my life.*

Besides, twenty-pence pieces are heptagons, and that means there's a good chance you'll be poked in seven different ways by the same object, should you choose to carry one about your person.

The village folk of Marrowpleaze made an unfortunate home in that Staffordshire town for it was such a long distance from fresh water that all the women (and even some men) had to travel many miles each day to fetch pails of the stuff. One year there was a dreadfully parching summer that baked even the nearest streams into trenches of dust, and the winter that followed was so bitter that whatever water remained was frozen quite solid. The villagers were near their wit's end when a stranger appeared in their town, promising an end to their ordeal. For the mysterious be-ragged traveller presented them with a great oak barrel and declared that they need never fret again.

'This fine black barrel,' proclaimed the traveller, 'shall supply limitless water, as if from the freshest brook.'

The villagers gasped. One old spinster walloped her thighs with joy. The crowd cheered, but Mrs Mynnder, a shrewish and incredulous old floor-wiper bawled:

'I do not believe, ye! 'Tis some sorcery!'

'Nay, madam. See for yourself!' replied the stranger.

And with that, Mrs Mynnder picked up her skirts and tottered over to the water barrel. She twisted the iron tap and water rushed forth in a torrent that filled a hollow in the nearby field, whereupon it became a lake of glittering pure water.

The traveller laughed jovially, which annoyed the old woman tremendously. The applause from the gathered company was tremendous, but Mrs Mynnder, cross at having been made a fool of, hobbled off to her cottage complaining darkly of witchcraft. The villagers, overjoyed at this magical bounty, cared not for how these things came to be, and celebrated instead their deliverance from thirst. One-eyed Arthur, the village elder, began to dance with happiness, although his jig was halted when the traveller climbed upon his horse and announced in a loud voice:

'The water shall be yours in perpetuity. But beware: for you must never prise open the lid of the barrel to discover how the water flows so plentiful and abundant. A terrible fate awaits the curious who do not heed my words!' Having said that, the traveller kicked his mare and galloped off over the hill.

Over the next fortnight the villagers made great sport in the new ponds and lakes that gushed from the magic barrel and brewed much beer, which was imbibed in great abandon. But Mrs Mynnder was still sore from her humiliation and she was determined to discover the secrets of the keg, regardless of the warnings from the village's enigmatic benefactor.

One March night, Mrs Mynnder waited until the villagers were snoring in their cots before creeping over to the barrel by the meadow gate. Removing the flesh-hook and skimmer spoon she had concealed in her cape, she ground and twisted the utensils until the lid of the water cask opened with a sigh. Upon doing this, the old crone be-heard a great, sorrowful sobbing coming from within the keg and peered into its depths to espy the source of the melancholic blubberings. Within the tub she was most dismayed to see the tiny shrunken forms of four dozen weeping and withered hags.

One of the doll-like faces turned to Mrs Mynnder and said 'O! Another! There is another!'

'What devilry is this?' cried Mrs Mynnder.

'Why,' whimpered the shrivelled little woman, 'the devilry is in you! We all once pried as you have done, and now we are cursed to remain here forever! Our tears make the water, and the water is so bitter it is quite unsalted. You must join us too!'

Mrs Mynnder, seized by a panic, tried to reach for the barrel's lid at her feet, but as she did so the thing lifted itself up and batted her into the firkin before plugging itself firmly back on top.

The water flowed more plentifully than ever the next day when one-eyed Arthur turned the spigot.

After trying to enter into Grandma Berrial's attic one Sunday afternoon, I was very solemnly slippered for this offence and made to listen to this story as my grandmother shouted it though an ear-trumpet at me. Quite why the curious are always scolded (or in poor Mrs Mynnder's case diminished and imprisoned), is beyond me, as all scientific endeavour surely comes from such a natural instinct. This story has affected me for nearly my whole life, and even to this day, I am very wary of opening a tin of soup and use the can-opener very timidly. I often think of Mrs Mynnder when I run a bath or wash some cabbage leaves. I tend to salt the water when I'm boiling the leaves as well, so it's not uncommon for a whole half-hour to go by when I'm thinking just of Mrs Mynnder and nothing else. This usually results in me totally ruining the supper I'd planned as the water boils over and the cabbage dissolves.

Twenty-Noses

Imagine if you will, finding yourself in a hypothetical world where you were forced to relinquish one of your senses. I'm sure most of you would quickly surrender your olfactory faculties (or 'sense of smell' to the laymen amongst you). People these days are so busy trying to mask one scent with that of another that no one knows or cares about what a real smell is anymore. Once, I was lucky enough to spend a day at a sewage treatment works and found the whole experience remarkably honest, as it's a hapless task trying to spray the place with lavender air-

freshener. The men who worked there were very straightforward and practical, and I really admired their integrity. It may be surprising to hear that most sewage plants have wonderful visitor centres, although they are quite interactive, so I would recommend bringing along your own detergent hand-cleanser. The short story that follows is full of wonderful smells – it is greatly enhanced if you acquire something that has been evacuated by a meat-eating mammal and place that next to yourself whilst reading. For a fully evocative and sanitary experience, a bar of antiseptic soap should be close at hand too.

A wicked woman called Esther Hands consorted with the Devil and became pregnant with his child. Being an unmarried woman, she bound her fattening belly and took herself into the woods when it was time to give birth to the damned kelpie. Esther died with shock upon looking at the ghastly baby when it finally emerged from her womb, for it had no features on its face except for twenty snorting noses. The infant crawled from where its mother lay and took its nourishment from inhaling strong smells, as it had no mouth to feed from.

Twenty-Noses snaffled about the forest floor drawing in the rich scents of the woodland, all the time growing steadily stronger. One day when Twenty-Noses had exhausted all the odours of the leaf mulch, he staggered into the nearest town and gloried in the dung-heaps; it was not long before he had drawn out the smell of manure so completely that he was ravenous to find new odours to feast upon. The best of these were unwashed children, for they stunk so strongly that Twenty-Noses would creep into their rooms at night and terrify the grubby babes with his nocturnal sniffs and wheezes. Even clean children were not safe, because if they used too much soap to wash with, Twenty-Noses would seek them out too, scratching at their soft skin to release the scent of carbolic.

One young lad called Robin McDunnock grew so tired of Twenty-Nose's intrusions (whether or not he was clean or soiled) that he followed the monster after one night's prolonged sniffing down to the coal shed where he liked to sleep because the smell was so strong. He lit a match and yelled, 'Here be an end to you, Twenty-Noses!' and set the coal shed ablaze. The Devil appeared in the flames of the fire and snatched his child away, cursing at what the small fellow had done.

Grandma Berrial used to like telling this story to me because it was a useful way of admonishing me if I was too dirty after playing in the garden. 'Scrub your hands, Kitty!' she used to say, 'Or Twenty-Noses will be after you tonight!' Not only was that an effective deterrent, but, it was also a handy way of berating me for using too much soap, as the same threat of this dreadful night-time visitant would be levelled should I have been less than thrifty when washing myself. It was a terrible double bind, but at least it taught me the value of thriftiness. I can cut slices of Spam thinner than anybody else I know and my Austin Allegro still has the same tank of petrol that I pumped into it in 1981. It's true to say that the corollary of this is that I cannot actually drive my car anywhere, but it does allow me to enjoy the many pleasures of walking. One such pleasure is bumping into old friends on the pavement. Now, if I bumped into friends on the pavement whilst I was driving, that would be quite a different story. I really do thank my late grandmother for instilling the virtue of frugality in me at such a young age.

The Brilby Marriage Stone

Brilby is a pleasant, if somewhat marshy market town in Lincolnshire. Prior knowledge of medieval marriage customs is not strictly necessary to make sense of this story, though it might be useful. I would urge you to make a visit to your local municipal library and do some research, as these places are a veritable mine of information. A small note of caution, however: if you do borrow a book from the library, you must return it on time or you will be liable to a penalty fine and your minor crime will be in the government database forever. This electronic information will most likely outlive you, and your execrable conduct will stand as a damning testimony to your character for generations to come. If you do not have children it does not mean this blot on your character will necessarily be forgotten either. People are very keen these days to trace their family trees. It would be embarrassing for you if this stain against your name re-emerged in the twenty-third century.

During the reign of King John in the early 1200s, marriage had been prohibited by the Pope, so courting couples used to make their vows by holding hands through a large eight-foot aperture in a gigantic standing stone next to Brilby Priory. The Abbot of the monastery was a kindly man who tolerated this symbolic union, but he warned all who chose to make their vows there to be on their guard. For there was another holed stone nearby, somewhat smaller, whose orifice was just large enough to permit the passage of a small person's body (people were much smaller then, more like twenty-first century toddlers, so moving through the hole wasn't as tricky as it would be today). This stone had the rather blunt name of the 'Evil Stone'.

One warm summer night, an amorous fellow named William and his darling Sarah were truly intoxicated by mead and pledged themselves to be married at the Brilby stone. Unfortunately, in their inebriated state, both mistook the Evil

Stone for the good one. Laughing, they both wrestled their way through the small stone's breach and they were instantly transformed into lapwings, before being netted and then drawn down under the stone into the faerie kingdom for an eternity of torture.

I strongly suspect that a Catholic supporter of the Pope may have been behind this sordid tale, but it is also strongly didactic about the perils of alcohol. I have become something of a collector of smaller holed-stones (sometimes referred to as 'hag-stones') and often wear them as talismans when I am feeling especially apprehensive about leaving the house (muggings are sadly rather common in Shadwell). I have even attached them with superglue to my old service revolver, which I carry with me in my handbag. The charm has certainly worked, as I have never once needed to threaten a villain with my gun. I would have absolutely no compunction about shooting a robber in the head if such violence was called for.

The Pineapple

When I desire something, I ask myself why I do, and then I deny myself that thing I so ardently wish for. The next thing I do is to find something similar but a great deal cheaper and buy that instead. This technique has worked very well for me over the years, and I think, as a result, I'm a good deal more stable than the rest of the consumers on this planet. I'm almost always in a state of partial satisfaction, whereas others spend their lives passionately desiring something, then either being hugely disappointed that they can't afford it, or deeply upset when they do buy the thing and it breaks - leaving them out of pocket and miserable. The following folk story illustrates the dangers of covetousness and the wickedness that often attends it. At the very least this story should make you think twice before you fork out for a pineapple again.

A grand manor house used to stand in the town of Mosset-cum-Sagley and its sole occupant for many a long year was an exceedingly wealthy man called Antony Bladdermine. The manor house itself was most singular on account of its enormous tower and Bladdermine would spend hours watching from the top of the turret as he waited for his goods to arrive.

Bladdermine was an obsessive collector of exotic foreign items; there was not a corner of the globe that he had not sent his servants to in order to acquire more precious things for his collection. The townsfolk had never paid much heed to the wagons of cargo that often thundered through Mosset-cum-Sagley on their way to Bladdermine's manor; truth be told, he was rather feared – not for anything he'd done but there were many rumours about the terrible and frightful things in his private museum. The residents of the town were content for Antony Bladdermine to privately get on with his hoarding in the dark cells and corridors of his large home.

Normally, Bladdermine's acquisitions would arrive under the cover of great sheets or locked up in enormous boxes, but that was to change one fateful day.

Unusually, Bladdermine had one day ordered two of his servants to paste a quantity of large posters around the town square, seemingly to advertise his latest imported purchase. This is what the poster read:

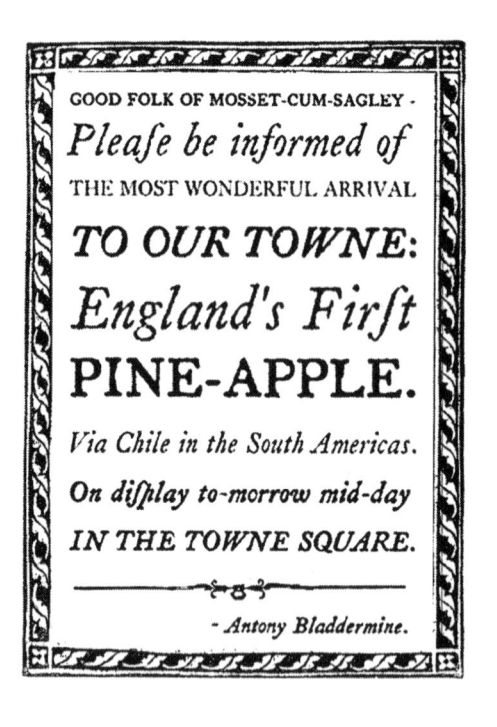

> GOOD FOLK OF MOSSET-CUM-SAGLEY -
> *Pleafe be informed of*
> THE MOST WONDERFUL ARRIVAL
> **TO OUR TOWNE:**
> *England's Firft*
> **PINE-APPLE.**
>
> *Via Chile in the South Americas.*
> *On difplay to-morrow mid-day*
> *IN THE TOWNE SQUARE.*
>
> - *Antony Bladdermine.*

Before long, the whole town was excitedly talking about the arrival of the mysterious fruit. Many of the folk were not rich and had never tasted anything more fantastic than an occasional wild strawberry and the residents of the town began to slaver in anticipation of the exotic pineapple's arrival, even though they knew full well that Antony Bladdermine would never allow them to take a bite of the fruit.

True to his word, at midday a large cart clattered onto the town square's cobbles and Bladdermine, who had made a very rare appearance amongst the townspeople, was there to untie the hessian shroud that protected the package beneath.

Bladdermine held aloft a bright red box before theatrically undoing the gold clasp and lifting the hinged lid. He then ceremoniously placed the box back down onto the wagon seat below. The crowd were in a frenzy of excitement; children clung to their mothers' skirts, men stood with their arms crossed pretending to be unbothered and the women giggled nervously. Bladdermine bent down over the large box and seemed to discourse or whisper to the concealed fruit within. This caused much merriment amongst the people, though Bladdermine seemed either not to notice this or to care. He reached down into the box, adjusting the thing inside most carefully then held an enormous prickly pineapple high in the air.

The crowd roared with appreciation, as if Perseus himself was displaying the severed head of the gorgon Medusa. When the noise had died down, Bladdermine addressed the throng:

'Ladies and gentlemen, boys and girls! Here in my hands is England's first pineapple, as fresh as the day it was picked in Araucanía in Chile.' He patted the spiny fruit tenderly and swept his gaze over the crowd.

'They say that the flesh of this pineapple is like liquid gold! Can you imagine?' he asked. 'No. No, I suppose not – after all what would any of you, or indeed I, know of such a heavenly taste, when we have all made do with a few withered and frost-soured berries at best?'

The crowd nodded in agreement.

'But, do not accuse me of meanness. I wish to share some of this fruit with but one of you – just one slice. This is what will happen: first, the pineapple must mature for four days. Its taste will be all the better. On the fifth day I will invite one of you to dine with me at the manor house, and we shall share in the nectar that pours forth from this jewelled fruit. What say you?' asked Bladdermine.

By now the crowd was almost out of control – they cheered and stomped their clogged feet and hugged one another – this was certainly the most thrilling prospect any of them had ever experienced.

'Good,' shouted Bladdermine over the din. 'I will now away with my pineapple to the manor. My servants will take down your names on the scrolls of parchment they bear, for I fear you are all too illiterate to write your own names. I go now; good luck to each and every one of you. For someone standing amongst you today will taste this divine pudding in five days. Farewell!'

Bladdermine's cart drove off as he gently replaced the fruit in its red box, attended by cheers from the people of Mosset-cum-Sagley. Dutifully, his two servants began the long process of recording each and every name of the waiting townsfolk.

Four days passed, and the good folk of the town could barely contain their excitement. They wondered and chattered about whom it would be, and were making guesses about which name would be chosen in the lottery that they had heard would be drawn that very night.

However, there was one young man called Fabian Gristleby, a bean seller, who wanted so desperately to be the one, that he prepared himself to do a terrible thing. After days of agonising, he had won the battle with his conscience and had decided that that night he would break into Bladdermine's manor and eat the entire pineapple for himself.

When night fell, Gristleby donned his father's cloak and stole into the dark of night. He was most anxious not to be recognised, so he had smeared his face in cow dung before he left his cottage. The night was still and warm and the sharp hoots and calls of night birds only served to prove to the young man how uncomfortable and nervous he was. However he was resolute: the pineapple had to be his. He reasoned that someone would have to win anyway, so it might as well be him. As for Bladdermine – he could easily afford a dozen more pineapples.

Fabian Gristleby was somewhat surprised at how easy it was to gain ingress into the manor house – the door was not even locked. Even more surprisingly, he found that the red box surely containing his prize, was sitting on a long table in the great hall, quite unguarded.

Gristleby licked his lips as he crept silently over to the table. The fool Bladdermine had even been remiss enough to leave a candle burning which only served to help the thief and deepen the scarlet blush of the box. He was about to open the catch of the case when he saw the two scrolls of names lying just behind the box, almost out of sight. Gristleby could not resist finding out who the intended winner of the lottery had been, as he would enjoy the wordless and private gloating this would afford him.

He unfurled the first scroll and noticed how each of the names had been scored through on that sheet. He flattened out the second sheet of paper and gasped with astonishment – all names but his had been scratched out: he was the winner!

Gristleby could not resist a quiet laugh at his good fortune. But then a strange thing happened. There must have been a weird echo in the manor house, because he had stopped laughing and yet he still heard sniggering. No matter, he thought, it was time to taste his quarry. He lifted the lid and caught a glimpse of the precious, sweet-smelling pineapple nestling inside the box. He was just thinking how large the box was in comparison to the fruit inside when he froze with fear.

Something had wound its arm around his waist.

'Good evening, Master Gristleby,' said the voice that belonged to the arm and the rest of the body it was attached to.

It was Antony Bladdermine.

'I see that you could not resist my pineapple. How adroit you are,' Bladdermine continued, 'to have guessed it was you I had picked – quite by chance, and in secret.' The last word was laced with such a depth of menace that the young man shuddered. He tried to swallow, but it felt like his mouth had turned to cinders.

'Well,' said Bladdermine, as he moved to stand in front of the boy, smiling rather genially, 'it would seem that you have saved me the trouble of finding you tomorrow. How…convenient this is,' said the older man.

'Oh, sir, I am most sorry to have walked into your home without knocking! I swear by almighty God that I was not going to touch the pineapple! I just…I just wanted to look upon it, before I ate, I mean, before it was eaten!' said Gristleby, rather unconvincingly.

'Of course; do not be nervous. Here, rest your feet and sit upon this chair,' said Bladdermine, as he drew out a seat for the quaking young man.

'Would you like a bite of the pineapple now, Master Gristleby?' asked Bladdermine.

'Oh, sir, indeed I would,' said Fabian, forgetting his shock and growing more excited at the taste ahead of him.

Bladdermine walked over to the sideboard and collected a large china plate that depicted some scene of oriental warriors, and a great sharp knife, its handle all embroidered in strange patterns – surely another of the man's romantic foreign purchases. He placed these in front of the boy; next, he reopened the red box and, as he done that day in the town square, appeared to find something intensely curious to look at within, which seemed to inspire his lips to move and a feint whisper to escape from his thin mouth.

Carefully, almost paternally, Bladdermine lifted the pineapple from its box and placed it on the china plate.

'There,' said Bladdermine, 'why don't you cut yourself a slice? Make it as big as you like, but do be sure to leave some for me.' The boy was too eager to notice the fixity of the older man's stare – he was not gazing upon the boy or indeed the pineapple – instead he kept his small, piercing eyes locked onto the red box.

Fabian Gristleby grabbed the knife and sawed a great wedge from the pineapple's bristling orb. He crammed the chunk into his mouth and allowed the wondrous flavours to surge and swirl around his palate. Noticing for the first time how Bladdermine was not watching him, he cut off another, even bigger yellow hunk from the fruit and delighted once more in the glorious taste.

The boy was about to risk a third cut from the pineapple when he noticed that Bladdermine was now gazing at him, but in a queer way. The older man forced down Gristleby's hand that clutched the knife, causing it to clatter in a syrupy puddle on the plate in front of him.

'Do you recall,' said Bladdermine slowly and lowly, 'where I said this precious pineapple had come from, young man?'

The boy paused for a moment, wiped his sleeve across his lips and said 'Oh, I think it was from Chilsby, was it not?'

'No. I fear you misheard me. It has come a long way. It comes from Chile,' said the man.

Gristleby returned a blank expression; it was clear he was still savouring the taste in his mouth.

'The problem is transporting something as delicate as this pineapple across the oceans without it rotting in the damp sea air or ripening too quickly during the voyage. Was it not fresh and wonderful?' said Bladdermine to the boy.

'It was, sir. I should like another slice, if I may.'

'No, not now. You have had enough. It is time to settle your account,' said Bladdermine.

'I don't understand you, sir,' said Gristleby.

'Let me explain. I had to take measures to ensure my pineapple's safe passage and its…integrity, on arrival,' said the man.

'For certain, sir. Whatever you did, it was worth it,' said Gristleby.

'Indeed. My pineapple did not come alone. It was accompanied by a guardian of sorts. It's still in the box. Would you like to see what it is?' asked Bladdermine.

'I would, yes,' said Gristleby.

'Chonchon,' said Bladdermine.

'What was that, sir?' asked the lad.

'Chonchon!' said the older man again.

There was a strange scuffling noise in the box for a moment, followed by the unmistakable sound of something wet crackling. A sudden burst of movement shook the box so violently it flipped onto its side and something dark and swift flapped momentarily, before taking to the air and flying off into a dark corner of the hall.

'What was that?' asked Gristleby.

'That was the Chonchon. I made a bargain with it. In return for the safe conveyance of my pineapple, I promised it human blood at the end of its long journey.'

'But won't that hurt you when it bites?' said the boy.

'It won't hurt me, no. But it will hurt you!' said Bladdermine before he began to laugh most demoniacally.

And then, for the first time, the Chonchon swooped down towards the table where Fabian Gristleby was sitting, and was lighted by the flickering candle. Most hideous the Chonchon was, too. For this odious beast, created by the wicked kalku sorcerers of Chile, was but a single human head whose ears had been transformed into giant bat-like wings, its snapping jaws bearing row upon row of pin-sharp teeth.

Young Gristleby had just enough time to shriek with terror before the Chonchon champed into his pulsing white neck.

Mr Bladdermine, chuckling with amusement, cut himself a slice of pineapple and luxuriated in the sweet feast as he watched the foolish thief of a boy being chewed to death by the crazed and rapacious demon of the Chilean jungle.

It's exciting getting one's hands on something exotic once in a while. Like Antony Bladdermine's pleasure in pineapple acquisition, I'm thrilled to have presented to you a monster that doesn't originate from some dreary English bog for a change. I can't help feeling that we've really rather found ourselves at the end of days as pineapples no longer excite us. Anything that can be tinned ceases to be at all exciting. Once upon a time, just like the townsfolk of Mosset-cum-Sagley, a pineapple really must have been a complete marvel. Now they're just cut into chunks and shoved in cans. The supermarkets inflate the prices of pineapple to make them seem special, but I know their game. There simply are no more new fruits to discover; I've tried guava, I've been disappointed by a custard apple. There's nowhere else to go. It's ridiculous really, as we've got to the end of all fruits yet we've barely seen anything other than spheres and ovoid shapes. Sometimes I despair at our vegetable kingdom, I really do.

The Sunday Nail-Cutter

This story was often told as a treat on Sunday nights before television was invented. It's hard not to overstate how boring life without television was and how even the most tedious tale would enliven a drear evening after supper. I do adore the TV, and much prefer it to folk-tales. I would ask you, before you read this story, whether or not there really is nothing on the box that you would like to watch, rather than reading this. There are so many channels available nowadays, that it really is worth a look. You don't even need to get up from your chair anymore because of remote controls. I really do like television.

One evening a lonely old man called Mr Dderwen, who lived in a large house in Llandwrog, was preparing himself for bed when he felt his fingernail snag on the fine silk dressing gown he was removing. Looking down at his nails he was surprised to see quite how long they all were and rang the bell to get his maidservant to bring him his nail scissors. Gwenfrewy was moderately new to the house and had proven herself somewhat clumsy, so it was with a sense of dismay when he espied the girl enter his chamber proffering the scissors. The old man had no time to listen to the girl for he was eager to be abed and reading his novel – he quickly silenced Gwenfrewy upon her declaration of 'Oh, but, sir, it's –' for he did not need to hear how late it was. He was perfectly well aware of that.

Relieved when the infernal creature had left, Dderwen sat upon the edge of the counterpane and began the job of trimming his fingernails. He enjoyed cutting them for himself so much, that he removed his slippers and docked his toenails also. Satisfied, he swept the clippings onto the floor for the chambermaid to clear in the morning.

For some reason, the old man did not enjoy his book so much that evening, especially as there seemed to be a wretched tree tapping against the window in the stinging winds that were gusting outside. He closed the book, blew out the candle and settled his agitated head onto the pillow.

Sleep came quickly, but, unfortunately for Dderwen, it held a vivid, repeating nightmare that kept waking him with a start. Each time he regained his composure and drifted off into sleep, the dream came billowing back, and he found himself verily soaked through with a foul, cold sweat.

Every time he had fallen into slumber and began dreaming once more, he fancied that there was the sound of something stealthily opening the sash window and thudding softly onto the rug beneath. A little later, a flash of lightning would illuminate the room whereupon he would clearly see something, alarmingly tall, standing at his toilet. He was upset to ascertain that the figure was not a man at all, on account of the fact that he had a goat's head and wasn't wearing any shoes. That is because shoes don't fit easily on cloven hooves, which is what the figure had for feet. On each occasion the vision returned, Dderwen noticed, to his discomfort, that the figure was doing something akin to a jig, or merry dance, to some absent music. The overall effect was somewhat eldritch and dispiriting to watch.

After dancing, the goat-like man leant over the foot of the bed and whispered: 'Only a wicked fellow would cut his nails on a Sunday. I shall vex you for a week.'

Indeed, Dderwen was troubled every night by similar night-phantasies, though the odd thing was, he seemed to be enjoying a string of most uncommon good luck through the course of the week's daylight hours.

On Sunday morning the cook announced that a large delivery had been made of some very expensive meats and two cases of exceedingly fine Pierre Chabanneau & Cie Fine Champagne cognac also. The old man fell upon these with great relish and rather reckless abandon.

On Monday, the man's sour old cousin Irwen cancelled her visit, which delighted him greatly.

Tuesday brought him great surprise when he discovered his father's old fob watch that had been missing for decades.

On Wednesday, he won over two hundred pounds at a game of picket.

Thursday continued the happy streak when he fell into a conversation with a most attractive lady outside the church. She called on him later that day and seemed most keen on his hasty marriage proposal.

By Friday, his happy week got even better when he read a letter from his solicitor informing him that his widowed sister-in-law had left him his rich brother's estate in Ireland after she'd died in a waterfall accident. He had never liked her anyway.

Saturday proved to be the turning point, and the old miser's luck ran out, like a brook dried out by the parching summer heat. The case and-a-half of cognac was stolen from the butler's cupboard after the backdoor was broken-open in the night.

His cousin Irwen informed him that she would indeed be coming to stay, but for twice the expected length of time; his father's fob watch was knocked from his bedside table whilst Gwenfrewy was dusting, which shivered it into pieces (she was promptly fired in spite of the inconvenience that that caused).

The woman he had started courting developed a distemper, which ended her life, and his brother's Irish estate was burnt to a cinder after a lightning strike. Dderwen was feeling very sorry for himself; he went to the public house, which was entirely empty, so he drank and drank until he fell asleep in the armchair. The ghastly, tall goat-man returned during his noontime nap, laughing rather too fiercely for his liking. Roused into wakefulness by the awful howls of mirth, the old man hurried home to find his house had disappeared. There was nothing there, save the feint odour of sulphur in the air. Dderwen, who lived in a lonely part of Llandwrog, wandered many hours until he came upon a slate quarry on the outskirts of the Penygroes. He lay down on the wet rocks shouting and bawling at God for allowing this to happen.

Two policemen appeared and promptly arrested him for breech of the peace and vagrancy. With great celerity, he was taken to the local gaol where he remains to this day. He is instantly recognisable as he has enormously long finger and toenails.

This slightly more modern tale is almost inconceivably stupid, but I find it rather amusing. In order to make it relevant to a contemporary audience, we must look at it in strictly figurative terms, as clearly the prohibition of nail-cutting on a Sunday stretches the Good Lord's doctrine a little too far. Even Great Grandma Berrial was inclined to say that it's a touch too dogmatic, and that's coming from a woman who wouldn't even have peacock feathers in the house, because of the Evil Eye, you see. On the other hand, she certainly wasn't a Christian. I'm sure of this as she spent her Sundays sorting through seashells and getting up to things in the loft. I was never allowed in the loft, but of a Sunday I often heard great gales of laughter issuing from the rafters and quite a lot of squeaking too. Whilst my grandmother never explicitly called the narrow fellow with a goat's head 'the Devil', I assume we are meant to perceive him as such. I am often struck by how much time the Devil seems to spend working on individuals in a very intensive manner. It's a shame he can't put his skills to better uses – he would make a super gym instructor or window salesman. Quite what use the Devil would have for a country mansion in hell, remains a mystery. Maybe the Evil One needed the bricks for some social housing project he was co-ordinating in Hell. It certainly makes you think.

Captain Pickerel's Companions

Birds are fascinating creatures as there's such a wide variety of them. On the one hand you have wrens, on the other there are ostriches. Please don't take this illustration literally because you would have a real ordeal trying to balance these beasts on separate hands in a real-world scenario, and the RSPCA would certainly be after you with some form of animal cruelty charge, unless this was part of a licensed circus act. The folk tale that you are about to read, unless you have chosen to find something more interesting from the contents page, features a species known as a psittaciform. This is not a variety of pub-nut: you may know it as a 'parrot'. I once looked after a friend's pet parrot for twelve days, and its holiday ended with marked wasting and total immobility. This is sometimes known as 'death'. Please take a course in parrot care before helping out a needy friend who wants nothing better than to escape their domestic chores and flee to the indulgences of Portugal.

A retired seafarer by the name of Captain Pickerel was a popular man about the town of Crebbley, for he told very witty stories and was generous with his time and kind with his advice. He lived modestly in a weatherworn cottage that overlooked the ocean, but most of the time he was to be found entertaining the good folk who supped in The Brown Whale Inn with his rakish ballads and tales of adventure.

However, two companions forever accompanied Pickerel wherever he went. The first was a remarkably bad-tempered green parrot called Barnacle who sat perpetually on the captain's shoulder, hissing and screeching, and always ready with a painful nip should anyone get too close to the captain. His second companion was altogether more peculiar, for it was a silent boy whose face was concealed behind a beautifully painted mask. Whilst Pickerel wove his impressive stories through the fug of pipe-smoke, the child would sit wordlessly by his side with neither a nod of the head nor the slightest chuckle, no matter how amusing or arresting the tale. All that the captain's many audiences could ever ascertain was that the child was named Muldoon and he had been badly burnt in a fire whilst saving the captain's life. The garrulous gentleman had adopted Muldoon, or so he said, and consequently the boy followed him everywhere. The men and women who so adored Captain Pickerel tolerated his strange companions, but they always made the atmosphere slightly uneasy and there were many dark mutterings when the captain was out of earshot: 'Pickerel would be better off w'out them others' or 'Lovely fellow, the captain. Don't care so much for his bird though – and as for that horrid little fellow!' &c. &c.

Well, one night Pickerel was telling a fine story about his escape from a terrible maelstrom when the spiteful parrot suddenly flapped his verdant wings and spoiled the story with his infernal squawks and proceeded to ruin every subsequent narrative by mimicking his master's every utterance. Barnacle's shrill echoes were so annoying, that everybody lost their interest in the stories and retreated to other, less discordant, corners of the inn. That night, as on many others before, some of the bolder listeners had attempted to swat the troublesome parrot, but before anyone had struck the braying bird, the captain had restrained them with a grip from his calloused hand. 'Please! *Please!*' he had said, with a look of awful dread on his deeply lined face. All the while the silent figure of Muldoon, in his perfect white stockings, had sat and watched the captain from behind his gay china mask.

That evening, a young lad named Ben Barfold, emboldened by booze, followed Captain Pickerel and his strange company home, with the intention of giving the racketing parrot a thorough hiding or at least a wicked pinch. He hadn't quite decided at that point exactly what else he might do (because he was so drunk) but he was set on stealing into the captain's cottage and giving the bird a wallop at the very least. Tottering up to the window of Pickerel's small home, he watched as the old fellow dressed for bed, before setting the irksome Barnacle on his perch by the headboard. Muldoon did not appear to have a bed; instead he had settled himself on a rude stool by the fireplace, so that he could continue to gaze at the old seadog as he slept.

Barfold was so committed to spanking the parrot that he waited a good hour for the fire to die down; the captain was snoring and he assumed Muldoon was asleep too as all was quite still in the cottage – even Barnacle had fallen into a feathery slumber, with his head tucked under his wing.

Barfold clenched his teeth and opened the door to Pickerel's cramped home, tiptoeing over to the parrot by the bed. With a sudden lunge, he grabbed the bird, intending to silence it with his right hand; alas, in his drunken state he used such force that with a terrible wet snap he broke Barnacle's neck. In a panic, he dumped the bird on the floor and was on the point of leaving when he heard a ghastly sniggering from behind him. He spun round and saw with horror that Muldoon had stood up from his stool. The child's gurgling laughter grew louder and louder and was so frightful that the young intruder was quite frozen to the spot in terror. The squealing laugh grew so intense that Captain Pickerel was awoken by the din and lighted a candle on his bedside table.

The instant he spied the body of Barnacle lying on the flagstones Pickerel let out a pathetic whimper and began to shake most violently:

'Undone!' he cried, 'Undone!' Muldoon scampered over to the captain's bedside, continuing to laugh most horribly. Pickerel, clawing at his sheets, fixed Barfold with his wild eyes before screaming:

'What have you done? Oh! What have you done?' Before the drunken youth could answer, Muldoon's chortles stopped with fearful suddenness, filling the air with a dreadful silence. The child reached behind its ears and unclipped the delicate pale mask, which fell onto the floor and smashed into pieces. What was revealed was not the countenance of a child disfigured by burns at all: this was the face of the most loathsome devil imaginable – the skin was filthy wrinkled leather with eyes like glowing opals set deep in its hideous, lumpen skull.

'At last,' yelled Muldoon with a shriek of jubilation, 'you are mine! The parrot is dead! The bargain is fulfilled! Come!'

With that, Muldoon picked up the sobbing captain as if he were as light as a ship's biscuit, and carried him from his wretched bed and out into the night.

Barfold dashed after the pair, but the instant he stepped over the door's threshold into the warm midnight air, he perceived that the ghastly couple had quite vanished.

Legend would have it that every girl likes a sailor, but received wisdom is often misleading. I've never met a sailor, so I remain open to being persuaded. Open people are much more receptive to surprise than closed ones. The captain in the above narrative seemed like a nice man, but he was clearly the progenitor of at least one ghastly atrocity. It's very tempting to make a bargain with the devil or one of his miserable acolytes, and I've certainly been driven to the point of acquiring a Ouija board in the past, just to make ends meet. I remember very clearly a most dreary month when all I had in my cupboard was a box of sea salt (a gift from a fanciful relative) and an unopened packet of Weetabix. Not only had I absolutely no recollection as to how I acquired these terrible cereal lozenges (which meant I regarded them with some awe and reverence), but also they were quite useless as a meal with salt alone. In a rage against my impoverishment, I declared that I'd sell my trousseau if only the Devil would give me a pint of milk. Now, whether or not it was the milkman's error, that morning I found a bottle of milk on my doorstep. I was so shaken by this dairy manifestation, that I put the milk in my chest freezer, and there it remains until I decide what to do with it. You may be interested to hear that later that day I found a five pound note in my tumble-dryer which I spent on five multipacks of baked beans, which saw me through until pension day. The imaginative amongst you might suppose this was also an enticing but conditional gift from Satan, although I am sceptical on this matter. Tumble-dryers are certainly an invention of Jesus Christ.

The Worm Garden

What do you fear most in the world? Is it spiders? Is it being lost in Calcutta without a mobile phone? Is it waking up one morning to find that you're American and stuck in Calcutta without a cell phone? I really don't know. For some people it's worms. It certainly is for the lady in the story you're about to read. My late husband Desmond was once pronounced clinically dead for a quarter of an hour after succumbing to the effects of a particularly tenacious tapeworm. He was lucky enough to die at a bus stop, falling right into a proctologist who was waiting for the 339 to Stepney. Desmond recovered because of the proctologist's quick actions, which I understand were somewhat public and embarrassing for my husband. I never pressed him on how the thing was removed but I understand a bit of bacon on a string will do the trick. I still keep Des's slippers by the bed. Not for him to put on, should he come back from the dead, but to throw at him, as I don't want another ghost in the house.

Miss Pinkfinger lived all on her own in a small tree house on the outskirts of the town of Shanksleeve. The reason that she didn't live in a normal house was because she detested earthworms so much that she had to be as far away from them as possible. As she was not a rich woman she could not afford a cob house let alone a weaver's cottage (she envied these greatly as they have three floors), so she spent much of her miserable life living in a cherry tree.

One day she was making ready for bed when a magpie landed on the branch outside her window. In its beak it carried a beautiful gold ring that it had obviously stolen from some unfortunate soul.

Miss Pinkfinger let out a gasp of astonishment at the wondrous ring; this frightened the bird so much that it flew away, dropping the ring as it did so. The gold band rolled down the length of the branch, through the window (it had no glass because she was so poor) and right into her trembling hand.

The next day Miss Pinkfinger took the ring into town and sold it for five shillings. She was very foolish to sell it so cheaply as it was worth fifty pounds at least, but that is what happens when you spend your whole life in a tree.

However, Miss Pinkfinger was very happy. She employed two workmen to remove all the earth in her garden and replace it with salt, for earthworms will not travel through the stuff. She paid them two bob each and a shilling for the salt, which left her with a broad grin on her face and no money in her purse at all. For days afterwards her garden was most striking and lovely – it glowed white as snow and sparkled as the sun travelled through the sky. The old lady danced for joy in her reclaimed garden, delighted that she need never fear a loathsome earthworm again. She would no longer have to dread March when the first worm casts would appear all over the lawn, and she would never again move a stone to be appalled at the slithering things beneath.

Another day passed, and Miss Pinkfinger sat in her cherry tree smiling to herself when she noticed that there was something wrong with the tree. All of its leaves had sickened and hung limply from the twigs. She plucked a handful of cherries from the branch and they turned to mush in her hand. She hurried down the ladder and saw that her tree was dying. Her meagre crops too were black and odious when she pulled them from the salt.

She stood in the centre of her beautiful white garden and wept, but her tears only added to the poisoning salt. She had no money; she had no food.

Her garden was dead.

Within a week Miss Pinkfinger's well had dried up completely and her cherry tree crashed to the ground.

She died a week later, friendless and penniless. Shanksleeve's vicar, who, like all the other townsfolk did not care for the strange woman, was good enough to afford the wretched woman a pauper's grave at the edge of the churchyard. There was no money for a coffin, so Miss Pinkfinger's corpse was rolled in cloth and set down in a narrow grave by a large flint wall that obscured the glorious vista of the hills beyond.

It did not take long for the worms to find her. They soon burrowed through the cloth shroud and ate her up completely, save for her bones – bones that were as white as purest salt.

I ought to despair of a noodle-head like Miss Pinkfinger, but in a strange way I can empathise with her. I have been guilty myself of constructing great follies in my garden. Back in the 1960s I became an enthusiastic amateur sculptress after having seen some of Barbara Hepworth's extraordinary pieces at an exhibition and I fancied having a go myself. As I soon discovered, I didn't quite have the same artistic panache as the late dame and I populated my small Shadwell back garden with a series of brick-built monstrosities that not only looked abominable but were incredibly dangerous too. There was a dreadful gale blowing round the garden one night and the whole lot came down like a terrifying set of dominos. These days I mainly stick to knitting woollen dollies or creating my own rose bushes. The cultivation and hybridization of roses is much safer than sculpture on the whole, but it has led me to create some abhorrent mutant aberrations. Alas, the world is not yet ready to hear the story of the unstoppable Brown Rose Floribunda of Shadwell.

Joan and Thomas

The narrative that follows is a rather bleak one. I wouldn't read it while you're in bed. It's the kind of story that's best read when it's interrupted by telephone calls so that you don't really have to think about it. Set a time in the day when you've arranged for friends to call (if you have any – if you don't get some salesmen to call – insurers will do), staggering the calls so that they arrive every couple of minutes over the course of approximately two hours.

One very fecund year in the village of Herald Hem, there were five women pregnant at the same time. The villagers were dearly praying for boys as the farmers were all old men and the wives spent most of their evenings rubbing unctions and salves onto their husbands' throbbing bunions and calluses.

Well, the folk of Herald Hem were delighted when all five mothers bore five fine sons (although one of the ladies was not strictly a villager but was in fact a slave who was already pregnant on arrival and was sent away in disgrace the moment she had birthed).

Of the four mothers remaining, one in particular, Joan, was determined to get her son working on the fields and learning his father's ways before any of the other children. At twenty-five, Joan was an old mother and earnestly longed to have her son look after her in her old age. She was already planning his marriage so that she would have his future wife in the home to clean the cottage and tend to her aching bones.

First, Joan was desirous that her son should be walking before the other babies could even crawl. And, after much work and chiding, her son, Thomas, was striding about when his friends were not yet even slithering on the floor.

Next, Thomas's mother set about making sure her son was the first to talk, and this she effected by prattling at him all day long. She particularly liked to talk to him about her nightmares as she knew full well that her harried dreams would bother him and he too would get little sleep for all the ghastly stories she put into his dear, innocent mind. The plan worked; Thomas rarely slept and, as he was awake, his mother would continue to jabber at him. Soon, the young boy, not even a year old, could converse better than most men in the village, although it was clear that he was a rather melancholy child. If any of the other mothers dared laugh at the garrulous youth, Joan would upbraid them most severely and do dreadful things to them whilst they slept. She often released the mocking mother's pigs from their pens at midnight or even neutered their cockerels so that the hens would no longer produce chicks.

Within two years, Thomas was moving hay-bales in the barn and had become adept at skinning rabbits quicker than his father could catch them (there were a lot of rabbits in Herald Hem and his father was very skilled at trapping them, so this is more remarkable than it seems). Joan was always with him while he laboured in the barn, spanking him for any tardiness and bitterly complaining if he took too long to eat the pottage his mother had given him in the smallest bowl she could find.

Aged five years, the boy had mastered the family's belligerent old shire horse and the great plough it lugged behind itself. Joan was cheered beyond measure that her son was working the land and threshing the crops before the other women's children had even managed to wash their own faces. She enjoyed proclaiming her son's merits at every opportunity, so much so, that the other womenfolk would avoid her lest they had to endure another series of tales extolling her only son's virtues. Joan cared not a fig for her encroaching isolation, for she knew that soon she could retire to her bed; in less than nine years she would have him married to her mute friend's daughter in the neighbouring hamlet of Herald Fen.

One year later, Thomas was found lying, quite still, in the carrot field by his harassed father, Thomas (they both had the same name). The boy could not be roused, so his father carried him back to the barn, out of sight of his mother, and called for the physician (also named Thomas, but we shall call him Dr Blacksmith even though he had no surname to speak of and was not a qualified doctor, but it helps with the clarity). Dr Blacksmith was, alas, of no use. The child had expired. Through tears, Thomas's father asked what ague had taken his son, and the goodly physician replied: 'Sir, he died of old age.'

When Joan heard what had happened she dashed over to the barn and castigated the youth, demanding that he stand up and set about his work. And yet the boy was still. Eventually the woman accepted the boy's death and hanged herself from a beam in the barn in a great fury.

Thomas's father did not remarry but was tended to most lovingly by the other three recent mothers in the village. Their strapping sons, who laboured on the widower's farm, planted and harvested the land well, and the three kindly mothers served him bread and honey until he himself passed away aged two hundred years old.

When I first heard this account from the lips of dear Aunt Vulna, I wondered why the women didn't just use a vinegar rag on the men's toes – that would've solved a lot of problems. We've all met women like Joan, but typically for a folk tale like this, her end is always rather swift, whereas in real-life they tend to go on and on and spread their malaise into their nineties at least. I often tell this tale with some embroidering of my own. I rather fancy that Joan would not have killed herself, but would have moved underground and lived with moles. The king of the moles would have then used her as a sort of fleshy radiator in his lair, to warm up the burrow. I have been advised that this rather detracts from the pathos of the original format, so I present Aunt Vulna's version here, as I was told it. Returning to the narrative, I suspect the main theme here is the danger of pride. I do not suffer the affliction of self-worth myself which is why I am often to be found in charity shops and only purchase groceries from Tesco supermarkets.

Bad-Mouth Peppermere

Reverencing the dead is a widely practised custom, and one that I certainly observe. However, I'm sure we've all felt the need on some occasions to visit an enemy's grave and do a quick clog dance on it. It's nothing to be ashamed of and, if anything, it helps to aerate the soil and allow the forget-me-nots to flourish. The following story has a rather perverse ending so don't be worried if you end up feeling rather confused or indignant. If the sensations of bewilderment persist, do go and see your GP, as it could be an early sign of incipient dementia. If that's the case, I'm sorry to say that all that can be offered to you is palliative care, as scientists have not yet found a cure for this accursed affliction. After reading this story, please make sure your will is up-to-date, as you don't want to start fiddling with that when you're thinking is impaired.

Many years ago there was a small coastal town called Little Wartley that was threatened by the Great Pestilence that swept across the land. In time, the plague finally reached the township and many hundreds of people died most agonising deaths as buboes erupted under their arms and their skin turned as black as coal. In desperation, it was decided that all the corpses of the recently deceased would be ferried over to a small island known as Cranny Mound so that the townsfolk would not be imperilled by the cadavers' poisonous miasma.

As soon as the bodies were removed to the island, the Pestilence diminished rapidly and before long it was gone altogether. Although the people of the town were sorely bereaved, they celebrated the end of the disease and made merry now that the contagion had been conquered.

One night, a fisherman was returning to the shore with his catch when he was disgusted to see that a strange man had set up a dwelling on Cranny Mound and was cooking the bones of the dead to make soup. The townsfolk soon heard of this appalling sacrilege and mustered as many boats as they had with the intention of rowing over to the island to slay the abominable man who was eating their loved ones for his obscene feasts. However, as the boats got close to the island, the filthy wretch, still gnawing bones, would shout 'I am Bad-Mouth Peppermere! Try as you might – you shan't land here!' After bawling this oath he assailed the boatmen with such a quantity of rocks and stones, that they were all forced back to the mainland, bleeding and cursing.

Upon every subsequent attempt to land on Cranny Mound, whether by night or day, in fine weather or foul, the valiant men were always pelted with missiles, and they would retreat back to the shore howling in pain and rage.

The best baker in the town, a Mrs Potley, assured the men that this evil blight would not last forever, because, as any cook knows, no matter how good the ingredients are, one day they will dwindle to nothing. It was little comfort to know this, but it was all that could be said.

Two men always kept watch through every hour of the day and night at the sea's edge, waiting for a sign that the nauseating repast of the island's sole inhabitant was coming to an end.

Well, the people of Little Wartley waited four years for the cankerous scourge known as Bad-Mouth Peppermere to run out of stock for his pot, and they were certainly ready for him when he swam to shore one night, grumbling in the plashing waves about his hunger.

The instant he emerged from the brine, the two patient men leapt on the stinking man and struck him on the head with a ditch-shovel. On hearing the commotion, the townsfolk ran down to the beach and dragged the odious tanned body of Bad-Mouth Peppermere up to the crossroads where he was strung from the gibbet and dashed to pieces by clouting stones.

Every hunk and strand of meat that spilled from the swinging corpse was eaten raw by the baying crowd that fumed and jeered below it.

As a young girl, I was often berated by Auntie Vulna for biting my nails; I was caught in the act of toenail-chewing one afternoon, so I was sat down and had the above story conveyed to me in no uncertain terms. My aunt told me that if I continued to eat myself then I would give birth to what was known as a 'Nail Baby'. Thrilled with apprehension, I asked what such a thing was. 'A Nail Baby,' said Auntie Vulna, 'is a clawed infant with a hoof for a head and covered in hard, white scales. It has a hole for a mouth, and from that whistling aperture comes just one entreaty: 'Eat me! Eat me! Eat me!' The wailing only stops when the miserable mother eats the bairn. Now think on that, my girl.' I was so frightened by this dismal prospect that not only did I stop biting my nails for good, but I also vowed never to have children. I'm not sorry about this, as I have several impressionable nieces and nephews of my own now, and I've enjoyed terrifying them with lurid stories of the Nail Baby.

The Ivory Comb

The following story takes place during the Crimean War, but that's not really important. If you have a favourite war, you can put a line through anything faintly Crimean in this story and replace it with words particular to your preferred conflict. I once tried inserting some Nazis and Falklands War elements into this story when I told it to strangers at an evening of story-telling at the local community centre. This was purely imaginative on my part, but it offended several veterans in the audience who had served in the skirmishes I'd alluded to, and they clearly thought I was being overly whimsical. One of them threw a bottle of olive oil at me. What sort of fool brings olive oil to a night of storytelling at a community centre? He wasn't even Italian.

The renowned and fearsome Royal Navy commodore Sir William Evermow was one day preparing to set sail to the Baltic in order to join the Crimean War. He was very much looking forward to blasting as many Russian seaports as he could. This august man was exceedingly fond of his new wife Beatrice and was saddened at having to leave her just three short weeks since their marriage. However, Sir William was a jealously possessive husband and he was reluctant to leave his pretty young bride alone, lest other men should try to steal her heart in his absence.

'Winsome little dove,' said Sir William, 'I must set sail to-morrow and I may be gone for many months! I dread that you shall forget me, and you will make me a cuckold. How shall I know your love is true?'

'Oh, Willy! My love for you will always be true!' replied Beatrice.

'You say that too easily, my dear,' said Sir William.

'Love is not a memory. Love is now and forever in my heart. My love for you will never fade,' replied Lady Beatrice.

'And yet I am doubtful. If only I could speak to you each day to hear you say that, then I should believe you more,' said the Commodore.

'Wait, Willy! I have something for you,' said Beatrice. She opened her handbag and deftly removed a delicate ivory comb from it before placing it in her husband's hand.

'Why should I need a lady's hair comb? How can such a small thing prove your love to me? Do not say that I have married a half-wit!' cried Sir William rather cruelly.

'Sweet Willy! Listen to me now: I have a story to tell you. Come sit with me at the fire.' The good Lady led her husband over to the ottoman by the hearth and said this:

'When I was just a child, I was looked after by the kindest woman I have ever known. Her name was Nurse Furmer. Sadly, after many years of caring for me, she began to grow old and weak. I said to my dear nurse, whom I called Furmy, 'I cannot live without you! My heart is breaking! You cannot leave me alone!' and Furmy said this to me: 'Sweet Bea, you know I will always love you, whether I am here or not.' Like you, dear Willy, I doubted her. How could she love me when she was passed away? Well, she patted me tenderly on the head and handed me this comb. 'Pass this comb through your hair,' she said, 'and ask it one question. Be sure it is the right question, for you shall never be able to change it. You may ask that question to the comb for as long as you shall live, but it will always have to be the same one or bad luck will befall you.' So, I took Furmy's comb and ran it through my hair as I asked the question 'Does Furmy love me?' I cried for joy when I heard the little comb speak to me! It said 'Furmy loves you dearly.' My dear nurse went back home to Heaven later that week and every morning since then I have combed my hair and asked it the same question. Always it answers the same: 'Furmy loves you dearly.' My darling, I want you to have the comb.'

'This is some nonsense! You mock my affection for you,' said Sir William, gruffly.

'That is not so. Come,' she said, 'pass the comb through your locks and ask it one question. Be sure it is the right one, for you will never have another chance, and I can never ask my question to it ever again!' said Beatrice.

'Very well, Bea, if it will make you happy.' So, Sir William passed the comb over his scalp and said: 'Does Lady Beatrice love me more than anyone else in the world?' The comb replied straightway: 'Lady Beatrice loves you more than anyone in the world.'

The Commodore was most amazed and asked the question a dozen more times. Each time, he received the same true answer. Sir William and his wife embraced and, for the first time in their marriage, he was certain that his bride's love was pure and profound.

The next day Sir William Evermow, ready for battle in his uniform and shining gold epaulettes, parted company from his beloved and set sail to the Baltic. There were many tears at his departure, but the Commodore was happy to be carrying the ivory comb in his pocket so that he could be appraised of his wife's true love every day.

Every morning, when Sir William was at his toilet, he combed his thick, wavy grey hair and asked the question 'Does Lady Beatrice love me more than anyone else in the world?' and the comb would always say the same: 'Lady Beatrice loves you more than anyone in the world.'

The Crimean War dragged on and the battles were relentless. One day, some nine months into the conflict, Sir William was readying himself to guide his fleet towards Helsinki and rain down more punishment on its benighted dockyards when he took out the ivory comb from his pocket and asked for the affirmation one more time.

However, this time the comb had another reply.

'Does Lady Beatrice love me more than anyone else in the world?' asked the Commodore and the comb replied: 'Lady Beatrice loves another more than you.' Each time the man asked the question, the comb gave the same, horrible answer. Sir William's fury rose. All the fears and jealousies he had harboured came back to him now with new vigour and colour. That day, the Finnish capital was the victim of the Commodore's rage and spite.

To everyone's surprise, Sir William resigned his commission and sailed directly back to his home to meet with his dishonest and wanton trollop of a wife.

When the Commodore eventually returned home, he arrived in the middle of the night and woke only the dozy maid Charlotte when he hammered upon the door. Charlotte tried to speak to the maddened man, but he pushed her aside and raced up the stairs to his Lady's bedchamber. A small nightlight flickered dimly in the room, just illuminating his wife's soft, delicate face as she slept soundly in her bed. Sir William took the blasted comb from his pocket one more time, drew it through his wild hair and between clenched teeth hissed the question once more: 'Does Lady Beatrice love me more than anyone else in the world?'

The comb could only whisper: 'Lady Beatrice loves another more than you.' Upon that dismal declaration, livid with anger and consumed by wrath, he asked the comb 'Why?' This time there was no answer. 'Why?' he repeated, but the comb was silent. He strode over to the bed, his heavy footsteps waking Beatrice from her dreams – and she gasped 'Oh! Dear Willy you have returned!'

Without a word, the Commodore wrung the woman's pale, throbbing neck until she lay quite still and lifeless (she was dead).

The moment that Sir William had extinguished his wife's life, he was startled to hear a strange, unexpected noise from the corner of the room. A thin wail that steadily grew louder and louder. The man picked up the feeble nightlight and hurried over to where the sound was coming from. Lying there, in a small cot bedecked with laces and bows, was a baby, his baby, crying for its mother, who had loved it more than anything else in the world.

If there's ever been a folk story that really makes me cry, it's this one. I short-circuited countless word-processors just trying to get this committed to print. Many years ago, on my birthday, my sister June had given me a present all wrapped up in fancy paper with a big yellow ribbon. I opened the box and inside found a boring old key. I was so disappointed and angry (I was only six years old) that I scratched her face and pulled her pigtails. She ran off upstairs crying her eyes out and I was given a right spanking from Aunt Vulna. She pulled me by the arm out into the back garden and pointed to a big wooden box sitting on the middle of the lawn. Auntie then used the key June had given me to open it. Inside were a white bunny rabbit and a big cake, which had been iced (in a naïve style) by my sister. Yes, the rabbit had eaten a third of the cake, but the thought was there, and I was left feeling very guilty. Whilst my mother dabbed iodine on my sister's bleeding cheek and forehead, I was sat down on the Hard Chair and told the story you've just read by my aunt. I learnt several lessons that day - one about animal management, another about the surprising diet of rabbits, and one about the perils of a quick temper. Unfortunately, like most things I've been taught, I forget half of it – in my lifetime I've killed several pet rabbits by mistake and I continue to react hastily to problems.

Crossing the Stobley

The numbskull in the following story makes a catalogue of mistakes, but we shouldn't be too quick to judge: very often a clumsy blunder can lead to great invention. Only this morning I made the error of brushing my teeth with a popular brand of antiseptic cream and rubbed toothpaste into a wound I acquired when chopping a beef tomato. I fully intend to repeat this 'mistake' in future because my teeth have never felt so clean and my cut now has a wonderful minty odour.

Stobley River was a fearsome course that thundered across the Gybbart Valley. Most of the villagers of Gybbart had houses that clustered near the only bridge for many miles, except for one man called Edgar Babley. This fellow, who was remarkably stupid, had built a flimsy cottage very far from the town and this meant that every day he had to travel almost twelve miles to cross the river to sell the chalk that he mined himself.

One day, Babley's horse fell lame and the prospect of hauling his chalk sacks over to Gybbart Bridge without help was too much to bear, so he decided that he would build his own bridge. First, he dragged ten hay bales over to the river's edge, but as soon as the first bale was lowered into the speeding water, it was swept away. He repeated this nine more times and on each occasion the result was the same – the bale was snatched by the swirling flow and dragged down by the currents.

The next scheme that Babley hatched was to lower rocks into the river to create a rude crossing. He supposed that the rocks would be heavier than the bales and that he would enjoy success this time. Well, he spent several hours lowering as many rocks as he could find into the waters, but as soon as he had heaved them into the river the water spilled over the tops of the stones and drew them down-stream. He soon ran out of rocks and threw the last pitifully small pebble he had gathered into the spiralling eddies and sat down on the bank, beating his fists into the sand.

All of a sudden he had another idea as he was gazing upon a mighty oak tree that towered above him. He raced home to fetch a saw because he had a plan to create a wooden bridge from the planks he would cut out of the oak's trunk. He hurried back to the riverside as soon as he had found the biggest saw that he had (which was still rather small) and he began to cut into the gnarled girth of the tree. But because Edgar Babley was so doltish, he sawed into the tree in such a way that meant when the great oak was felled, he would be beneath it. Of course he did not realise this and on hearing the sound of splitting timber, he looked up at the enormous oak with great satisfaction before its giant trunk collapsed on top of him and killed him instantly.

The tree was so tall and so wide, that it made a convenient bridge from one side of the river to the other, although Edgar Babley was never able to make use of it.

Over the years, the village of Gybbart grew into a prosperous town and new bridges were needed; the felled oak by the dead man's cottage allowed workmen to easily construct a stone bridge next to it, and it was named Babley's Bridge. According to many passing tradesmen, once a year Edgar's ghost can be seen running in circles at the riverside, still trying to cross the Stobley River.

There are far too many people these days who are so busy trying to save the trees that they don't for a minute sit and think about what a nuisance they are. The slightest wind and they topple over, ruining people's cars and demolishing bedrooms. I'm well aware of the fact that we need plants to survive on this planet, but I really do think that shrubs are much better than trees. It's the inherent laziness of most people that allows what could have been an attractive hedge to grow into an egregious mess like a tree. I have written to the National Park Authority to argue the case that the New Forest needs to be clipped right back so that holidaymakers in Brockenhurst can enjoy unspoilt views of Southampton, instead of having such a pretty vista spoilt by swaying trees. I have supplied them with some naïve watercolour artist-impressions to represent what my vision is. I have not heard back from the NPA, in spite of me going to the trouble of supplying them with a self-addressed envelope.

The Weather Vane

The following narrative anticipates some of today's technical innovations in weather forecasting. Never forget that today's occult practices are tomorrow's science fact. I don't waste time watching the weather forecast any more as England's twenty-first century climate is so unpredictable that you're far better off thinking about yesterday's weather. At the end of news bulletins, I mute my television set and reminisce about past weather events. For example, today I set my mind to recall a day back in

1949 when it rained slightly in the morning, cleared up for two hours, before it started raining again. It's a super pastime – why not go and buy a desk diary today and keep your own weather journal? You can surprise all your friends with unerringly detailed knowledge of really remarkably insignificant meteorological moments from bygone days.

For many years the little town of Fleck-on-Wornley had been supervised by a most interfering and querulous cleric called Parson Pryvene. Everybody who lived there (and a good number of residents who were now dead) had suffered the parson's complaints and cantankerous fussing; he held such power that no one dared to defy him, and he was quite capable of meting out terrible punishments to sinners who disobeyed his commands.

One day, after his Sunday sermon, Parson Pryvene proclaimed that Fleck-on-Wornley was to have a very special visitor in one month's time.

'Parishioners!' said the parson, 'Listen carefully because I have a great and important announcement to make. We are to host King Edward on the first day of April. I shall receive him in this very church that you are now standing in.'

He delivered these words with such solemnity that it drew a collective gasp from the congregation and Mrs Rimmbly fainted with shock. The parson continued:

'Every man, woman and child in this town will now set about making sure everything is in order for his Royal Highness's visit,' he said. 'Hedges will be trimmed! Doorsteps will be scrubbed! Walls will be painted! Livestock will be brushed and perfumed! And that is just the beginning of your work for to-day!'

Again, the crowd gasped, and Mrs Rimmbly, who had just revived from her first upset, fainted once more.

'When His Majesty visits this town, he will marvel at its beauty and tidiness. Now leave this holy place that I might confer with my God and pray for King Edward's safe passage to this town,' said Parson Pryvene.

With that, the townsfolk were ushered out of St Harold's Church into the cold, biting March winds to set about their preparations for the royal visit.

Later that day, the parson had returned from his round of inspections and stood outside St Harold's wondering what improvements he could make to the building. It was far too squat and Saxon for his tastes, and he began to consider what could be done to make the edifice more impressive, as the thing he besought most was the approval of King Edward.

It did not take him long to conceive of a very fine plan indeed. What the church needed, he told himself, was a weather vane. Not just any weather vane; it had to be the largest and most glorious weather vane the country had ever seen. This was a perfect idea in the parson's opinion as it would not only serve as a compliment to the king, but it would also belittle all the other weather vanes in Fleck-on-Wornley, making his the most magnificent and illustrious.

The town had an unusual number of quite elaborate and beautiful wind vanes already, as the blacksmith, Alfric Slabb, had been one of the most adept metalworkers in the county, perhaps even the kingdom itself. Alfric, an unmarried man who had lived with his mother, Agnes, had been driven from the town some three years previously, accused of witchcraft and sorcery by none other than Parson Pryvene himself. Alfric and Agnes escaped with their lives and were fortunate to flee before Pryvene was able to arraign them formally. Whether or not the imputations against the Slabbs were true or not had long been a matter of quiet conjecture amongst the townsfolk when out of earshot of Parson Pryvene.

What was certain, however, was that there was no longer a blacksmith in the town, and the men would often have to travel miles when a blacksmith was needed. Pryvene's reputation was such that any potential blacksmiths were sorely put-off moving to Fleck-on-Wornley lest they too were to fall under the suspicious and dangerous gaze of the parson of that town.

Pryvene hurried into the church, and climbed up into the pulpit, as if he were about to begin a sermon. Instead of eulogising, he turned over a sheet of paper on the lectern and began to draw a sketch of his idea for a weather vane.

And so the parson worked all night on his design – and most ornate and immoderate it was too. As soon as the dawn chorus began to fill the air Pryvene sent for the church sexton, Godwin, to make haste to London with his design.

'Now, Godwin: you understand how important this document is? I know you are new to this town – are you sure you can find your way to London from here?' asked the parson.

'Yes, sir, I know the way,' replied Godwin.

'Good. When you have reached our capital, be sure to pay the best master blacksmith a bag of these gold coins in advance, and the other two bags on completion of the weather vane. I am entrusting you to make sure the design is exactly as I have specified. You will stay with the fellow for the duration of the wind vane's construction. You must return before three weeks have passed. Do you understand, Godwin?' said Pryvene.

'I do, sir,' replied the sexton.

'Off then! Off!' shouted the parson, and the young sexton gathered up his reins, squeezed his colt's belly, and rode away. Pryvene watched the horse and rider gallop over the heath, and turned back to his church when the pair was out of sight.

The days of the following three weeks seemed to pass by interminably slowly for the parson of Fleck-on-Wornley. He was becoming ever more agitated as the day of the king's visit drew nearer and he had still heard no word from Godwin. Much of his frustration had been taken out on the townsfolk, and he had become ever more barbaric in his upbraidings with those residents he considered too slow or lazy to tidy the town properly.

On 28th March, Godwin returned with his horse and cart. The parson tore off the hessian sacks covering the weather vane, before weeping with joy at the glorious thing that lay beneath.

'Oh Godwin! I was going to have you flogged for being so late, but this wonder of craftsmanship undoes all my old ill feelings! This is a thing of such beauty! Well done, sexton, well done!' said Pryvene.

'The blacksmith was most determined to do his best, sir. And indeed he refused two bags of gold because it was work for the Church and Crown! See, sir, I have them here,' said Godwin as he pulled the two pouches from his jerkin.

'Good, good,' said Pryvene. 'But first, gather up some men to hoist this wonder up onto the tower.'

Shortly, a group of men were gathered and the glistening weather vane, the height of three men, was hoisted gently up onto the flinty tower of St Harold's. Before long, the weather vane had been fixed onto the stout and sturdy belfry. The afternoon sunshine reflected off its scrolling curlicues, and the gigantic crown at the centre of the vane dazzled all who stood beneath it. There was no doubting this was the finest weather vane in the town now.

An hour or so later, and the whole town had gathered about St Harold's church to marvel at the new addition to the tower. The parson turned irritably towards Mrs Rimmbly who was pulling at his cassock rather insistently.

'Cease your tuggings, madam! What is the matter?' asked the parson.

'Reverend! The weather vane! It's not right!' said Mrs Rimmbly.

'What nonsense, woman. It is perfect.'

'No, Reverend! Look – the arrow's pointing north. But it's a southerly wind to-day! See all the other vanes in the village – all pointing south 'cept yours!' said Mrs Rimmbly.

She was right. A shudder of apprehension shook the parson.

'Oil, men! The new vane is stiff. It needs oil. The thing is pointing in the wrong direction. Sexton! Oil it immediately!' shouted Pryvene.

The weather vane was oiled, but it made no difference. The arrow on its crest moved most smoothly, but still it pointed in the wrong direction.

Parson Pryvene let out a great bellowing roar and snatched the oil can from the Godwin's hands when he had returned from the tower. He threw the can at the lad, who fell to his knees, clutching his winded stomach.

'The blacksmith made a pretty thing indeed, Godwin, but it doesn't bloody work!' screeched Pryvene.

The crowd gave a collective gulp and Mrs Rimmbly fainted, for she had never heard a clergyman swear before.

'Tell me, boy, whom did you employ to make my weather vane?' asked the parson, as he pulled the boy to his feet.

'Ah, well, I did not – I mean to say that it was a very skilled man,' said Godwin, quavering with fear.

'His name! I will find him this night and drag him here to fix that abominable skillet basket up there! His name, boy!' repeated the parson.

'Alfric Slabb, sir,' said Godwin.

'What?' cried Pryvene. 'Alfric Slabb? That iniquitous degenerate? No wonder the vane moves not with the wind – it is cursed! You fool, Godwin. That man and his craven-hearted mother are witches. Tell me where in London you found them!' shouted Pryvene.

'Well, sir, that's just it. I didn't need to go to London – halfway there I stayed the night in a village called Darglowe. I met the blacksmith – Mr Slabb there. I saw his smithy and the wonders within! I did it to save you money, Reverend, truly I did!' cried the sexton.

'Nay, you have been spellbound,' said Pryvene, before slapping the boy's cheek, which sent him tumbling onto the ground.

'You turnip-pluckers,' said Pryvene, pointing at a group of four men nearby, 'saddle your horses. Darglowe is seven hour's ride from here. We shall drag the Slabbs from their beds and execute them forthwith. We shall teach these witches to play a joke on the Parson of St Harold's!'

Pryvene began to walk away to his stable with the other men, before he turned around and paused. He glanced up at the glistering weather vane before moving his gaze back down to Godwin, who was sitting on the ground, rubbing his reddened cheek.

'Mr Pinngage,' whispered the parson to the butcher who stood next to him at the church gate, 'cut off Godwin's ears and thumbs for disobeying my orders and consorting with the Devil.'

Mr Pinngage, who had a surfeit of muscle and a deficit of intelligence, pulled the knife from his belt and walked up to the sexton, as Pryvene and his men strode off to collect their horses.

It was in the early hours of 29th March that Pryvene and his band of turnip-pickers arrived at Slabb Forge in Darglowe. It was the custom then to leave the front door unlocked, so the humid bedchamber of the Alfric and Agnes Slabb was easily entered. The son and mother were quickly roused – Pryvene was further prickled by the way that the pair seemed to be expecting them and showed no sign of surprise.

'Alfric and Agnes Slabb: I accuse you both of the foulest witchcraft – to wit - the enchantment of a holy weather vane. I ask you now –'

'Yes, yes, yes! You're the wicked one amongst us, Pryvene,' said Agnes. 'I'll admit – that weather vane is enchanted - but by good magick, not ill. If you'd only listen we'd tell you about its real power.'

'She speaks the truth,' said Alfric. 'My mother is a good woman and has only ever used her powers to heal and bring happiness. You are a minister of great evil, Parson Pryvene,' said Alfric.

The Slabbs indeed spoke the truth, but their words sealed their fate. In a few hours, Pryvene, in a great fury, had woken a local Justice of the Peace and the testimonies of the turnip pickers, alongside the declarations from the lips of the Slabbs themselves, only confirmed their guilt.

Within six hours a great bonfire had been constructed and Alfric and Agnes were burnt at the stake, their mouths stuffed with linen to prevent them casting about any more witchcraft. Pryvene was pleased to finally rid himself of his nemeses, but he was less than satisfied with the Slabbs' deaths. They emitted not a sigh or a murmur as their skin burnt away, but they kept their sad, doleful eyes fixed on his, until they were turned to glowing charcoals.

Upon returning to Fleck-on-Wornley the next day, a terrible north wind had started to batter the town. Unlike all the other weather vanes on nearby buildings, the one atop St Harold's was rotating on its shaft so fast and wild, that no one could go near it to dismantle it before the King arrived in little over a day's time. Pryvene had given orders that the weather vane be either removed or fixed in the direction of the prevailing wind, so that the king would not notice its ungodly indications. All such attempts failed, and the giant crown ornament spun like a daggered cartwheel as the winds howled and moaned through Fleck-on-Wornley.

Parson Pryvene was in a very dark mood indeed on 1st April. The town was littered with leaves and sticks; tiles had been sucked off the church and lay smashed on the ground. The roofs of cottages had had their neat thatches all ruffled, or worse, torn off completely. And still the winds roared and buffeted through the town. All the weather vanes in the town still indicated a ferocious north wind; and yet the weather vane on St Harold's Church indicated a south wind. Pryvene had noticed this, but he was more concerned with tidying the wrecked town than attending to that carbuncle of a weather vane any more.

At midday the king arrived. The crowds of well-wishers were so thick, that the king did not notice any disorder, and for that the parson was greatly relieved. He fawned and genuflected around the king and led him to the church for a feast he had prepared.

King Edward was most pleased to spy the enormous regal weather vane at the top of the belfry:

'Pryvene! We are delighted to see our weather vane. We have heard much about it's magical properties,' said the king.

'Indeed, your Highness?' said Pryvene.

'We heard word of its construction in Darglowe – surely Mr Slabb is the greatest blacksmith in all the land! We awarded him a royal charter in January! A magnificent fellow. We had the man and his mother visit us in our palace in January – and that wonderful old lady saved the prince's life – he was dying of some terrible distemper. And look,' continued the king, 'do we not have thick hair, old parson? Before we were bald and half blind – Mrs Slabb cured us of those afflictions also!'

The parson was unable to speak.

The king continued: 'Mr Slabb sent us a letter promising us that he was sure you would soon make a most wonderful gift to us. A weather vane that *predicts tomorrow's weather!* See,' continued King Edward, 'the vane points south, yet today there is this dread north wind. Tomorrow we shall enjoy calm, sweet airs from the south. It is foretold!'

Realising everything, Parson Pryvene began to make a great pretence that he knew this, although he had not ten seconds earlier.

Pryvene, continuing his duplicitous act, and never mentioning how he had had the Slabbs executed only a day before, invited the king to the feast, where they ate well and drank merrily.

'Your Highness,' said Pryvene, when the banquet was over, 'I shall fetch your weather vane for you now. To show my gratitude, I should like to personally lower the device from the tower myself.'

'Excellent, Pryvene, excellent. Well, set about your task, we must be off soon,' said the king.

There is little left to say except that the parson scaled the tower alone and the crowds gathered below watched with mirth – the king included – as Pryvene made an obsequious bow as he stood at the castellated tower top. It was most strange, then, that everyone below distinctly saw *three* silhouetted figures atop the belfry. At first it looked like Pryvene was receiving help from two others, even though no one else had been seen climbing the tower with the parson.

All of a sudden, a sharp cry was heard and Parson Pryvene seemed to fall backwards over the edge of the tower, followed by the weather vane, quite untethered to any rope, which landed on top of the cleric and severed his head from his body, as clean as any executioner's axe could ever have done.

The king was the first to laugh, and soon the whole town was in a fit of convulsive amusement.

'What a terrible man that parson was,' said the king. 'We had word this morning about what he had done to our dear Agnes and Mr Slabb. We swear to you, good townspeople of Fleck-on-Wornley, we were preparing to have him clapped in irons for his wicked deeds. We see that God has chosen to deal with Pryvene for us.'

The king clapped his hands together and then beckoned poor Godwin over.

'We hereby appoint young Godwin, formerly sexton of this parish, as your new vicar. May you and your town be blessed forever more, for you are to-day freed from the tyranny of the malicious Parson Pryvene!'

The crowd cheered and Godwin forgot the pain of his bleeding ear and thumb stumps altogether. Mrs Rimmbly was overcome with such joy that she fainted into the arms of the King of England.

*The clergy do come in for a bit a bashing once again in this folk tale; please don't think I'm in any way trying to encourage you to turn your back on God. I rather fancy that yet again the trouble is with men. If this world were a china shop, the men would surely be bulls and the women would be gluing together all the bits and pieces in their wake. I can't help but wonder whether or not the world would be in the mess it is today if some women priests had been ordained earlier than 1994. Though having said that, I did write a science fiction novel of my own once (*Venus Amen, 1968*) which imagined an alternative earth that was run by female bishops. It was a complete disaster - not in terms of any cataclysm that befell my fictional parallel society, but with regard to the storytelling. The plot was absolutely devoid of conflict – everybody was kind to one another and talked through their problems. It was the most boring novel I've ever read, and I say that as the author of the book. Every publisher that I sent it to, apart from a small communist publisher called 'Hammer and Tickle' (whose main lines were socialist erotica and humour), rejected it. I was desperate to get my manuscript published, so sadly I complied with Hammer and Tickle's editorial demands and added a number of whimsical 'sex scenes'. It was an absolute mess – I was pleased in the end that the company folded and very few copies of my novel were ever sold. Margaret Thatcher once said that the problem with socialism is that eventually you run out of other people's money. Now, I don't agree with a lot of what she said, but on this score she had a point when I think about Hammer and Tickle's business. My friend Valerie* *(who's very computer literate) said she saw one copy of* Venus Amen *changing hands on eBay recently for £15.99 (post and packaging was free).*

Hole-in-the-Head

The Buddha once said 'what's done to the children is done to society,' so please bear that in mind when you read the story below. I flirted with Buddhism for a time in the 1970s, but I was bothered by how fat Buddha appeared to be and how this could be reconciled with his history as a modest travelling beggar. I went to a Buddhist centre and asked them to explain this conundrum and I was told by a little Sri Lankan fellow that this was something the Chinese had done. Unsatisfied, I looked up a Chinese Buddhist centre in the Yellow Pages and undertook a three-hour train journey to Liverpool. When I arrived I asked the Chinese chap why the Buddha was so plump and he told me it was because the Blessed One had reached Nirvana. I argued with this viewpoint as I found it very difficult to believe that anyone could be perfect if they were so fat and indulgent. The Chinese man told me I still had a lot to learn.

Prunella and Roland were disheartened to see that when their first-born was delivered he had a large hole in the top of his head. At first they were very ashamed of him and wished him dead because he was not the same as the other children in the village.

Hole-in-the-Head was completely silent, so Roland picked him up by the legs and gave him a shake to see if he would cry out like babies should do. However, upon shaking him, he did not utter so much as a squawk; instead, a quantity of seeds issued forth from the hole and scattered onto the ground below. Prunella picked them up and planted them in a pot, and she was most amazed to see how quickly the seeds sprouted into two-dozen blooming mustard plants.

Roland put Hole-in-the-Head down and plucked a mustard seed from one of the stems. He chewed on the pod and declared it was the finest mustard he had ever tasted.

For the next five years, come springtime, Prunella and Roland would hold their son upside down, give him a gentle shake and seeds would pour from the hole in his head. Each year the seeds were different, so the family were able to enjoy all sorts of crops that grew to full size in less time than it took to boil an egg.

The whole village was able to share in his remarkable gift and Hole-in-the-Head was rattled day and night for his kernels, nuts and corns. The older Hole-in-the-Head became, the more seeds he produced from the top of his big open crown from the months of March to May.

One day, the evil Prince Pephredo heard of this boy's strange talent and took a retinue of men to the village to take the child back to his castle on top of Gulwin Hill. In spite of Prunella and Roland's pleadings, Hole-in-the-Head was snatched from their arms and taken to the castle. He was locked in a small, damp room in one of the castle's towers until it was spring and time for the boy to be shaken.

After almost half a year of waiting, Pephredo was keen to see the boy produce the seeds he was renowned so widely for. The prince took it upon himself to pick up the boy and shake him, such was his eagerness to reap this remarkable harvest.

However, upon shaking Hole-in-the-Head, only clouds of dust billowed from the cavity in his pate. Pephredo shook the boy more violently, but the air became so dense with clouds of smoke, that all those who had assembled in the hall of the castle to witness the spectacle had to run outside to breathe.

Like a belching chimney, more and more smoke poured from Hole-in-the-Head's hollow until a thick, grey fog choked the whole castle.

Pephredo, sore embarrassed by this humiliation, rode off to his father's palace in the north, abandoning Gulwin Castle altogether.

Hearing the stampede of horses leaving the castle, Prunella and Roland left their cottage to go and see if they could find their son on the hill. When they climbed the steep slope and arrived at the castle they were amazed to see that every wall was all covered over with great, fleshy mushrooms. Prunella picked one of the mushrooms from the wall and chomped on it. She announced it was the most delicious fungus she had ever tasted and encouraged her husband to do the same. He too ate one and agreed – it was most moist and tasty.

The pair soon recovered their son and invited all the villagers up onto the hill to take a share of mushrooms for themselves; the bounty was so remarkable that there was enough food there to feed the villagers for the next year.

Prunella and Roland congratulated their clever son on smoking out the wicked prince with clouds of fungus spores. Feeling sorry that they had perhaps mistreated and used their child badly, they made the decision at last to plug Hole-in-the-Head's bonce with a great cork, and they swore they would never jerk or joggle their sweet son again.

In a week or two the open gorge in Hole-in-the-Head's skull healed over and he learnt to speak and to work in the fields like every other son in the village; his parents renamed him Kasen because it meant 'the helmeted one'. The hole in Kasen's head that was no longer there was never mentioned again and everybody lived long, happy lives.

Child abuse aside, this is a rather fun story that seems to anticipate the invention of anti-caking agents in table salt that paved the way for the creation of salt shakers. I cannot bear the sight of table seasonings because I was once trapped for twenty-four hours in a Cheshire salt mine and became badly dehydrated in the briny atmosphere. Unfortunately for me, on making my eventual escape, I stumbled straight into a neighbouring pepper factory and was only saved from sneezing to death by an opportunistic pepper robber who had chosen that evening to secretly fill her sack with pilfered peppercorns. After thanking the kind condiment-thief, I felt it was my civic duty to report her to the police; this I did, and I'm pleased to say that I still continue to write letters to her in Peterborough Prison. Returning to the folk narrative for a moment, I would suggest that this story is a good one to tell to any alcoholics in your family or circle of friends, as the resolution actually involves putting a cork in a vessel to solve the problems, rather than uncorking a bottle to alleviate your feelings of self-loathing.

Two Lace-Makers

Many traditional industries and their accompanying folk narratives have sadly died out over the course of the centuries. Lace-making is one such industry. Today, the town where this story is set is home to more modern forms of enterprise such as second-hand car sales and sofa retail. The only lace on sale there today is to be found either in a doily and tablemat shop (sadly in terminal decline – the merchandise offered within has a somewhat narrow market appeal) and another, less salubrious establishment, which I will not give the oxygen of publicity to. The depth of depravity in that benighted outlet ought never to be experienced by anyone. Two hours in there was quite enough for me.

In the town of Wendleton there once lived two lace-makers: a good lace-maker and a bad lace-maker. The good lace-maker was sore aggrieved as no matter how hard he tried and how well he paid his employees, he could never compete with the bad lace-maker who produced a miraculous amount of fine filigree. Each day the good lace-maker became steadily poorer and would go to bed most lachrymose. His wife was so discomposed by her husband's sorrow, that one evening, she stole into the bad lace-maker's lace-mill to discover the secret of his production methods and to divine how the man seemed to be so rich when he appeared to have no workers toiling for him. Luckily for her, she found the backdoor unlocked and she proceeded up the stairs to the workshop. To her great surprise, she found a goblin within, twirling and twisting bobbins so fast that a strong wind blew with mighty force around the room. The goblin, still working, turned to the lady and sobbed 'I cannot stop making lace! That black-hearted lace-maker has my feet! I can never leave until I have my dear paws back!'

'But what has he done with your feet?' the kind wife replied.

'He has chopped them off with his Damascus knife and wears them about his neck! I am powerless to leave until they are returned!'

The good lady saw how infernally miserable the poor creature was and swore she would retrieve the goblin's feet. Being a canny woman, she knew of the Old Ways: a sprinkling of valerian in the bad lace-maker's pipe would soon send him off into a deep, dark sleep.

She carried out her plan the very next day, by bribing the wicked lace-maker's maidservant with a few hunks of bread and pheasant's wing. Duly, the maidservant made sure the valerian was surreptitiously sprinkled into the bad lace-maker's tobacco and when the cruel old man was fast asleep she had the girl open his room. The good wife retrieved the goblin's feet, which were about the man's neck in the form of a grotesque neck-chain, and she hurried back to the stricken goblin and handed him his missing body-parts. The instant the feet had been restored he dashed the spindles on the floor and jumped for joy on his returned pads. The spell was broken and his heart soared with joy at his renewed freedom.

The bad lace-maker soon went out of business as no one in Wendleton would work for him, such was his malignant character. The good lace-maker prospered, for he paid the goblin well for his work, and he slept like a child betwixt husband and wife, content and dearly loved until the day the man and woman died. Thereafter the goblin was seen no more and lace-making soon stopped altogether in the town. On a rainy night, some say that one can still hear the sound of the little goblin wailing in grief for his lost friends.

It's no surprise to any of us that lace-making has all but ground to halt on this sceptred isle. I suspect that the goblin – if he did exist, and had had the nous to do so – would most likely have relocated to China where the industry is booming. After reading this tale, my grandma Joyce Berrial used to remind me that it is not good to sleep with a child in the bed – not only does it stifle the natural course of lovemaking between a sanguine young couple but there is also the hazard of rolling onto and compressing the infant. I asked her whether I should have the same concern regarding a shape-shifting bug-a-boo like the goblin invading my bed, and she said in this case I was quite wrong to harbour this worry. Such goblins, Grandma Berrial told me, were at liberty to mutate into the form of a flannel, thus avoiding the unpleasant death of being flattened by a dozing, languid pair of buttocks. I have not yet had a goblin as a bedfellow, but should this ever come to pass, I feel I should not need to panic at the prospect of smothering it during the course of my nocturnal tossings.

Boastful Master Kelly

Ask anyone in the street what England's most haunted town is, and they will probably say they don't know. If you're lucky, you might meet a paranormal investigator, and they will most likely tell you that it's Pluckley in Kent. This is the point where I like to inform the ignoramus that Pluckley is a village, not a town. The town mentioned in the following story was certainly once England's most haunted, though it seems no longer to enjoy this accolade on account of the fact that most of it is now a car-park for a nearby airstrip. That's not to say that there is anything about a car park that precludes ghostly presences, but turbine engines do tend to dislodge spectres and blow them into the next county. As you might imagine, one of the least ghostly places in England is Heathrow Airport, although the absence of ghosts there has not stopped it being a truly horrible, horrible place.

Reputedly, the most haunted town in all of England was Forby St Vera and for many tedious years it was also home to an irksome youth known as Master Kelly. The young man was always bragging about his exploits and would try to beguile women with his fantastic tales of heroism and courageousness. The older men (and most of the young ones too) tolerated these extraordinary tales, but as soon as Kelly reached the age of thirteen, he became an even greater nuisance for he was now permitted to sup in the town's taverns. Alcohol only served to amplify the youth's boasts and claims, and the townsfolk were becoming far less willing to suffer his inflated indulgences.

One rain-blighted night when the wind was howling down the chimney of the Black Bull Inn, an elderly man named Martyn challenged the young braggart to prove his steel. For he had noticed that the boy never betook himself to engaging in chatter about ghosts and imps, even though this was most common talk in the streets and parlours of Forby St Vera. Martyn interrupted Kelly's latest tall-tale with an invitation to spend a night with him in the Mallow folk's haunted barn, where a ghastly phantom was said to manifest every night as the bell tolled two o'clock. The boy's ruddy face drained somewhat, but he was unwilling to admit his fear of ghosts to this old man. He agreed to this supernatural caper, and that very night the pair, to the great amusement of the patrons of the Black Bull, sat down in the chilly barn and waited for the chimes that heralded the spectre's appearance. Surely enough at the appointed hour, the phantom did appear, and most alarming it was too – for it was the shade of a mighty white horse that stamped and snorted with all the fury of hell. Old Martyn stood his ground, but young Kelly shrieked and dashed out of the barn at great speed.

The next evening, Master Kelly returned to the Black Bull, although his hands were shaking most terribly. Martyn sidled up to the lad and said:

'Ah! Master Kelly! So you were scared of the spirits after all!'

The boy was not yet ready to admit to his fear, so he said in reply:

'Nay, sir, nay. I merely hastened to be away, for any fool knows that to see a white horse is unlucky. I crossed my fingers and ran to find a dog, to expel the misfortune.'

Martyn was maddened by this, for the boy certainly knew his country-lore well. He could not deny that the boy had been sensible, though he knew most assuredly that the crowing lad had been scared by the ghost and was covering his shame with a lie.

Not willing to be beaten by this, Martyn challenged the boy a second time, for he was annoyed by the smug grin spreading over Kelly's victorious face.

'Very well,' said the old man, 'come with me tonight to the Forby Castle ruins and prove your mettle there.'

Young Kelly was reluctant, but Martyn would not relent until the boy agreed. And so, that night, they settled amongst the chill stones of the castle and waited until the bell had chimed twelve, for the spirit would surely appear at that time.

The older gentleman was not wrong: as the last chime echoed about the hills, a thin wailing was heard and the misty shape of a new-born child swept over the broken castellations and floated towards them, begging to be shown the way to church.

As he had done the previous night, Master Kelly leapt up with a piercing cry and sped back to the town below before the glowing infant vanished, as if the ghost had been a candle flame snuffed by unseen fingers. Martyn was somewhat discomfited too by the apparition, but he was firmer than the youth and when it had disappeared, he strolled back into town rather more slowly than the boy had.

The next evening Martyn was keen to exult in his triumph and besought to tease the boy for his lily-livered timidity. However the youngster was so late in arriving at the pub that the old man supposed he might not show at all. When Kelly did appear, he was shaking more than he had been the day before and took to drinking only strong liquors.

'Scared, were you, lad?' laughed Martyn, enjoying the boy's evident discomposure. But, as ever, the callow youth had a quick reply, albeit through quivering lips:

'Nay, sir, nay. I fancied that the child was unbaptized. I was in search of a minister.'

Martyn was dismayed at how the boy had again found a reasonable excuse, and dared not question Kelly's judgement, for the Good Lord is most wrathful to those that doubt. After draining their cups, the old man walked the shivering boy home and was on the point of suggesting another test of the youth's bravado, when they were both shocked to see a small shadowy form ambling towards them.

The dark little man ahead all of a sudden paused on the path and forced the pair to verily brush alongside it as they passed. Young Kelly glanced at the countenance of the newcomer as he walked by and saw, to his absolute horror that the face of the figure was that of his own –

for he had seen his own fetch and this prophesied only one thing – his imminent death.

The boy jumped into Martyn's arms and sobbed 'I am afraid of ghosts, I am! I am!' As he held the terrified boy, Martyn finally understood the teenager's greatest fear was not ghosts at all, but himself. He feared the lies he told; he feared the consequences of his own falsehoods and he feared the damnation he would suffer for his perjuries.

The fetch walked slowly away and Master Kelly gurgled abominably before falling lifeless to the stony ground.

According to Grandma Berrial, a fetch is the ghostly double of oneself that always augurs ill for those who see it, for it signals that death is near. Grandma was very superstitious and her fear of seeing her own doppelganger was so extreme that she would never allow anyone to take a picture of her, lest it hasten her demise. Back in the 1950s when she was a very old woman, Grandma Berrial discovered from a friend (who worked as a film-splicer in Shepperton Studios) that she had inadvertently been recorded as a passer-by in the forthcoming Norman Wisdom farce Take That Hat Off Indoors. *She was so worried about this that she managed to force entry into the cutting-room one night and destroy the entire film with a pair of pinking shears. Needless to say, the loss of the negatives was all hushed-up by the studio and that's why no-one's ever heard of the film. Even to this day*

Norman Wisdom doesn't talk about it, and that's beside the fact that he's dead.

The Wolves of Wodlesham

These days parsley has been relegated to the status as a garnish on top of fancy meals, and most people discard the sprig as if it were ornamentation and nothing else. In fact, growing this mystical herb can be very hazardous indeed. A friend of mine once grew some parsley and died six years later in a car crash in Puerto Rico. I have spent many years drawing out a complex map of causality that demonstrates how the parsley sowing led to her downfall, but it is too large to publish here, so you'll have to take my word for it. Please do not grow your own parsley, as it is fraught with dangers. It's fine to purchase it from your local greengrocer, as if there was a mistake in propagating the crop, the shop-owner will perish, not you.

Many years ago, long before helicopters crossed our blue skies, there was a family of wolves (called the Synnershins) that lived happily in the village of Wodlesham alongside their human neighbours. It would not be true to say that the villagers did not fear the canine kin, for such beasts can be quite unpredictable and vicious, but these wolves had never so much as harmed a hair on anyone's scalp in all their long years of residence in Wodlesham. The wolves were tolerated because they grew prodigious quantities of parsley, which the villagers made good use of and, in return, the wolves took a share of the beef that the villagers produced.

This equitable relationship was very good for the villagers because parsley helped heal the swollen rheumatic bones of the old folk and there was not a man in the village that did not have a thick mop of hair, because the seeds of the herb, when sprinkled about the pate, cured the horror of baldness. The growing of parsley is always left to those of an evil disposition, as it flourishes when nurtured by the hand of a witch or by the paw of a fearsome beast. Many a fool in the village's past had tried to propagate the plant and had met with an untimely death.

One afternoon, a local woman was hammering on the Synnershins' door begging for parsley, as her new-born son could not see from his milky eyes. The panicked woman thanked the wolves as she left and handed them a hunk of meat in return, sure that when she had mixed the herb in storm-water and doused her son's unblinking eyes, he would see her at last. Moments after she had departed, there was yet another knock at the door, and Papa Synnershin walked up to the entrance to speak to the visitor. Standing on the step was a tall man dressed in the pelts of murdered wolves, brandishing a mighty silver sword. Before he could do anything, the warrior plunged the blade into the old wolf's heart, and he fell to the floor dead. The killer then dashed into the cottage and slew Mama Synnershin and her four cubs. The warrior roared in triumph and skinned the six wolves before depositing their pelts in a canvas bag.

It didn't take long for the villagers of Wodlesham to discover that the Synnershins had been slain, and their hearts were broken at the wolves' gory deaths. The warrior, whose name was Richard Slatterkid, upset the villagers all the more by taking up residence in the Synnershins' home, hoarding every last floret and stem of parsley for himself. The Wodleshamites were so terrified of the wolf-executioner that none of them would go near the place lest they too meet with a gruesome end for their friendship with the wolf family.

However, Richard Slatterkid had never come across parsley-cultivators in wolf-form before, and he was ignorant of the dangers of the herb. For many weeks he had feasted on parsley and made great pies and sausages from the Synnershins' larder.

About three weeks into his occupancy of the cottage, Slatterkid decided that it was high time to dig up one of the parsley beds and plant some new seeds, so that he could continue to bake with the tasty herb. Unfortunately for him, he planted the seeds on a bright morning in May; even the simplest dunderhead would warn against such a folly - for a mortal man ought only to do this on Good Friday, when the bad earth is recovered from Satan's ownership. Slatterkid used a fine golden spade from the Synnershins' outhouse to dig the earth, but as soon as he started toiling, he felt something roll in the crumbling soil. Bending down and brushing the greasy fringe from his pinched face, he soon discovered what was beneath the earth: it was a wolf-cub (for all wolf cubs are delivered from parsley beds); the grey pup snarled as it leapt from the muddy bed and snapped so savagely at Slatterkid's throat, that he bit the man's head clean off.

The last of the Synnershins grew to be a powerful and kind old wolf and redeemed the land that was his; he worked hard for the villagers of Wodlesham for the rest of his long life. As a mark of respect and gratitude, the village was renamed Wodlehound, and it still bears this name today.

A long time ago, my husband Desmond and I were on holiday in Dalby Forest in North Yorkshire when we came across what we took to be an abandoned puppy. When we had returned to Shadwell, we brought the dog with us, but as it matured we started to realise that it was a wolf as it grew to an enormous size and would howl at the full moon. It also developed the uncanny ability to walk through solid walls unimpeded, which was quite discomfiting when one was spending a penny on the lavatory. One sad night, the wolf walked through a supporting wall straight into my two-bar electric fire and was killed instantly by the surging current. Thus ended the legend of the Last Wolf in England.

Uncle Darwyn

Once again, you are about to be plunged into conflict at the heart of a family. It's familiar ground to all of us, but I have to say that when you reach my age, a greater peace descends because many of the people you argued with in your youth are dead. Having said that, I remember going to see a psychic medium once and she declared that Grandma Berrial was coming through, across the ether. The first thing she said was 'Where's my watch?' followed by 'You never polish your shoes.' I found this infernally irritating as the whole séance experience is very one-sided; I tried telling Grandma that I sold her watch as I couldn't stand the ticking and that shoe polishing is a luxury for those with good hips. Of course the medium just 'shushed' me and I left later that evening annoyed and dreared by the prospect of more arguments when I get to heaven.

There were once two brothers called Adam and Darwyn Underbind. Adam was a good husband and father who worked hard to make a living on his farm in Bunnpenster. Darwyn was not a good husband (he was exceedingly naughty for he had four wives) and he lived a decadent life on Bunnpenster Rock where his lighthouse was fixed. Darwyn was often so drunk or so busy cavorting with his wives that many ships were lost on the savage rocks because he had not bothered to light the tower beacon.

On the mainland Adam would toil day and night on his fields whilst his wife tended to the chickens and geese as his daughter milked their only cow.

A mean trick that Darwyn had been playing on his brother for years was to creep onto the farm once a week, when the family were fast asleep for a few short hours, and steal half of their supply of butter. As if this wasn't enough, Darwyn would also liberate half of the farm's store of beer. The bad brother would put these pilfered things onto a barrow and quietly wheel it to the shore, before rowing back to his lighthouse. When he had returned to

Bunnpenster Rock, he fried his fish in butter that was not his and then he would wash this down with beer that was not his either. And so this had been going on for many a year.

Adam and his wife Mildred were not over-encumbered with intellect and had never wondered why they always had such a spare larder, in spite of their hard work. Their daughter, Elizabeth, was as equally block-headed as her parents, but she had an affinity with animals that was to become of great help in the poor family's plight.

One day, Elizabeth was washing her aching hands in the stream and muttering about how hard she worked and how little her family had to show for it. She was rather startled when the little bush next to her seemed to say this:

'Worry not, Elizabeth. I can help you.'

Elizabeth dried her hands on her apron and said:

'How can you help me? You are just a thicket of thorns.'

'Nay, I am Dunkpot and I be right caught up in this snaggle-trap. If you can release me, I'll be true to my word and help you,' said the little voice.

Elizabeth knelt down by the bush, parted its prickly branches, and saw a narrow little ferret, with a very big head, caught in the spiny twigs.

'Do you see? I am fairly stuck in here!' said Dunkpot.

Elizabeth carefully teased the thorny branches apart and pulled the little fellow from the bush.

'Thank you, Elizabeth,' said the ferret.

'How do you know my name?' said the girl.

'Oh, it was a guess. You look like an Elizabeth,' said Dunkpot.

'How did you come to be here?' asked the girl.

'My mistress died, and ever since then, I've been a-wandering. So, you have no butter and no beer? That's not very good,' said Dunkpot.

'I cannot understand it as our cow makes much milk and father brews such a lot of hops – yet we never seem to have anything in the larder to eat or drink,' said Elizabeth sadly.

'Where do you live?' asked Dunkpot.

'Over there, on Bunnpenster Farm,' said the young woman pointing at the barn peeping over the top of a hedgerow.

'Very well. Meet me back here in one month and I promise I shall be able to help you,' said the ferret.

Just then, the bell rang out, and Elizabeth said she would be having to get back to her butter churn or her mother would be cross with her; she ran back to the farm and pledged to find Dunkpot in a month's time.

After a month of scurrying around the farm and its outhouses, Dunkpot's spying had proved to be worthwhile. On four occasions he had seen Darwyn come into the dairy and steal the butter and beer and he told this to Elizabeth when they met again.

'He is such an evil man, Uncle Darwyn,' said Elizabeth. 'I would tell my father about this, but I fear he would get into a fight with my uncle. I cannot let that happen as he is twice the size of my father and has a terrible temper – he might kill my dear old daddy! Oh, whatever are we to do?' she cried.

'I have a fair idea, Elizabeth,' said Dunkpot with a swish of his little brown tail. 'Your uncle will be due back tonight for more of his thieving. Let him have his butter; let him have his beer. Do you trust me?' asked Dunkpot of Elizabeth.

'Oh, I do!' said the young woman.

'Good. Promise me this: keep out of the dairy and the beer store this evening. I have things to prepare. The wind is with us tonight. There is a storm coming,' said Dunkpot.

'What do you mean?' asked Elizabeth.

She did not receive a reply, because the ferret had already scurried off into the grass, towards the farm.

That night, in spite of the growing winds and hail, Darwyn moored his boat on the beach, slunk into the dairy and beer store and stole once more. He took an even greater supply this time, as he too knew there was a storm coming and Bunnpenster Rock would likely be cut-off from the mainland for many days. The evil uncle even stole bread and mutton and rowed them all back to his lighthouse where his wives would be waiting.

When Darwyn had gone, Dunkpot scampered up to Elizabeth's bedroom window and tapped on it with his paw. She let him in and dried his soaking fur with her blanket and then sat with the shivering little beast by the fire.

'Your uncle has gone,' said Dunkpot through chattering teeth.

'Yes, but what have we gained, for he will be back,' said Elizabeth.

'No, he will not,' said the ferret as his hair bristled with excitement.

'Why not?' said the young woman with a thrill of curiosity.

'Because,' answered Dunkpot, who then broke into song:

> 'I've salted his butters,
> I've salted his beers,
> I've salted his bread
> As salty as tears!'

'Goodness! Have you really?' said Elizabeth, clapping her hands with delight.

> 'I've salted his mutton -
> Tell me what do you think?
> When he's back on his rock

He'll have nothing to drink!

'And the storm's just come in,
Like your Dunkpot had said.
When the waters are calm
He will surely be dead!'

Well, Dunkpot was quite right. The storm lashed the coast hard, but it beat against Bunnpenster Rock even harder – and the thrashing went on for a fortnight. In that time Darwyn and his four wives all died of thirst, as they could not leave their lighthouse.

Dunkpot stayed with Elizabeth Underbind for the rest of her life and taught her many things, until she was a very wise woman indeed.

Folk tales can often be quite bold when it comes to pulling the curtains open on some taboo. This time I'm talking about polygamy, and sadly the curtain never really gets opened in this narrative - just tweaked slightly. I remember sitting on Auntie Vulna's lap asking her how a man could marry four wives. I can't quite call to mind what she said, but I do recall the very hard-to-describe face she made – something like a mixture of disapproving, saucy and sly. Dunkpot the ferret is a recurring character that you can find elsewhere in this volume of folk tales – I think Auntie Vulna included him in these stories, as she was rather fond of polecats. When she was dying, I had to look after her last ferret, Foalgin. As you may have heard, these animals are extremely intelligent but also highly mischievous – not only could it operate the remote control for the television set, but I still swear to this day that it completed an entire crossword puzzle whilst I was out of the room engaged in scrambling an egg. Curiously, Foalgin then appeared to have eaten half the evidence of this magical feat, because I had to take him to the veterinary surgery after he went off his biscuits and a ballpoint pen was retrieved from his colon. It was a very mysterious episode.

Mr Willow

If you're poetically inclined, you may have spent some time underneath the boughs of a willow writing some turgid lines of doggerel without the slightest notion of the folklore of the tree itself. The following story may be illuminating for you. The idea of sitting beneath a willow tree and writing some verse is a rather lovely one, but when I tried this myself, I found it to be most uncomfortable. I swiftly terminated my artistic endeavours because the whipping motion of the sticks was akin to being in a Victorian flogging machine. I've no idea whether such a device has ever existed, but if it did, I'm sure a Victorian would have invented it. The following story requires the suspension of disbelief for the more empirically minded amongst you. I suggest a suspension of roughly ten fathoms if you're underwater, or sixty feet if you're on dry land. If you're in need of metrical measurements, I recommend you locate a Frenchman and ask him, as I've no idea what a centimetre is.

Once upon a time Cleaston Clessard was renowned as one of the most heavily wooded towns of all of England. Being so deep in amongst the trees can give folk a queer outlook on life and there certainly were some odd men and women who lived there. Strangest of all of them was a man called Mr Willow. An old song, whose music has long been forgotten, used to run thus:

> He's welcome in winter,
> He scares in the springtime,
> He's shocking in summer,
> He's ails in the autumn,
> So who is this fellow?
> He's Old Mr Willow!

You see, Mr Willow looked like any other man when winter visited Cleaston Clessard, but when spring came, buds would burst through his skin, giving him the look of one suffering from a terrible green pox. By the time summer came around, his whole body would all over be covered in verdant leaves and his fingertips would sprout waving sticks. When autumn arrived he would look most appalling, for he was a mass of shivering brown fronds, smelling of rot and decay. However, when it was wintertime, Mr Willow would look quite normal and the folk of the town would even deign to talk to him in the inn.

However, no matter what time of year it was, Mr Willow could never afford to stay still too long or his aching feet would sprout roots and he would be fixed to the spot. The poor man would forever keep pacing, lest he thereby become anchored to the ground.

Sadly, nothing stays the same for long, and gradually any affection the people had for Mr Willow began to dwindle. New fears and anxieties troubled the townsfolk – chief amongst them the horrors of witchcraft. One harsh winter in the middle of the eighteenth century, when Mr Willow was looking quite normal, he found that he was barred from entering the inn.

'Please, sir! Let me enter!' said Mr Willow to the publican, 'it is a most cold night.'

'We don't want you here, Willow,' said the innkeeper. 'You are a devil, sir! Up with your sticks and off my doorstep, fiend!' bellowed the innkeeper.

'Oh, sir, I thought you were a friend,' said Mr Willow despondently.

'Christ's toes! I swear if you do not leave now, I'll chop off your wicked head and throw it on the fire,' replied the other man as he waved his clenched fist at him. The door was duly slammed shut on Mr Willow, who began to weep as he walked back over the frost-hardened ground into the forest.

He knew of one woman whom he could trust to offer him a warm spot for the night, so he walked into the deepest part of the woods towards the cottage of Miss Hardneck.

Mr Willow was most sickened to see that his true friend was not in her cottage warming herself by the hearth; instead, he saw that her limp body was swinging from the branch of the old aspen tree outside her garden wall. Her house was but a smouldering black wreck and he could see, in spite of the gloom, that small rags of cloth with the word 'witch' had been tied painfully all over the extremities of her bloodied body.

Stricken with grief, Mr Willow let out a howl that would have frozen the blood of the boldest she-wolf. In great sorrow, he stopped his pacing, hung his head, and began to feel his shoes split open. As the hours passed and the night grew darker, his roots coiled deeper and deeper into the soil until he was stuck fast in the lonely woodland.

When spring arrived Mr Willow's skin had already become cracked and grey and he soon sprouted glistening green buds that rapidly erupted into cascades of bright green foliage. From his mouth grew two great branches, so he was no longer able to talk. By the time autumn crisped his leaves he was no longer like a man. He had become a tree.

One hundred years later, on a sweet day in May, a young girl called Milly Marton came wandering into the forest. Her dear face was streaked with tears, for she had been forsaken in love. It was still the custom then, as it had been for many centuries, for a lover whose beau had deserted them to find a willow tree and wear a garland of its leaves as an emblem of their sorrow. She followed the little stream that ran through the woods, up to where the ivy-strangled ruin of Miss Hardneck's cottage was, and at last came upon a mighty willow tree, whose mournful branches swung gently to and fro in the breeze. Milly dabbed her face with her lacy sleeve then reached up and plucked one of the willow's strands. It was a beautiful branch for it was smothered with delicate, pale catkins. She wound the sprig around her head; the instant that she had done this Milly heard a low, deep sigh. Looking up into the hanging boughs of the tree she saw what looked like a pair of doleful brown eyes at the top of the trunk. She gasped and placed her hand to her mouth, after touching it's burning-hot bark.

Milly felt sure she must have brushed her hand against something in the forest, for her skin felt strange. When she examined her hand, she saw that it was flecked all over with glowing green shoots.

Milly Marton was not afraid, for she was a canny lass. She knew she had found her one true love; she embraced Mr Willow's trunk and became as one with him.

Much of the mighty woodlands of Cleaston Clessard are now lost, but it is said that if a rambler is determined enough, he or she might find the tumbled ruin of an old house, next to which are a pair of willow trees, twined and wound together like a lover's knot.

One of the soundest bases for a good marriage is shared grief. Happiness is fleeting but bereavement is profound and long lasting, so it's a great way to bind two people together. I met my late husband Desmond in one of London's first dedicated pet cemeteries. He was burying a Dalmatian bitch and I was committing the body of a cherished Elkhound to the earth. Desmond tripped over a tiny headstone for a guinea pig (the correspondence between size of the deceased and size of headstone is unique to animal graveyards); I helped him up and we went to the cafeteria over the road for a chat. Apart from the time he went swimming with a female business client, we had a very stable and loving marriage. However, if Des had ever asked me to become a tree, I would have had to put my foot down. It's not so much the fixity of life as a tree that I find frightening, but the thought of being the host to so many animals, many of them of a burrowing nature. Can you imagine the horror of an Asian Longhorn beetle chomping its way into your hindquarters and being powerless to stop it? I certainly can.

The Poacher and the Devil

Game pie is not a dish just for the nobility; poor people who steal can enjoy this rich and flavoursome meal too. There's a certain romance to the notion of poaching that is very hard to resist, but any would-be rabbit-catcher needs to think long and hard about the consequences of getting caught in the act. I was a once good friend with a woman who had bought a huge Winchester double-barrelled shotgun on the black market with the intention of acquiring some ptarmigans for her supper. The expulsion of the first two cartridges caused such a loud report that she was momentarily deafened and could not hear the approach of a nearby family who were netting butterflies. In her confusion she shot the entire family dead and almost broke her back burying them in a muddy trench. You really are better off going to one of those expensive farm shops and paying through the nose for game, rather than risking imprisonment for theft and murder.

A devious poacher called Willard Bottlebrush was scampering home one evening cursing to himself, for the hessian sack slung over his shoulder was empty save for a couple of bony stoats.

Bottlebrush had just got to the crossroads that signalled that he was almost home in the village of Tockton Oggley; he had traversed this path hundreds of times, but on this warm night there was something rather unexpected waiting for him on the road. A tall fellow in a dark hooded cape was standing in the middle of the track and waved at the poacher as he approached. This was not altogether pleasing, because the poacher preferred to go about his business unseen, for obvious reasons. Most disconcertingly, the cowled gentleman seemed to know his name.

'Good Friday morning, Willard!' said the strange figure in an altogether too familiar manner.

Upon hearing this, Bottlebrush remembered that it was indeed Good Friday, and grunted

'Good Friday to thee too,' before hastening his pace to be away from the man. Before he could pass, the tall man beckoned him over and asked him how fine his night's yield was.

Bottlebrush replied with a snarling 'What business is that of thee?' and the stranger laughed softly.

'Willard, I could make your nightly haul so great that you would need two sacks to get it home. Hand me your bag.'

Bottlebrush was normally an unobliging fellow, but something about the newcomer compelled him to pass over his paltry sack. The moment it was in his hands, the hooded gentleman up-ended it and out tumbled half a dozen fat partridges and six roundsome geese, all plucked and ready for roasting. Bottlebrush's eyes glittered and he licked his lips with great relish.

'Oh, sir! This is most wonderful! Tell me your secret!' demanded the poacher.

'Alas,' replied the strange man, 'I cannot do that. But, for a small price, I can promise ye that every night's hunting forthwith will be as bountiful as this one.'

'Oh, d—n!' said Bottlebrush. 'I am a poor man. All I have is this farthing.'

The dark fellow laughed again and put his arms around the poacher's shoulders and drew him close – his breath was like old Stilton and pond-water.

'Sir, I do not seek for money! What I desire is not to be found in your purse. No, I require but one tooth from your dishonest mouth,' said the stranger.

Bottlebrush assented and opened his jaws, allowing the other man to reach inside. There was a sharp twist and then a tug, before the poacher was looking most excitedly upon his tooth as it rested in the centre of the stranger's hand.

'Tomorrow's harvest shall be plentiful,' said the tall fellow, 'although I ask you to rest inside your cottage until dusk. Do not go to church. In the evening you will enjoy your reward. Farewell.' The caped man walked away from the direction of Tockton Oggley, and whistled a mournful tune to himself, before he disappeared around the curve of the road.

Willard Bottlebrush did exactly as he had been instructed the next day, and when night fell, he stole into the coppice at the edge of the town and caught some exceedingly fine birds and sixteen plump rabbits. He was overjoyed at his successes and scurried home after only half an hour, with two full sacks.

When he was back at his home, Bottlebrush emptied the contents of the bags onto the floor with his skinning knife clenched in anticipation between his remaining teeth. The knife clattered to the floor when he saw what the sacks had contained.

Instead of a hoard of juicy game, the stinking bodies of a hundred loathsome rats slithered into a putrid jumble onto the flagstones.

From that night onward, every midnight sortie the poacher made into the woods was accompanied by the stranger's nauseating whistling tune, and upon returning home, every beast he'd caught had been transformed into gruesome, filthy vermin.

Willard Bottlebrush soon cast off his former life of poaching and betook a more honest trade as a carpenter. He never missed church ever again.

An old family favourite of mine was Bottlebrush Pie, and I recall asking Auntie Vulna how this name came about. The story you have just read is the same as the one I was told. It was only in later years that I realised that we had all been eating a rat-tart when Bottlebrush Pie had been served. Whilst many amongst you might find that appalling, the most important thing to me was that it was made with love. Any meal made in anger tastes bad, no matter how many onions you put in it. I had a terrific row with one of my neighbours once about stinging nettles that grow at the bottom of my garden (I grow them for medicinal purposes), and my neighbour was complaining that they were an eyesore. Imagine my surprise the next day when I found that she'd gone to the trouble of making me a lamb casserole, and had placed it on my doorstep as a token of appeasement. I was horrified to discover that when I ate it that evening, there was a quantity of broken glass in the stew that would have been quite dangerous, had I not fished every last bit out. A meal made when one is harbouring ill feelings will always be a culinary disaster.

Daddy Coppernut

Anyone who's ever had a Tarot reading will recognise the singular thrill of having one's future read out to oneself. I'm ashamed to say I often had my future told by Great Grandmother Berrial before I choose to follow the somewhat narrower path to Heaven in my teenage years. Yes, the cards often made some startlingly accurate predictions, but the one thing they didn't anticipate was quite how disappointing my life would turn out to be.

There is a deep gulley in a forgotten part of Biddlegate that leads to a cave known as Crabbett Hole. A wrinkled old man called Daddy Coppernut used to live there; he was greatly revered by all in Biddlegate, for he could tell anyone their future through the arcane practice of gut-reading. All that Daddy Coppernut required was the body of a recently killed animal, from the smallest Jenny Wren to the biggest heifer, whereupon he would slit the cadaver's belly open and divine the signs that lay in a looped agglomeration on the ground before him. For many years, whenever a child was feverish or a husband starting wasting, the villagers would climb to his wind-blown crevice to hear the fate of their loved ones. And the old gizzard-scryer was never wrong.

One bleak January, the mother of a Biddlegate barmaid climbed the steep hills with a heavy poke in her shaking hands, desperately worried about her daughter who was bleeding most terribly after a kettle had fallen on her head. The mother was so concerned that she had brought two dead piglets, just to be sure. Daddy Coppernut welcomed the timorous lady into the Crabbett Hole and calmed her with a warming broth.

'Ease your mind, madam,' said the gizzard-reader, 'and we shall see what we see.'

The mother anxiously withdrew both piglets and Daddy Coppernut sliced them open from gullet to navel. The innards spilt onto the cave floor in two sticky mounds and Coppernut sat himself down next to them, muttering to himself. After five minutes, the old man stood up and placed his hands on the woman's cheeks and drew her closer, so that their noses were almost touching:

'One shall live; the other shall die, for so it is written in the coils,' said the man.

The woman gasped and stepped backward.

'But,' she cried, 'I have but one daughter and no sons!'

'Then why two piglets?' asked Daddy Coppernut.

'I wanted to be sure, in case one of the hogs slipped from my bag on the way as my hands are trembling so, and I was fearful that I would lose one!' said the mother.

The gut-reader was horrified, for he knew what had come to pass.

'You must leave me now, woman. Go back to your child. If she survives this harsh night, she will live. Be gone!'

The puzzled mother fled the cave and was relieved to see her daughter sipping water and making jests with a kindly neighbour on her return. By the next day the girl was recovering her strength, and the mother was so delighted that she climbed the hills that afternoon with a bundle of food for the mystic in Crabbett Hole.

When she had clambered into the gloomy hollow, she was saddened to see that there, upon the ground, was the cold, dead body of Daddy Coppernut. For, unwittingly he had been tricked into foretelling his own demise.

In future, the people of Biddlegate put their giblets and viscera to better use (in the form of sausages and pies) and no longer sought to know what fate awaited them.

A tale like this always makes me wonder how Daddy Coppernut came by a skill like gut-reading, if indeed he was ever a real person. When I was a much younger woman, I did a stint in a butcher's shop and I saw all sorts of extraordinary things going on there, I can tell you. The owner of the shop had the striking name of Paul Stalk and he had a very trim physique on account of the fact that he was a professional boxer. I once went into the refrigeration room at the back of the property and found Mr Stalk and his apprentice Harry Parsons using an entrail as a skipping rope. Before I knew it, I was drawn reluctantly into a game of 'Copy the Fox'. The trick, as I soon learnt, was never to squeeze the gut-rope too tightly or a rather unpleasant excretion would emerge from one or both ends, surely splattering the game-players in a rather odious mush.

The Lady Who Lived in a Pinecone

The following story is about the effects of lateness, but it also features a lady who lived in a very unusual abode. The strangest home I've ever seen was on a holiday resort in Malaga in Spain. I was sat licking an ice cream very close to Midnight (this was both the time of day and the name of a discotheque) and noticed that a man was emerging from the fibreglass nose of a dinosaur on a children's adventure playground. He was carrying a bag (of what I can only assume to be his own discharged waste) that he dropped into the bin, before climbing back into one of the great flared nostrils of a fibreglass stegosaurus. He seemed very happy and I was cheered at how public-spirited he was being by not just emptying his excreta onto the ground. If I'm being honest, I suppose I was a little bit jealous of his lifestyle choice.

Alma Gussey was the most unpunctual woman in the land and she was forever getting into trouble for arriving late.

When she was young, Alma was beaten by her schoolmasters for her tardiness, although her perpetually sore bottom never taught her the lesson it should have done.

When she was a young woman, Alma fell in love with a very patient man, but he broke off their engagement when she failed to turn up to the wedding on time.

As an older woman, Alma burnt every meal she ever cooked over her lonely stove, as she could never properly attend to the timings of boiling, frying or baking.

Eventually, Alma Gussey was booted out of her cottage by her landlord as she always forgot to pay her rent on time, so she ended up with nowhere to live.

After a while, Alma came across a large pinecone in the forest that was just about big enough to squeeze into, so she made this her new home. It was a very cramped way to live, but it more or less suited her needs, and the pinecone had a lot of useful nooks and crannies in which to store her few possessions.

One day, when Alma was sitting on a hummock next to her pinecone home doing some knitting, a village watchman walked up to her and told her to be wary as there was a big storm coming and the field where she lived in her pinecone would most likely be flooded.

'Now,' said the watchman, 'don't you forget what I told you, Miss Gussey. Don't be slow about making preparations for the flood. If I were you,' continued the man, 'I'd ask a neighbour for shelter.'

'Oh, I will,' said Alma. 'Thank you for warning me.'

The watchman walked off to warn others of the coming trouble, and Alma continued her knitting, humming gently to herself as she did so.

In a while, it began to rain. The weather worsened and before long great forks of lightning shattered across the sky.

'I'd best be getting into my pine cone in a moment,' said Alma to herself, 'but I think first I'll just finish off this row of stitches first.'

Alma was so behindhand that she didn't even notice the waters rising about her until it was too late. The flood was almost up to her knees and her knitting was soaked through.

'Oh my,' said Alma, 'it is very wet. I'd better get into my pinecone and out of this rainwater.'

But Alma had been far too slow. The pinecone had closed up tight and there was no way of getting inside, no matter how hard she picked and pulled at the wooden scales.

'I'm too late!' cried Alma Gussey, as the water swept her away, and sent her tumbling towards the sea.

Whilst Alma Gussey was no doubt a very irritating woman, it's hard not to like her for her complete rejection of society's obsession with timekeeping. In the 1960s many women liberated themselves from patriarchy's grip by burning their brassieres; I took a different route and burnt my wristwatch. The benefit of this was that when the second wave of feminism had died down and women started buying breast-supporting undergarments again, I still had all of mine and my watch only needed to have the soot cleaned off it before I could start wearing it again. I saved myself a lot of money. I've subsequently realised that female emancipation is more intellectual than simply setting fire to clothing – these days I make sure that I say 'no' to at least one man a day, and this has worked very well for me since I first started doing it in 1979.

The Singing Bastard
of Cobley Penn

If you're a parent, you doubtless think that your own children are the most talented offspring that have ever lived, but I'm afraid to say that after reading the next story you may have to revise your proud convictions. Let's not forget that pride is a deadly sin. Sometimes every youth needs to experience the terrors of deprivation – it's actually very good for them. Withhold the next lolly you buy for their insatiable lips and give them a glass of water instead. No one can fail to be disappointed by a glass of water in place of a treat. Lock them in their room for twenty minutes and enjoy the lolly for yourself. My favourite lollies are toffee-flavoured ones.

In the days before tractors there was a king by the name of Hedric who lived in a great castle in the wolds of Cobley Penn. He was apt to seduce any woman whom he took a liking to and several women whom he did not like at all. The result was that the surrounding village was populated with hundreds of bastards, many of whom grew up sorely resenting their fornicating father and his madge-poking ways. The wretched mothers had all been warned by Hedric that should they utter a word that revealed who the children's true father was, they would all be slaughtered.

The latest maiden to be deflowered was Rosy Banley who had been cleaning a fireplace when the unscrupulous king seized her and made her with child. After nine months, Rosy birthed a vigorous babe whose piping lungs never wheezed and bellowed like all other infants; instead the bonny child sang most beautifully both day and night and the good folk of Cobley Penn would gather every evening to listen to the sweet music.

Well, King Hedric soon heard about the strange child and ordered a retinue of his soldiers to sequester the baby and imprison him in the castle dungeons, for the king was greatly afeared that the singing would draw attention to him, as the baby was growing to be most lyrical in its melodies. Incarceration did not bring a stop to baby Banley's singing; in fact it only seemed to deepen the beauty of his pretty songs. Every sundown, when the nights were still, the Banley infant's singing would draw the beasts from the forests, which were quite beguiled by the glorious strains that escaped from the bowels of the castle. Hedric was half-pleased with this, for he would rain down arrows upon the creatures and stock his pantries with boar and deer.

One night, the singing was so exquisite, that even the tetchy brown bears were drawn to the castle walls, bewitched by the euphonious airs that drifted from the subterranean chambers. As we all know, a brown bear will brook no impediment to its pleasure, so they trampled over the footbridge and smashed the door down with their clawed fists, desperate to steal into the vaults of the castle and be close to the glorious song. Any man or woman who stood in the bears' way was mauled most terribly, and it did not take long before the bears had torn apart the dungeon door.

Little Banley was overjoyed at his rescue, and his singing grew even lovelier. He leapt onto the biggest bear's back and clung to his bristled pelt, singing yet more mellifluously. The animals, with their new friend, thundered up the cold stone steps and emerged into the Great Hall where there was one man standing in their way. For King Hedric stood in the doorway, armed with his bow and arrow. Banley's singing faltered for the first time, fearing that he was in terrible trouble. But before he could even discharge his first arrow, Hedric was felled by a wave of wild boar, maddened by the king's spite, who swelled up from behind him unseen. The king was dashed to the floor where the beasts quickly ripped him to shreds. The Banley boy was returned to his mother and the whole of Cobley Penn celebrated as one – men, women, children and beast – for they had all been delivered from the tyrannical yoke of the most evil king in the land.

I was curious to learn from my aunt what became of the remarkable singing boy in this story, and she dutifully provided this charming coda to the tale: he became a monk and committed all of his beautiful song to the praise of the Good Lord. Apparently, until Henry VIII demolished it, the corpse of the Banley monk continued to sing even in its priory tomb. Henry was yet another king who was a dirty great philanderer. The damage that that man did to some of Britain's most beautiful buildings is an absolute scandal. I'm ashamed to say, that I was so angry about Henry's destructive ways that I once vandalised one of his chairs during a visit to Hampton Court Palace by sawing away at its legs with a penknife I always keep in my handbag in case of emergencies. My *revenge backfired slightly as I later discovered that this was a 20th century reproduction and was intended for room guides to sit upon. The lady steward who did eventually rest on it was injured so badly in the chair's collapse that she needed two splints and a neck-brace before she was shoved into an ambulance. Fortunately, this shameful episode in my life was in the days before CCTV, so I eluded prosecution. It's quite astonishing how the monstrous effects of that Tudor king are still being felt to this day.*

Brownie Blackbonnet

I once persuaded my friend Mary to come with me to the Cotswolds to find the source of the River Thames. I was dreadfully disappointed to discover that it was just a soggy field crawling with hikers in primary-coloured waterproofs. One woman had even brought along her triplets, who not only made the scene unbearably uncanny, but it also filled the air with wailing demands for ice cream. If you have children, please don't take them to river sources — children much prefer to pound against the glass prisons of frustrated gorillas than being wheeled two miles up a hill to look at a dribbling hole.

The River Ormens was once the most beautiful river in all of England; it was said that many people used to stand and weep at the sight of the gentle river as it meandered through the flower-filled countryside of Drumpston. One day, however, the Ormens dried up and everybody complained that the unusually hot summer was to blame. A fellow called Gabriel Goodcup would not accept this excuse, so he decided that he would start the long, arduous journey to the river's source to discover why the Ormens failed to flow.

The forty-mile journey was indeed a difficult one, for it was all uphill and the sun beat down harder and hotter with every day that passed, but Gabriel Goodcup was a hardy chap, and he pressed on tirelessly until he finally arrived at the Ormens' dusty source in the Massley Mountains.

The brave adventurer found himself in the midst of a thick, dark forest that seemed to seethe with odious creatures that always kept hidden in the shadows but made hideous screeches and menacing growls. Undeterred, he pressed on, taking faith in the map that his wise uncle had drawn, feeling sure that he would soon find the towering white stone from beneath which the nascent river ought to have been trickling. Before long, Goodcup found himself in a mossy clearing and, in spite of the thick mist, he was overjoyed at finding the white stone that was the very image of the sketch his uncle had drawn for him on the map. Even though the forest itself was quite damp, not so much as a drop of water oozed from under the great stone. Goodcup could just about discern a track that must have once carried the virgin waters down the mountainside, though this was now just a reedy ruck in the soil.

Beneath the mighty white stone was a small crevice, just big enough for a man to crawl into, so he fell to his knees and poked his head inside. Almost the instant he did so, he recoiled in terror, for sitting inside the crude cave was a small coal-coloured creature with enormous black eyes, ears like elm-leaves and a lank white beard. The creature hissed as Goodcup fell backwards in shock. From a yard's distance, he could see that the beast was sitting upon a large, square rock that seemed to cap the top of the spring. The monster unfolded its arms and clung to the stone whilst a whistling sound issued from between its peg-like teeth. Then it spoke.

'I will eat you,' whispered the cave dweller.

'What is your name, creature?' asked Goodcup.

'My name is Brownie Blackbonnet and I will eat you.'

Goodcup had recovered his wits somewhat, and decided to call the brownie's bluff.

'Very well,' said the young man, 'come hither and eat me.'

The brownie snarled and said 'I will eat you later. I am guarding my spring. Be gone before I squeeze you into paste!'

Goodcup was a canny fellow, and he soon understood the greedy brownie's ways. It was clear to him that the beast would not shift from its rock, for fear of losing his magic stone that had quelled the bounty of the spring. This was to young Gabriel's advantage for he knew that eventually the brownie would have to drink water or he would perish. As Blackbonnet would surely eat him if he got too close, he realised that all he had to do was wait.

The days got even hotter as the summer wore on and all the mosses and ferns in the clearing wilted and died. And still the brownie clung to his spring stone like a limpet. Gabriel grew concerned, for his water was running out and his last flask was almost empty, save for the bottle of mead he had been given by his uncle.

Blackbonnet had grown thin and agitated by the time that Goodcup uncorked his mead three weeks into his vigil. In desperation, the brownie screamed: 'Water! Give me water!'

'Why, you would have plenty for yourself if you would only share it, Blackbonnet!' said the man.

'God's blood, give me water, you persecuting swine!'

Goodcup was almost on the point of telling the brownie that this was no water, when he realised he had had the perfect trap in his knapsack to catch Blackbonnet all along. Feigning pity, he passed the bottle – at arm's length – to the wailing creature whereupon it was quickly snatched and the parched brownie guzzled the entire bottle before throwing the spent vessel hard at Goodcup, hitting him on the hand. But, as the young man had gambled, Blackbonnet, being a forest sprite, would never have sipped so much as a thimble of an alcoholic brew before, and he knew that soon the mead would take effect. In a few moments, the hob's saucer-like eyes began to swim and he started swaying on his rock; Blackbonnet's limbs stiffened; he let out a great bubbling burp and fell from his enchanted stone in a faint. The moment he did so, Gabriel Goodcup heaved the great boulder from its place and water began to trickle out. Minutes later, the trickle was a torrent. As the water gushed forth, the pathetic spindly-limbed brownie was swept away.

Goodcup, having restored the great waterway, followed the stream all the way back home where he was celebrated for the rest of his days as the saviour of the River Ormens.

Back in the mid-1990s I made some extensive plans to establish a folk story theme park. It even had a name: Kitty Brownbelt's Folk Story Fheme Park. I had dreams that my name would be as famous as Mr Disney or Mr Alton Towers. The centrepiece of my park was to be the Massley Mountains trail up to a huge white stone made out of fibreglass. Sitting beneath this monolith would be an employee of mine dressed as Brownie Blackbonnet, whose job it would be to scare children before being pushed violently into a man-made watercourse, presumably to the delight of those who'd bothered to make the trek up to the site. I was sure the actor playing the brownie wouldn't mind, as he or she would be so drunk on mead (fed to them as part of the role play) that it would all seem like fun. However, my bank manager soon put an end to my business plan when he declared that it contravened virtually every health and safety law in the kingdom. 'Kitty,' my bank manager said, 'actors with liver disease are not rare, but you'd only be making the problem worse – and that's beside the fact that many of them could very well drown – we should never get to see their Hamlets.' His reasoning was immaculate; I left the bank suitably chastened and abandoned my theme park idea for good.

The Frenchman's Ghost

An area often overlooked by paranormal reporters is the topic of foreign-speaking phantoms. I have a job trying to understand most foreigners, let alone dead ones. My sister Eleanor was once kicked in the throat by a pregnant Friesian cow and was the talk of the town after she spontaneously started to speak Spanish, even though she'd never so much as eaten a Satsuma in her life. Alas, when a (now sadly very dead) Spanish pen-friend of mine, Nuna, came to stay, she reluctantly revealed that my sister was not speaking Spanish at all. Nuna was multilingual and swore that Eleanor was speaking no known language. Before we could transcribe this wonderful if painfully-acquired new parlance, my sister gave one great bellowing cough and returned to her native speech.

Dunton Becket in Shropshire was the home of a wealthy squire whose manor house was plagued by the ghost of a Frenchman. Most nights, the gruesome spectre would rouse the whole house with its dreadful clitter-my-clatter, fairly scaring the family of Squire Tyms out of their wits. Oftentimes, the continental revenant would breach the locked doors of the family's bedchambers and rave at them in its ghastly foreign tongue (even though it had no tongue to speak of). Squire Tyms was so fatigued with these nocturnal disturbances that he elected to build a facsimile of his manor house next door to the haunted one, with the avowed intention of abandoning the original to the mischievous shade's rattles and moans.

A ditch was soon dug to set the foundations of the squire's new residence, but the plans were sorely hampered when the grisly discovery of two skeletons, locked together in a death-grapple, were revealed lying in the loamy earth.

The squire, who was an ambitious man, was keen to disinter the cadavers and continue the work. However, the pit-diggers laid down their tools and refused to dig any more. Old Robert, the most elderly digger, explained to the squire that they had doubtless unearthed the body of the Guard of Shropshire whose valiant body was known to lie in the vicinity. The wise old shovel-smith explained that local lore spoke of this fabulous mortal who was buried alive after he fought for a whole year with a marauding foreigner. Their struggle was so protracted and untiring that they both worked themselves into the soil with their indefatigable exertions, until the walls of their trench tumbled down on top of them.

'Then which be which?' asked the squire, vexed by the delay.

'Why,' said Old Robert, 'them white bones on the right be our good lad. T'other is a stranger to these lands.'

'And how, pray, doth thou knowest that, sir?' replied the squire.

'Oh,' said Old Robert, smoothing his great red whiskers, 'that be easy. Any fool knows that a Frenchman's bones are black.'

The squire, who was a sagacious fellow, understood that there, clasping his foul bones to the dear Guard of the County, was the source of all of his family's woes and torments, for it was the inky skeleton of the restless spirit that troubled his manor. Delighted to finally avenge his persecuting phantom, the squire had the Frenchman's bones ground to dust in the mill, before feeding them to the finest swine in all of Shropshire. The unfortunate beast was then drowned before being burnt on a great bonfire in Dunton Becket's market square. As for the Guard, his good body was covered over with a fine slab of limestone, and the squire was cheered greatly to move back into his home, untroubled by the Frenchman's ghost, for it was never seen again.

I was an impressionable girl of twenty-one years when Aunt Vulna narrated this Gothic yarn to me. Unfortunately, I laboured under the misapprehension for decades afterward, that all Frenchmen's bones are black; my aunt was somewhat medieval in her outlook and her attitudes on most subjects were entrenched and inflexible. I would like to disavow any reader of the mistaken belief that foreign bones are any darker than those of a native Briton. Even Old Robert must have been young and open-minded once, before he swallowed this ludicrous fibula fib. I would also warn readers that not all house-ghosts are as alarming as the spook in this tale. I am occasionally visited by a poltergeist that helps me with the chore of washing-up. The technique it has developed to assist me in this bothersome task is quite singular but very effective: it smashes the crockery and I am compelled to purchase replacements from a high-street outlet. Nine times out of ten, shop-bought dishes are sold unsoiled and ready to use, thus avoiding the need to trouble myself with the tedium of soaping and scouring. If you are unconcerned by ecology and environmental disaster, then disposable plastic plates are a super innovation and can be bought at a fraction of the cost of their china equivalents.

Father Bloodwick
and the Cobbler's Cat

Any communists amongst you might be tempted to make a Marxist reading of the narrative that follows what with the themes of gigantic, oppressive consumers and honest, humble peasants. Be careful not to spend too long on identifying subtexts, though, or you'll get so bogged-down in theory that you'll never finish the story and you'll end up writing a PhD about it. There are far too many doctors in this country who don't have the first idea about how to use a scalpel let alone how to pilot a camera in a colonoscopy.

Samuel Stipples was a cobbler in a friendly little village called Hudley Hutch and for many years he had dutifully provided the villagers with very fine clogs. Every day, as the Hudley Hutchers went about their business, he would smile at the sound of the clacking shoes as they quickened over the cobbles.

Stipples was very fond of an enormous brown cat called Hazeltips who had been part of his houschold for many long years. Hazeltips was very sweet in nature and was more like a child, for she would assist the cobbler in his clog-making every day, apart from Sunday, when she would pad alongside the family and attend church. The churchgoers and the vicar were exceedingly fond of the cat too, and she was always fussed and petted by the congregation as she settled down on her very own pew and revelled in the Word of the Good Lord.

When Monday came, Hazeltips would begin her work, first sorting her master's nails from the buttons, then she would wax the leather ankle straps by proddling them with her soft paws. If Stipples ever mislaid his lasting-pincers, she would dive under the bench and retrieve them. In short, Hazeltips was a fellow worker to the cobbler, and not a day went by where she was not rewarded with a bowl of the dairy's creamiest milk for her good help.

However, one day a family of giants thundered into the village and declared that the villagers would all work for them; the giants brooked no refusals and any insolence was met with a horrible death. The family of giants were called the Bloodwicks, and very apt their name was too, for they would chomp to pieces anyone who resisted them.

The Bloodwicks, like all giants, particularly like to be the biggest people around, so anything that was too large was picked up and eaten, so that nothing approached their size and stature.

Even giants need shoes, so one rainy day Father Bloodwick stomped up to the cobbler's workshop and demanded he make him some shoes. As he was shouting through Samuel Stipples' window making this demand (for he was far too large to walk inside), he was jealously angry when he caught sight of the furry bulk of Hazeltips on the table who was busily lapping at a flank of leather to make it supple. In an instant he had reached his great hand inside and grabbed the mewing puss. Before Stipples could protest, the giant swallowed the cat whole.

'The same will befall you, cobbler, if you do not make all six Bloodwicks a pair of clogs before midnight!' boomed the giant, before stomping back to his great wooden castle at the top of the hill. In tears, the poor cobbler set about his task and made twelve new clogs, the size of horse-carts, before the clock struck twelve. His weeping was all the more bitter because all of his wood and leather was used up and he had no more materials to make a living. On hearing her father's cries, Samuel's daughter, Mabel, crept into the room to comfort her bereaved father.

'I don't know what to do, Mabel,' he stuttered, 'for Bloodwick will soon be back and I shall have to give him what he has ordered. And my poor, dear Hazeltips has been eaten!'

Mabel was infuriated about what the giants had done to her village: most of the crops had been torn down by the rampaging ogres and all but a few sheep remained, for the others had been gobbled by the Bloodwicks.

'Worry, not, dear Papa,' said the kind girl; 'for it is time we threw a feast in honour of our new masters.' Samuel was horrified at the girl's words, but she assured him that she had a plan. Mabel, ran out of the room and went to see the farmer who owned the last two sheep, and after that she asked her friends to help her make a salad to go with the mutton she had persuaded the farmer to give her.

Before the midnight bell had tolled, Mabel, with the help of her friends, had laid out six tables that were piled high with the last of the villagers' potatoes, cabbages, carrots and turnips. In amongst the salad, great flavoursome slices of mutton lay, peppered, salted and minted; the smell was so wonderful that many of the village children tried snatching at the delectable fare, but all who did so received a slapped wrist and a sharp scolding for their naughtiness.

The tired cobbler emerged from his workshop and wearily laid the gigantic clogs out on the street; when he saw the banquet his daughter had laid out he dashed over to her and was on the point of giving her a hiding, when the bell struck twelve. The ground began to rumble with the mighty thumps of the six Bloodwicks who were making their way down the hill from their fortified timber castle, and Mabel clutched her dear father's arm and asked him to be quiet. In a few moments, the ghastly family of ogres were in the street where the clogs and the feast lay waiting for them.

'Are these our clogs, cobbler?' shouted Father Bloodwick.

'Yes. But they are the last I shall ever make: all of my wood is gone now, and there are no more cows to provide me with leather. You have eaten them all,' said Samuel.

'I hope that is not a reproach, cobbler, or I will eat you!' As he said this, the other giants began to chuckle and lick their great drooling lips. Father Bloodwick pushed his filthy great feet into the clogs and got the rest of his family to do the same.

'They fit well, cobbler. You will make us each two more pairs.'

'But,' cried Samuel, 'I cannot! There is nothing left! Not a shaving of wood nor a scrap of leather!'

'D'you defy me, cobbler? I will eat you whole if you cannot make me more clogs!'

Sensing great danger, Mabel pushed past her father and shouted up at the towering man:

'Mr Bloodwick! There is no need to eat my father, for I have prepared this lavish spread for you!' and she pointed her finger at the laden tables. As soon as the giants had seen the food, they clattered over to the feast and swept up the meat and salad in their enormous hands and guzzled every last scrap.

'What a delight!' boomed Father Bloodwick, 'And now for you, cobbler!' roared the greedy ogre. But, as he turned to face the cowering Samuel Stipples, his legs buckled from under him and great pains seared across his swollen belly. The other Bloodwicks also fell to the ground and began writhing in agony. A look of triumph spread across Mabel's face and she glanced at her friends who began to laugh.

'Oh, Mr Bloodwick! I do hope you enjoyed your supper!' giggled Mabel.

'What is this wickedness?' snarled the giant, as his face contorted with burning pain.

'My friends and I gave you some good greens to compliment the last of our village's meat.

Henbane, monkshood, hemlock and foxglove! Larkspur and belladonna!'

Father Bloodwick bellowed a moan that was so loud it made the bells in the belfry toll, as if for a funeral:

'Poisoned!' he gasped, before he and all of the Bloodwicks stopped breathing altogether.

Mabel dashed over to the wicked giant and slashed his belly with one of her father's cobbling knives. A flood of slippery muck slid from his yawning gut along with Hazeltips herself who tottered over to her master, mewing like a new-born.

The giants' castle was shivered to the ground and Samuel used the wood for his new clogs. The Bloodwick's bodies were skinned and their tanned hides provided enough leather for the rest of the cobbler's long life. To this day, Hudley Hutch still manufactures the finest clogs in all of England.

There was something of a revival for the clog in the 1970s; it was pleasant hearing the sound of these sturdy shoes clattering down Britain's high streets once again. There's a good reason why this evocative sound is no longer heard and the fad died out – and her name is Eve Stevens. This foolish woman had a shop on Bond Street in the '70s and went too far – she started making thigh-length boots entirely carved out of wood and there were some appalling accidents – Eve Stevens was sued into obscurity. Of course you might be wondering why you hadn't heard of this before – and I can tell you why: it was all hushed-up. Samuel Stipples in the above narrative was also a victim of his own skill and his story is a timely reminder that you're better off being rather mediocre and dullish if you want a quiet life. As most people on this planet live lives I would describe as being of the 'garden variety', I have no doubt that most of you reading this have no need to worry. If you are brilliant and original then for goodness' sake keep your mouth shut and keep your ideas to yourself.

Nurse Cottishole's Surprise

Whenever anyone says a cruel thing about you, don't bottle the ire up inside; instead try some very practical ways of returning the cruelty. These days it's very cheap to order a short-run of leaflets that can be distributed at night-time through neighbours' post boxes. The trick is not to get recognised whilst mailing the inflammatory material, so cross-dressing is a good way to conceal your true identity otherwise you may be prosecuted for libelling your enemy. Half a bottle of sweet sherry is a good way to settle your nerves as you become accustomed to your new persona. The characters in the folk tale below carry such a freight of resentment around on their shoulders it's a wonder they can walk at all. Saying this, I remember now that one of them can't walk, which only goes to prove my point. I do hate metaphors. I never know what I'm really saying.

A solid old woman called Nurse Cottishole had spent most of her adult life caring for Lord Bedwax's family. A more loyal woman could not be found for she stuck to the family as a limpet does to a sea-lashed rock. Through scandal and death, through wealth and penury, Nurse Cottishole was there to tend to the family's needs. In the later years of her long and ascetic life she tended to the last of the now long-dead lord's children – a feeble and drink-ravaged invalid by the name of Bernard Bedwax.

When he had been a young man, Bernard was thrown from his horse in a thunderstorm, leaving him paralysed from the waist down. The horse, as if punished by God for its skittishness, was blasted by a fork of lightning and was found smoking gently next to its crippled rider. Ever since that day, Bernard was under the committed and indefatigable care of Nurse Cottishole; she bathed him, rubbed ointments into his pale skin and fed him, mostly by spoon, as a mother would a child.

Bernard resented his old nurse in many ways, but the thing he despised most was her perpetual desire to 'surprise' him. She would be in the act of feeding him a thick soup when she would pause and say, with a feint sadistic twinkle in her eye:

'Why, Mr Bedwax! Here's a surprise!' and she would fish a damp flannel from her apron and rub his face energetically with it, whilst chuckling with what appeared to be good-humoured affection, but with what Bernard knew to be ruthless pleasure.

On any other day, Bernard might be sitting, gazing out of the French windows when Nurse Cottishole would manifest soundlessly by his side and say softly, but perhaps with too much glee:

'Oh! Mr Bedwax! I have a surprise for you!' whereupon she would produce a great brown bottle of cream of magnesia.

'Away, with you, Nurse, away!' Bernard would shout impotently, but Nurse always won out.

'You haven't been for two days, Mr Bedwax. Two whole days! What goes in', she said, straining to open her charge's gnashing jaws, 'must come out! There you go,' she said, as the great tarnished spoon clattered into his mouth.

So went the poor invalid's days.

However, as Bernard had grown older and somewhat more infirm, he began to delight in surprising Nurse Cottishole with tricks of his own. For every unsolicited haircut and unexpected tooth brushing, he would return with even greater frights. One of his favourites was to stow a spider in his mouth – he would ring the bell, and in would patter the old woman. He would point in mock agony at his chin, and the moment Cottishole was close enough to see what the matter was, he would open his pursed lips, with a strangled exclamation of 'Surprise!' and out would tumble the frantic creature, which would send the nurse into shrieking hysteria.

Summer was Bernard Bedwax's favourite time of the year, for the house would always be hopping with invading green crickets – something Nurse Cottishole had a complete aversion to. Bernard found most inventive ways of getting them tangled in her hair. After eating one of the nurse's clotted dinners, he would hide crickets or centipedes under the domed lid of the salver, and would shake with mirth on hearing the crash of falling silverware in the kitchens below, attended by piercing howls.

Unfortunately for Bernard, the surprises he shocked Cottishole with, only served to increase the vehemence of her own. One day, after a particularly unexpected and very bristly scrub with an exotically large luffa, Bernard had arranged for a friend called Tomlin to hide in his bedroom until nightfall. When the old woman had taken herself to bed, Bernard dressed Tomlin in his pyjamas, and got him to slide into his bed, whilst Bernard hid underneath him on the floor. Suppressing their giggles, Tomlin rang the bell and waited for the dutiful nurse to make her nocturnal entrance. This she did, with remarkable haste, carrying a small candle. From beneath the bed Bernard cried 'Oh, Nurse! I have a surprise for you!' With this, Tomlin, indistinguishable from his crippled friend in the wan light of the room, pulled the sheets off himself and stood up, his arms outstretched. Cottishole took such a great fright from this horror that she squealed and bolted out into the hallway. In her frantic race to escape, she tripped on the stairs and tumbled to the bottom.

A doctor was called, but he merely confirmed that all life was extinct. Nurse Cottishole had broken her neck.

Bernard Bedwax stayed only two more months in the house. His new nurse said that the man had been complaining of 'disturbances' in the night. The young nurse, supposed the man was becoming mad, for every morning great scouring red marks would appear on his skin, and he had begun to rave and babble about 'someone' in his room. He was taken to convalesce in Brighton, but died not many months later during a most terrible seizure that visited him one cold night.

I once broke my shin whilst out ladybird hunting, and as I lay in my sickbed, Great Grandma Berrial told me this strange tale with rather too much relish for my liking. It would be flippant of me to say that being incapacitated is a super experience, but I really did enjoy having people bustle about me and attend to my every need. After the bone healed, I sank into a deep depression as I realised I would have to butter my own parsnips, and I found visits to the lavatory were a solemn and lonely experience after all the care I had received. I soon started going out of my way to put myself in danger, and for six months I acquired all sorts of maladies by drinking strange chemicals and imbibing water from the Thames, which was fearsomely dirty at the time. I did enjoy the mollycoddling that followed, but only after speaking to my good friend Margaret Stamen, did I realise that all of this was unnecessary. Margaret was attending acting lessons at the time, and informed me that by merely pretending to be ill, I could achieve the same effect as having a serious and very real illness. It worked very well for a time, but, alas, my theatrical illnesses ended when I grew a moral backbone during the Second World War.

The Toby Jug

If you ever want people to do something for you that you can't manage by yourself, then it's wise to remember that if you offer them alcohol, they're more likely than not going to be very willing to lend a hand. Whenever there's an emergency I never dash into the police station – instead I dive into the nearest pub and offer a round of drinks. Justice, as meted out by men lusting after a pint, can be very swift and efficacious, with the added benefit that one need not find oneself in the damnably slow-moving process of State procedure. I call this 'folk justice'.

Arthur Beardlace was a marvel to his fellow villagers for he kept the tidiest house in the district. In spite of his old age and not inconsiderable infirmities, his small home was always kept in apple pie order. He was a popular, good-humoured old fellow and he had many visitors. Indeed, many of his friends would delight in coming to sup with him at his home because it was so clean that it made for a pleasant holiday from their own domestic disorders.

Since anyone could remember, Arthur Beardlace's home had been free from bothersome cobwebs and the floorboards were always polished to such a shine that you could see your face in them.

It was something of a mystery as to how the old man kept such a well-ordered abode as he was stiff on his legs and his dear old hands were swollen with rheumatism.

'Oh, Arthur!' visitors would say, 'I wish I knew your secret!' to which he would always respond with a gentle chuckle and a wink.

For Arthur's secret was this: on the sideboard he kept a magic Toby jug. When the grandfather clock chimed three times in the morning, the little chap on the front of the mug came to life. He would detach himself from his ceramic chair and bring the brush that he was holding with him. For the next two hours little Toby would set about his work, sweeping, scrubbing and dusting. When the clock chimed five times, he would scamper back to his shelf with the aid of a small string lasso and take a well-deserved drink and draw on his clay pipe for the next hour. The arrangement was an equitable one, for Arthur would stuff Toby's pipe with tobacco and fill the jug with ale before bed, and this was all the sustenance that Toby desired for his travails.

As a child, when Arthur had first been given the Toby jug by a mysterious uncle, he had had but one conversation with the tiny man who lived on the jug:

'Hullo, boy,' Toby had said one evening.

'Hullo, Toby,' said Master Beardlace.

'Here's a fine deal for you,' replied Toby. 'You fill my jug to the brim with ale, and I'll keep your mother's house tidy for the rest of her days. And when she's gone, I'll do the same for you. I do love my ale, sonny,' said Toby with a broad smile.

Young Arthur took a measure from his father's keg and did as he was told, and from that day on, little Toby kept the house as clean as a whistle.

One day, when Arthur was an old man, he had been lying in bed laid up with the 'flu, whilst his cousin, Bella Tuckpin, had been nursing him through his illness. Poor old Mr Beardlace was so ill that he was in quite a stupor and, of course, the Toby jug was not being filled with ale anymore, as Bella knew nothing of her cousin's long-standing bargain.

Bella was a kind old soul but quite hopeless when it came to housework (her own cottage was like a hog's hovel) and without Toby's help Arthur's home became grubbier and filthier as the days passed. Cobwebs hung like sacking over the ceiling; the floors were all streaked with mud and cups and plates lay unwashed in the scullery.

Two weeks since the beginning of his illness, Arthur came to his senses and was immediately aware of the stink in his home. Bella was sat at his bedside knitting when she heard him take a deep sniff before letting out a pained groan.

'Cousin! You are back! I feared we might lose you!' smiled Bella.

'That smell – oh my! Draw the curtains, Bella, it is so dark in here,' moaned Arthur.

'Why, they are drawn. It's the soot on the windows that makes 'em so dark' said she.

'But they should have been cleaned – have you not been filling my Toby jug with ale?' asked Arthur.

'Oh, cousin,' said Bella, 'you are still a little in your delirium. I ain't sure you should be speaking yet. Rest, sir.'

'But my home – it's so fearfully dirty,' said Arthur.

'Well, is that all the thanks I get for taking care of you whilst you were ill?' said Bella, rather hurt by her cousin's complaint.

'I did my best to sweep up the worst of it, but my old knees aren't what they once were and besides I thought it better to look after you,' said Bella tearfully.

'Anyways,' she continued, 'this place is fairly alive with mice. What am I to do about that? You know how much I hate them. Why, only yesterday I heard such a frightful squeaking and wailing coming from that Toby jug on the sideboard and there's a mouse or something what lives right by it! I walloped it on the head with my old broom and nearly put my shoulder out doing that! Little rascal it was!' said Bella, getting more hysterical.

"Was'? 'Was'? What do you mean?' said Arthur.

'Oh, it was very late, I don't quite recall,' said Bella.

'Think woman!' shouted the old man.

'Oh yes - I bashed it with the broom and killed it. Queer lookin' mouse – I could've sworn it had a little jacket on,' replied Mrs Tuckpin.

'No! Please, bring me the Toby jug this instant!' cried Arthur.

'Ah, well, I'm sorry, cousin, I can't do that. I smashed it to pieces. You know how much I hate mice.'

'My little Toby!' screamed the old man.

'Shush! It's just an old jug. I'll get you another, Arthur,' said Bella.

But the old man did not reply, for his heart had broken and he was dead.

I'm ashamed to say that I once employed a cleaner to tidy my house after I broke my leg during a rather frivolous day that ended with my falling out of a tree whilst collecting conkers. I put a little card up in the newsagents and two days later a lovely woman called Anemarja came round to my house; she had a super set of references but I couldn't read a single word of them as they were all in Norwegian. I put her on probation for a week and relentlessly followed her around the house as she cleaned. She proved most effective and honest and I employed her on a semi-permanent basis. When my leg had healed I was reluctant to let her go; her blonde winsomeness seemed to bring a certain gayness back into my home that I was grateful for. We developed a very robust, if idiosyncratic, form of sign language and we seemed to have some very enjoyable conversations. I'm afraid I tended to do a lot of nodding and often wonder that I didn't agree too much with everything she said. One day I acquiesced with her so much I think I unwittingly dismissed her. I was really very sad. We still send each other letters. She's a prolific writer but I'm afraid I have no idea what she's saying. I find that if you turn Norwegian letters upside down and hold them against a strong light source (such as the sun or a 100 watt bulb) they tend to make more sense. Turning back again to the story you've just read, I'd imagine that most of you know of a clumsy relative whose visits to your home are accompanied by a very realistic sense of dread. My brother-in-law Howard is just such a man. Whenever he came over for tea I could expect at least one smashed saucer and a chipped vase. In the end I used to put a woollen housecoat on him when he arrived and sit him down in an armchair to which I had affixed strips of Velcro. This worked very well and I recommend you do the same. He was stuck fast to the chair and when it was time for him to leave, Des and I would tear him from the seat and bustle him out of the house. If you do follow my advice then be careful not to do what I once did which was to sit in the Velcro chair with the woollen house coat on when I was alone in the house. I was stuck in that armchair for the whole weekend whilst Des was away on business. This would have been quite restful and pleasant had it not been for the fact that the television was stuck on BBC Parliament with live coverage from the House of Lords. It was without a doubt the most distressing and disgusting period of my entire life, and I say that as someone who remembers experiencing the Blitz and all the rubbish piling up on the streets during the Winter of Discontent.

The Flea-Catcher
of Kipplenead

Parasites are terrible things, they really are. Every spring, before my dahlias have even had a chance, they're covered in aphids. I get so fed up with them, that I end up cutting the new stems off and I've barely seen a single bloom on one of the plants for as long as I've lived here. My friend Mary once picked up a tick after walking through a Somerset meadow; I think ticks must release some type of neurotoxin into the blood, because she became convinced that it was her friend. She told me how she used to find it a comfort to hear it squeaking at night as it drew on her blood. In fact, I often dream of one day going to Australia, just so I can be sprayed with insecticide on arrival. I hear that that's what they do there. What with that and those wonderful corks that swing on little strings off their hats, they've got the right idea about pest control. The following narrative features one of the world's most populous parasites. I do wonder what the world's most popular *parasite is. If I were forced to rank them, I'd say my favourite parasite would have to be the Guinea worm, purely because of its resemblance to vermicelli pasta; I absolutely adore Italian cuisine.*

The beautiful town of Kipplenead was afflicted every year with the most appalling plague of fleas that sent the good people there into great fits of scratching each summer.

Every January, expecting another uncomfortable season ahead of them, the men and women of Kipplenead would search their purses to pay for what had become known as the Pellitt Doles. The doles were paid to a man known as Peter Pellitt, who would undertake the task of ridding the town of the scourge of the biting pests each year. His method was really rather simple, although uncomfortable for him. What Peter Pellitt would do would be to cover himself with the skins of dead dogs and then to prick his skin all over with a pin so that he would be covered with beads of his own blood, which the fleas could not resist, along with the charm of dog skin. When he had finished pricking himself, he would enter every dwelling in Kipplenead and the fleas were sure to jump on him and begin their frenzy of bloodsucking. At the end of the day, Pellitt would be sore and weary and virtually unrecognisable because his body was a swarming mass of hopping black parasites. When he had walked about the last house in the town, all the men, women and children would cheer as the poor man hobbled down the high street towards the village pond, whilst the sexton of the town church would wheel a barrow behind him full of coins collected during the Pellitt Doles six months earlier.

Each year Pellitt would do the same thing at the pond's edge: he would be handed a freshly shorn bundle of wool, which he held between his jaws, before proceeding to walk slowly and solemnly into the pond. With each step he took into the green water, the fleas would leap further up his body to avoid drowning. The townsfolk would cheer when Pellitt's head disappeared beneath the water at long last, and all that could be seen was an agitated mass of fleas hopping and flicking about the floating island of wool. An even bigger cheer issued from the crowd when, as ever, Pellitt emerged on the far side of the pond wet and muddy but perfectly free of wretched fleas. On emerging from the pond, the tired man would then walk back towards the merry gathering and be handed a long stick of wood. Pellitt's last obligation would be to bat the blackened ball of wool beneath the water, thus despatching every last flea of Kipplenead to their watery grave. After he'd performed this feat of endurance the barrow of coins would be presented to him, and Pellitt would wheel the dole money back to his home in the woods.

Well, after fifty years of doing this, Pellitt was an old man, and an exceedingly rich one, too. But he so loved the money and adulation that he kept doing this year after year. Some people were even growing slightly concerned for the man as he was noticeably fatter and his joints were gouty and swollen from all fine food he feasted on. The year was 1790 and Pellitt's fiftieth year of flea-catching was upon him, but so too was the eighteenth year of life of one of the town's girls. Julia Ackles was a shrewd young woman, and for as long as she could recall, she had felt that there was something suspicious about Peter Pellitt and his seemingly philanthropic ways.

January 1790 had seen the collection of the Pellitt Doles and Julia was set upon discovering how the fleas came to infest the town that year, as they had done so many, many times before. When the weather improved and the sun started to warm the humble houses of Kipplenead once more, Julia walked out into the forest and secretly entered Pellitt's grand house.

As soon as she walked into the hallway, she heard the sound of many dogs growling and barking in the house's cellar. Intrigued, she silently padded down the stairs and peered through the keyhole of the door to the room where all the terrible canine noises seemed to be coming from. The room was bare, save for a large linen sheet that covered the floor. Upon this sheet were dozens of dogs of all types and every one of them was scratching and scraping at their coats with their frantic claws. A blur of hairy limbs were pawing at their own itching skin, and even from this distance, Julia could see the suspect black flecks of fleas hopping and leaping from one dog to another as they were kicked and dislodged by the antsy dogs.

Just as she was looking upon this dismal scene, Julia heard footsteps on the floor above her, so she dived into the shadows of the stairwell and watched as the portly figure of Peter Pellitt walked stiffly down the stairs. He was carrying a sack over his shoulder that clanked and knocked as he stepped arthritically down into the cellar hall.

'Here you are, my lovelies!' announced Pellitt, before crouching down where Julia had been moments before, and sliding open a small panel at the bottom of the door.

'Some juicy cattle bones for you today!' chuckled Pellitt as he emptied the open end of the sack into the locked room. Over the din of the howls, yaps and snarls of hungry dogs rushing for their bones, Julia heard Pellitt say this:

'Eat well, hounds, eat well. In two months Daddy will come to remove your dirty sheet and there'll be plenty of real meat for you all for the rest of the year!' Upon saying this, the old man slammed the hatch shut and hauled himself back onto his feet before disappearing back up the staircase.

Sure enough, two months later, Julia was waiting again in the gloom of the stairwell and, true to his word, a few hours after her arrival, Peter Pellitt was walking down the creaking stairs. This time, instead of opening the hatch, the saviour of Kipplenead produced a key and opened the door. The dogs seemed pleased to see him, but he did not stop to pet them. Instead he threw a bag of aniseed balls into the corner of the room, and the dogs gleefully fell upon these with relish. Whilst the animals were distracted, Pellitt gathered up the huge linen cloth that served as a carpet to the hounds' cellar room and stuffed it into another hessian bag he was carrying. Julia had watched all of this through the open doorway, so when Pellitt walked back to the cellar door, she dipped back into the shadows to avoid detection.

It was not long before the man left his house, and Julia followed swiftly behind. By now, night had fallen and all the townsfolk were fast asleep in their beds. As soon as Pellitt was past the town pond, she saw, by the light of the full moon, the duplicitous old man pull the flea-infested sheet from the sack and trail it all around the town. He crept into each house's garden and shook the filthy sheet onto the doorsteps of every abode, before nipping quickly over to the next house and so on, until every home had had scores of new fleas hopping through the door cracks and into the rooms of the unlucky houses again. When he'd finished his night's sheet-shaking, he bunched-up the linen and hurried home.

Julia was shaking with rage but she was jubilant too; for she had discovered that the very man who had rid Kipplenead of its unwelcome fleas was the very same man who had caused the plagues in the first place.

That year, Julia was the only one in the crowd who did not sing and cheer as Pellitt dourly swept up the town's biting insects.

However, the next day Julia made sure she told Magistrate Redrange what she had seen. He was horrified to hear this and sent a constable down to the house to see whether or not the 'dog cellar' was a fib or not.

Well, you can probably guess what happened next; the cellar with its flea-bitten dogs was discovered and it did not take long for the gossip to spread around town, and Julia Ackles was much in demand – she told her story again and again and the townsfolk were greatly angered by Pellitt's decades-long trick. However, the town was sensible, and they bided their time before exacting revenge.

The summer of 1791 came, and the villagers began to itch all over as their houses filled with the jumping black nuisances once more. One hot afternoon in late July, Pellitt had again performed his flea gathering and started to wade into the pond. 'Come, fellow,' shouted Pellitt as his ankles troubled the green mantle of the pond, 'where is my ball of wool?'

'He appears,' said Mr Redrange, patting the young boy on the head who was holding the wool, 'to have forgotten it.'

'What nonsense is this?' said Pellitt, irritated. 'He has it in his hand, sir! Give it to me now!' cried Pellitt.

'If you insist!' declared Julia Ackles, who was holding the batting stick that year. She swung the wooden pole at Pellitt and hit him hard across the belly. The strike winded the corpulent old trickster and he fell backwards into the pond. Mr Redrange snatched the pole from Julia and hit Pellitt hard on the head, whereupon he let out a whimper, before he sank, along with that year's haul of fleas, into the pond, never to be seen again.

In a way, it's a shame that wicked men like Peter Pellitt can't channel their genius and do something good with their talents. He certainly did exploit the villagers of Kipplenead, but then all the rich tycoons and businessmen of the twenty-first century do the same thing to us today. Apart from Richard Branson, whom I have complete blind faith in. However, I think that this folk tale is a reminder about the dangers of following tradition unthinkingly. Julia Ackles had the nous to look beneath the surface of things, and she saw the terrible truth of the matter. I have learnt to resist the pull of tradition too and I actively do things to disrupt patterns of behaviour that I have fallen into. For example, the other day, I had a call from Michael Angelo (from the hairdressers at 16 Chapel Street) who said 'Will I see you at the normal time today, Kitty?' I was so horrified by this I said yes, but made sure that when his car drew up, I called him on his mobile telephone and cancelled. I saw him punch the steering wheel in a typical expression of masculine-Italian frustration, but I knew it was healthy for me to put him to that bother and to save myself from the rusted cycle of tradition.

The Gossley Boggart

Many people who skip breakfast complain that they are 'starving'. If you have ever uttered a hyperbole like this, I would challenge you to say this again after reading the fable below. I was once hospitalised with pathological hunger, and it was not in the least bit funny, I can tell you. Even today, nearly sixty years later, my geriatric GP still sends me bundles of rhubarb through the post, even though it's quite ruined by the time it arrives. I really would write a letter to him asking him to stop, but

I understand that he's gone blind, and such a petition would probably fall on deaf ears.

A boggart who lived in Gossley woods was much feared by the men of the nearby town as he had the devil's own temper and, should a callow blunderer take one step into his demesne, the wrathful sprite would surely make all of the trespasser's horses fall lame. He lived in a circle of alders, at the centre of which grew a magnificent ash tree; the boggart had many hundreds of larders hidden throughout the wood, and each of those had a shiny golden key that was hung from the boughs of the great tree that he so jealously guarded. As with many other boggle beasts and bogies, The Gossley boggart had enchanted his ash tree by burying a tooth of his beneath the tree when it was just a sapling; as the growing tree's roots curled and laced around his bloody molar, the tree became a part of him, and he became part of the tree.

One year, the villagers were at the point of starvation when the harvest had failed and all of their crops withered on the stem. The villagers were fretting most terribly and dreaded the oncoming winter without any store of sustenance. The last cat had been eaten, so Mary Tallboy, an exceedingly cunning woman, made her way to the boggart, to beg him for some food from his abundant cupboards. Respectfully, she called from without the ring of alders to the bogey-beast, asking kindly for a small share of his stock. For her pains, she was hit most hard on the breast with a sharp rock and scolded for being so brazen.

Mary returned the following day and repeated her request, only to be met with worse pain when the boggart, scrambling from the branches of the ash, switched her across the face with a knotted twig from the tree within which he had been crouching.

Mary was persistent, for her hunger was by now gnawing at her belly, and she returned a third time, with the same entreaty. The boggart was even crueller on this occasion and up-ended his chamber pot over Miss Tallboy's head, sending her shrieking back to her cabin reeking of addled eggs and sour cider.

Much aggrieved at her treatment and maddened at the bogie's parsimonious hoarding, she worked hard all night to bake a bun with the very last of her flour, garnishing it with the village's only remaining cherry. She had ground-up several elder-seeds into the dough, knowing well that they had many magical qualities: chief amongst them was the property of transmutation. She spiced the bun with nutmeg and cinnamon in the hope that it would be so irresistible to the boggart that he would gobble it up the moment he spied it. Before bed, the wily woman cursed the bun with such malice that she fell into a faint and slept the rest of the night on the straw-covered floor, warmed only by the feeble glow of her fire.

The next day, Mary Tallboy walked into Gossley woods and left the bun on a linen cloth at the edge of his circle. The bogie quickly woke from his doze, for his senses were terribly keen and he spat words at her that would have made a sailor blush. Infuriated, he clambered out of the tree which rattled and jangled with all the keys hanging from its groaning branches, though this time he was too slow to abuse the woman any more - Mary fled before the boggart could catch her. Mary made sure that she didn't run quite out of the woods altogether. She peeped from behind a laurel bush, and saw with great delight that the bogie, after stamping the ground in a rage, snatched at the cake she had left for him and scoffed it whole. The instant he did so, Mary cried out with laughter for she knew she had won. The imp scurried up to her, pinching her most awfully for he did not have his feculence to shower her with this time.

'Cease your laughter, strumpet!' shrieked the malign little man. Mary paid no heed to this, for she was convulsed with mirth. The boggart, whose rage was now turning his grey skin red, dashed back to his beloved ash tree to find an even bigger stick to beat her with, but before he even climbed the tree, he gazed on it in horror. All of his precious keys had turned into seed-pods. Not a single sliver of metal remained. His larders, which were so deeply buried and so securely fastened, would nevermore be opened and he too should suffer the spite of hunger. He turned to Mary, but she, grown thin and weak from famine, had died of laughter. All of the other villagers perished too.

To this day, the boggart is still occasionally to be glimpsed in Gossley woods, desperately trying to insert the fragile winged seeds into the rusted locks of his hidden larders. On cold nights, his moans can still be discerned, echoing around the forest as his gaunt ribs clatter in misery.

Ever since this dismal event took place, the seed purses of all those noble trees have been called 'ash-keys'.

I'm tempted to side with the unfortunate boggart of this tale as he had worked very industriously to put aside enough food for himself, and it was only through agricultural mismanagement that the villagers came to such an unhappy end. Don't think I can't empathise with Mary Tallboy's plight – I'm sure she was famished, but that doesn't give every wanton beggar the right to claim a stake in my breakfast, mid-morning snack, lunch, tea, supper, pudding and midnight feast. Whilst I'm alarmed this does make me sound a bit like Margaret Thatcher, I think that every Briton should defend their right to sovereignty over the stowed goods in their own kitchen. Grandma Berrial told me this story when I was a small girl. She was eating a great quantity of Brazil nuts over the course of a very lean Christmas, and I had asked her if I might have one too. Instead, she recounted this narrative, ate the last nut and handed me the paper bag before ordering me to put it on the fire. I pretended to do this, whilst secretly stowing the bag in the pocket on my pinafore. Later that evening, ravaged by hunger, I devoured the splintered nut-shells along with a dried earwig that had foolishly found itself trapped in there. The following evening, I ate the paper bag too – which I found surprisingly wholesome.

Tomkin Teadwig's Toothache

Below is a cautionary tale for any of you who may have put off a visit to the dentist. It's not my place to be sending you a little card through the post every six months encouraging you to return to the surgery for a check-up, but I recommend you at least book an appointment with your local dentist before cancelling because you're too frightened. I no longer have a dentist myself as it's always people who've been brutally murdered beyond recognition that seem to have dental records that the police use to identify them by. My last dental surgery was destroyed by a gas explosion in 2002, so I feel very safe knowing that I cannot possibly be horribly murdered, as my orthodontic records no longer exist.

There was once a very clumsy man called Tomkin Teadwig who was too afraid of the dentist to have his rotten tooth pulled out, so he decided to find a way of dealing with it himself.

First, he waited three long months for spring to arrive, so that he could chew on the year's first fern leaf, as he'd heard this cured toothache. He went to the forest, found and ate the first fern leaf, but then a big, bony adder bit on the him on the ankle because such serpents are fond of fern leaves and are much beguiled by them in the springtime.

Tomkin then had to have his poisoned leg sawn off to save his life.

And still his tooth ached.

Next, Tomkin hobbled on a crutch over to a Miss Munkpaddle's house for she was a wise-woman and he had heard she could cure the pain of toothache. Miss Munkpaddle took a dried mole that was hanging by a string from one of her ceiling beams, snipped off its toes and tucked them into a pouch. She then tied this about the poor man's neck. Tomkin's pain disappeared, but she refused his payment of coins. Because she wasn't a very nice woman, she chopped off his hand with a cleaver as payment. Tomkin hopped home to find a bandage. On his way home, he fell over and all the mole toes fell out of the pouch and were lost in the long grass.

And his tooth began to ache again.

Next, Tomkin shuffled on his buttocks over to the churchyard. He'd heard that if you pull a dead man's tooth from his jawbone, the tooth would cure toothache. He started digging with his spade, but it was very dark and he ended up lopping off his only other leg by mistake. He crawled home with his last hand to find another bandage.

And still his tooth ached.

Next day, Tomkin dragged himself into the meadow to find a yarrow plant. He had heard that yarrow worn about the neck cured toothache, so he had brought along a knife to cut off some yarrow stems to make a necklace. Unfortunately he slashed so violently at the plant with his one shaky arm that he missed and cut off his own head.

He began to weep with frustration because all that was left of him now was a head.

And still his tooth ached.

Just then, Miss Munkpaddle came strolling through the meadow with a basket on her arm, looking for mushrooms.

'What have we here?' she said as she fixed her little red eyes on Tomkin's head.

'A fine mushroom for the pot!' she said with great glee.

'I am not a mushroom,' said Tomkin. 'Please cure my toothache!'

'Why of course I will', said Miss Munkpaddle.

And with that, she scooped up his bonce, put it in the basket, and took it back to her cottage.

'Here's your cure for toothache,' said the woman, as she dropped Tomkin's head into the bubbling pot over her fireplace. The old woman dusted her hands and went back to her runes.

I'm always surprised at how much dentists are feared – I always used to find visits to the dental surgery to be very relaxing. It's one of the few times in life when you can sit back and let someone else do all the work. The greatest difficulty I used to have when at the dentist was staying awake. Having said that, dentistry isn't what it used to be. Before all the anti-smoking nonsense came in, I used to lie in the dentist's chair, mouth open, ready for another extraction, and the dear little dental nurse would hold my cigarette for me. The moment the dentist turned his back to fetch another drill or mix a bit of putty, the nurse would pop the Silk Cut back in my mouth and I'd have a lovely draw. Absolutely immaculate customer service that today's cold clinicians could learn a lot from.

Vicar Pearnet's Yew Tree

When moving into a new house, people often like to stamp their mark on it, as if to try and rid themselves of the former proprietor's identity. When I moved into my current house, the previous owner had painted it bright pink and it looked like a giant fondant fancy. It was so garish that local schoolchildren seemed to mistake it for a huge confection and often stopped by on their way home to nibble it, as it looked so appetising. I'm quite sure that the reason why the house was so cheap was that it was suffering from subsidence, on account of the chunks of masonry that had been eaten by hungry youths. I soon put an end to this by painting the house black. Unfortunately, it looked so forbidding that not even the postman would come near and I had to set up a P.O. Box just to receive my letters. The following story looks with disdain at the consequences of trying to make too many changes when one moves into a new home.

The parish of Gowdthorpe enjoyed the happy reputation as being one of the most peaceful places in Northampton. The folk were polite and even in the depths of winter flowers bloomed; harvests were always abundant and it was said that even the ducks sang like nightingales. The place was exceedingly merry until the sad day came when the much-loved Vicar Nichols expired whilst attending to some cobwebs in the vestry of St Frideswide's Church one cold Tuesday morning.

However sad and tearful the vicar's passing, the parishioners knew that life couldn't stop forever, and in time a new vicar was appointed. The latest minister was Maurice Pearnet, and he was a young man with some rather robust changes in mind. However, the people of Gowdthorpe were so welcoming and trusting, that any schemes the young vicar had in mind did not perturb them – for they were happy in the knowledge that God's deputy was working for them, and had their best interests in mind.

Next to the old lych-gate, at the entrance to the church, grew an ancient yew tree, which many reckoned to be thousands of years old. Its mighty red boughs spread across almost half of the churchyard and arched elegantly over the pathway, as if protecting anyone who crossed the threshold.

Vicar Pearnet took a strange dislike to the old tree, and announced to his parishioners after his first Sunday sermon that he would require three men to assist him with coppicing the giant. There were over forty men in the congregation, but not a single one amongst them would offer their help in doing this. Some of the women began to whisper in an agitated manner before one stood up and declared that on no account must the tree be harmed. The first chord of discontent for many a long year was felt in the church that day, and after the parishioners had been sent on their way, Mary Cowton came over to the vicar and begged him to let the old yew alone.

'Dear lady,' said the vicar, 'I understand your fears. But the limbs of the tree are clearly a danger to all: the branch that overhangs the lych-gate is sore with malady. Have you not seen the scarlet sap that runs down its length? A bleed from a tree is a sign of *fracture*. It's like blood in a man's arm – it's only seen when there is broken flesh.'

Desperate, Mrs Cowton redoubled her pleas:

'Ye talked of coppicing, Vicar Pearnet! Thou intends to have the whole tree cut down to the ground! I beg of ye not to do this. If ye must, cut down the troublesome branch, but leave the rest be!'

'You are being most foolish and sentimental, madam. I fully intend to have that tree coppiced. It is most ungodly: the windows of the church are darkened by its infernal branches. The Lord's light must once again illumine the chancel,' he said, allowing a note of irritation to creep into his voice.

'Now listen here, vicar,' said Mrs Cowton, 'they say that that yew is a tomb-tree. Beneath it be the grave of Megwyn Maunders.'

'And pray, madam, who is Megwyn Maunders?' asked Vicar Pearnet.

'Ay, wouldn't ye like to know?' replied the woman.

'Come, Mrs Cowton, do not play with me as a child would with a pup. Why should a woman so many thousands of years dead be a source of concern?'

The woman sniffed and drew closer to the vicar's ear, as if unwilling to let herself be heard by something outside.

'Why,' whispered Mary Cowton, 'she were a very powerful woman in her time. She was good to those that were good to her and most foul to those that crossed her. As long as she is left in peace, so shall the town stay content. My grandfather used to say to me, he said 'Mary,' he said, 'know this: Megwyn Maunders 'ad that tree planted on 'er grave to make sure she would never die. It holds her spirit, so it does." And with that, Mrs Cowton picked up her skirts and hurried out of the church.

Vicar Pearnet was so irritated by the superstitious old woman that he betook himself that very night to the yew tree with a handsaw. With only the light of a candle to guide him the vicar began his work, though he was surprised at how hard the wood was; after half-an-hour of exhausting work, all he had to show for his travails was a small pile of ragged-cut branches lying by the irksome tree's roots. However, he was determined to do the same the next night; it did not matter to him if it took six months to raze the tree to the ground — he reminded himself that much of God's work was painful and arduous. Not willing to further upset his parishioners, the vicar took the bundle of eight small branches that he had sawn off into St Frideswide's north transept and placed them into a curtained alcove. He dusted his hands then made his way back to the vicarage for his supper.

The next day, Vicar Pearnet could hear the complaints of the townsfolk as he walked up to his church, well aware that their conversations were made deliberately loud enough for him to discern. But the new vicar was a wilful man, and it was with some pride that he passed through the lych-gate and saw the results of his handiwork the previous night. He was disappointed to see that Mrs Cowton was sweeping up the sawdust beneath the yew and mumbling something to the trunk when he strode up to her.

'What are you doing, madam?' enquired the vicar.

'Why, I be cleaning up the mess thou hast made,' replied the woman.

'There is no need. Please go back to your sewing,' said the vicar defiantly.

Mary Cowton carried on sweeping, and as the vicar opened the door to the church he turned around and saw the woman patting the tree and continuing her strange discourse with it. He tutted and walked inside the church. The first thing he did was to go into the north transept to retrieve the branches with the express intention of having them burnt in a prominent position in the churchyard. He was growing increasingly tired of the heathens that made up the community of Gowdthorpe, and they needed to be shown that the pagan ways were an abomination. The branches must be burnt.

Upon drawing back the velvet curtain to the alcove, the vicar let out a sharp cry, for there was no longer a pile of sticks lying there, but eight human bones all covered in ghastly gouts of congealed blood. He dashed out of the church and ran at great speed to the next village, wailing all the way about the 'eight bloody bones' that he had seen.

The townsfolk were greatly elated at mean Vicar Pearnet's hasty departure and congratulated Mary Cowton for her cunning as they danced about the churchyard. However, Mary was rather mystified, and said this to her gathered fellows:

'Vicar Pearnet is gone! At night, I entered the church and swapped our dear yew's cut branches for those of cow-bones! But here be the strange thing: I only laid down six cattle bones, yet our late vicar says he saw eight! What a muddle he must have been in!'

Intrigued, the good men and women of the town hurried into the church and crowded into the north transept and saw that there were indeed eight bones lying in the alcove, all covered with the sap of the yew, which looked so much like blood. There, though, amongst the cattle legs were two human arm-bones, cracked and brown with age. Too small for a man, they must have belonged to a woman. A very old woman. They quite crumbled to dust when Mary Cowton reached out to them.

There was a new priest who arrived at my church at the start of the 1980s who was altogether too keen on making swingeing changes to his predecessor's ways of doing things. He insisted on climbing the very narrow spiral staircase to inspect the church tower, being convinced that pippestrelle bats were the cause of the bells' muffled clangs. Unfortunately, this holy man was as fat as a Berkshire pig and wouldn't listen to my warnings about how tight a squeeze that stairway was. As I predicted, the priest became firmly wedged about halfway up and I had to use six blocks of butter to grease him with in order to initiate his release. This greatly displeased me as I had planned to make a chocolate parfait that evening and I had to use up every last ounce of butter to free the man. Worse still, after smothering him in the stuff, I realised I would have to clamber over the cleric in order to effect his escape. This was most undignified, and I only thank God that I'd chosen to wear dungarees that day. Well, I gave the parson a mighty shove and he rocketed down the stairs and tumbled out of the doorway covered in blood, with all the attendant howls of a new born. Moments later, whilst the priest was enjoying full unconsciousness, I scraped his vestments with a plastic spoon I usually reserve for my lunchtime yoghurt, and collected a sufficient quantity of butter to make some lemon tartlets later that evening.

Anne and the Shug Monkey

This is an old tale from Cambridgeshire. My Aunt Vulna grew up there (by about three inches) over the course of three summers. That doesn't equate to an inch a year, as she specifically told me that she'd had a growth spurt in the last twelve months of her stay. I am inclined to think this story is apocryphal on account of the fact that Cambridge is almost entirely flat and this story features a hill. If it did exist, the Victorians may very well have flattened it, as I don't think it's there now. I really can't be sure.

Anne was a headstrong young girl who worried her mother with her comings and goings. She was already working under her fourth employer, Lord Bersacks, even though she was only fourteen. Anne was a milkmaid, but desired more from her life than squeezing udders all day long and stirring the curd until her arms ached. The cows would often kick her and the goats would nip at her shoulders as she toiled at their teats.

Anne had fallen in love with a farmhand called John, and would think of him wistfully all day as she stirred the milk and thickened her cream. Before long, she began to shirk her work and she would run up to the wind-blown hill beyond Lord Bersacks's manor to meet with John in secret, where she would cover him in kisses. Anne was artful at deceiving the old hag Mrs Bannister, who ran the dairy, by dropping coils of mould, skimmed from certain cheeses, into her stout, which would send the wretched old virago into a torpor after lunch. One day, when Anne had absconded, she was hurrying up the lane toward the hill (known locally as Plum Pie Peak as the stone that topped it looked like a plum pie), when she heard a deep voice call to her from behind an old hawthorn tree.

'Who's there?' she called out, almost dropping her basket of raisins (she'd stolen these from Sir Robert's pantry which was a wicked thing to do as he spent hundreds of pounds each year having them imported from Umbria in Italy. Anne thought they were from Cumbria so we shouldn't judge her too harshly, although thieving is thieving).

The voice replied to her and said, 'Why, I am here!' and a gigantic black dog padded out from behind the tree, a large pink tongue lolling from its wet mouth. Anne did not shriek as she rather liked dogs – the bigger the better – especially as her carping mother had such a small one (she generally disliked everything about her mother). Anne straightened her petticoat and greeted the dog most familiarly.

'What's in your basket, my dear?' said the dog.

'Only a few raisins,' said she.

'May I have one?' said the hound. Anne thought of John who was probably on the hill bracing himself for more kisses and felt a certain guilt as she lifted the gingham cloth from the basket and put six raisins on her palm, but she supposed the poor dog must be very hungry indeed if it had to resort to speaking, so it wasn't all bad.

The dog looked at her offering hand and said, 'Have you another, to make seven? For that shall sate my appetite for a week.'

Anne glanced into her basket and saw only three left, but she felt generous that day and placed a seventh raisin on her palm. The monstrous dog lapped her hand with one stroke of his great flat tongue and the raisins were gone. He thanked her before withdrawing and vanishing behind the hawthorn tree from whence he came.

Anne met a shivering John atop Plum Pie Peak a little later and had a quarrel with him for being so late. He was dismayed to find his lunch was but one meagre raisin and upbraided her for her selfishness, accusing his sweetheart of devouring the rest of his meal on her journey. He was so angry that he refused to eat what she had brought.

'But, my dear,' Anne said, 'I gave them to a poor giant dog who was so very hungry.' John's face drained as pale as butter, for he realised his lover had fed the shug monkey.

'What is the shug monkey?' wailed Anne.

''Tis a hellhound, and you have been marked – examine your hand!' Anne opened her hand and saw that it was matted with dark, bristly hair. John fled down the hillside, stumbling in his haste to escape and fell over the side of the hill, before plummeting into a pond and drowning (he was later eaten by a pike but that is another story). Anne walked back to the hawthorn tree to bellow at the shug monkey; she re-traced her steps and found the tree again before calling him, this time by his proper name.

'Shug monkey! Come hither I wish to speak with you,' she shouted, sounding most perturbed.

There was a rustle and the oily black dog appeared again. If anything it had grown even larger and was now walking on its hind legs.

'Yes,' said the shug monkey, parting the hair on its crown so that his yellow eyes now met hers, 'what ails thee?'

'You are the shug monkey and you have soiled my hand with sprouting fur!'

'Only the hand of a filcher would thus be covered after a slug from my chops. The raisins offered to me where purloined. You will be fully hairy by noon tomorrow.'

Anne was appalled. 'Oh, tell me what should I do?'

The dog chuckled, before placing his paw on her arm. 'Why, you shall have to marry me of course.' Anne thought about this hard and then decided that that was probably the best thing to do. After all, she could not risk getting her new hairs in the master's cheese.

'Very well,' she said. 'But I have no dowry.'

'Look again in your basket,' said the shug monkey. She did so:

'Oh, but there are only a couple of raisins,' sighed the poor milkmaid. 'Yes, growled the dog, who now looked more manly than ever, 'One for you,' he said with a smile, 'and one for me.'

Anne and the shug monkey left the path and quickly eloped behind the tree. And they were never seen again.

Grandma Berrial, told me this one when I was being censured for stealing a hairpin to free a woodlouse from a crack in the floorboards. I am amazed at how I was so severely reprimanded over this incident, as any fool knows that nine woodlice worn around the neck in a small pouch will cure thrush and there was certainly a lot of that in our family. There was a need for woodlice, you see; it was often the topic of much discourse after midnight. Nowadays I always keep my carpet damp, to encourage the woodlice, although, fortunately, I have never yet needed them as a remedy. The story you have just read is a powerful polemic about the consequences of thieving whilst being somewhat ambivalent about pilfering at the same time. Yes, Anne got a hairy hand for her crime, but she also got married. I'm in touch with over a dozen spinsters who would gladly have a furry mitt just to be in with the chance of an engagement. Alas, it's too late for them; in fact, one of them died last week, un-husbanded, although, ironically, I think the cause of her desolate, unmarried life was because she was remarkably hirsute and had an impressive beard. As I explained in the introduction, I have tried to locate Plum Pie Peak, but in order to see one hill, one often needs to stand on another hill to see if there are any others about. And as there are no hills to speak of in Cambridgeshire, I gave up my search quite swiftly and went home.

Cup o' Salt & Bedderkin

These days it's very easy to discover if your partner is having an affair – you could set up a spy camera, trawl through their emails, or perhaps flick through their Filofax when they're in the bathroom applying make-up (female) or trimming their moustache (male) [I have had to gender stereotype here for ease of explanation, although I do recognise that many men apply mascara nowadays and there are some women – like my neighbour Lillian Bynster – who have to busy themselves with the shaving foam each morning]. The story you are about to read is a meditation on the perils of infidelity and the monsters that may visit those who have not shown integrity and faithfulness in a relationship. The beasts that feature in the story below might seem rather hard to believe, but that doesn't mean they don't exist, after all they only visit those who are unfaithful. Presumably most zoologists are very loyal and affectionate people, as I've never heard mention of such creatures in this story outside of this very folk tale that Aunt Vulna told me. In fact, I've never heard of a zoologist divorcing on the grounds of adultery. Please write to me if you have proof of this – I'd be thrilled to hear from you.

One day Margaret Whelk was busy plucking mussels from the rocks on the greasy black beach of Skombley Island where she lived. As she paused to wipe the sweat from her brow, she looked up and saw that a boat was rowing towards her. This was unusual because the boat that was making its way to the shore was not one she recognised and the island never had visitors. Even more strange was the helmsman of the vessel – a large elephant with two great tusks and one huge horn arching from its forehead.

Being a kindly woman, Margaret Whelk called out 'Ahoy!' but the elephant acknowledged this not and continued its frantic rowing. It soon lashed its boat to one of the rocks and walked straight past Margaret before making its way up the path to the small village inland.

Before the beast had quite disappeared, Margaret called out to it:

'Hullo, elephant! What is your name?'

For a moment the hulking creature stopped on its upward climb, turned its heavy, grey head towards her and shouted, in a deafening rumble:

'My name is Cup o' Salt.'

'I should be glad to offer you a place to stay. We don't often get visitors here, Cup o' Salt. My husband scarcely spends a night in our cottage these days. There's plenty of broth spare, if you like,' said Margaret.

Cup o' Salt lifted his lumbering trunk into the air, gave a great sniff, then said:

'Nay, thank you, madam; I shall find my own supper tonight,' before stomping off, and out of sight.

There were fewer than a hundred people who lived on Skombley and it didn't take long before word had spread about the mysterious and fantastical visitor to the island.

For reasons at that time unknown, Cup o' Salt began to chase a number of the women around the island. When the elephant had cornered these women he flung them up in the air with his mighty grey trunk and ate them whole.

For a time there was great mayhem and women were running and screaming. Some of the men folk on Skombley tried to fight off the elephant with sticks and clubs, but his skin was so thick it made no difference.

After two days, Cup o' Salt had eaten over thirty women, so he went to the tavern and demanded some ale to wash down his meals. The landlord gave the elephant exactly what he wanted as he was terribly afeared that his wife would be next, for he loved her more dearly than anything else in the world.

Cup o' Salt was soon very drunk and amenable to conversation rather than killing, so one young man called Jack Herring sidled up to the swaying beast and said:

'Cup o' Salt? Why have you killed near half of our womenfolk?'

The elephant looked at him, took another trunkful of ale and said:

'I eat unfaithful women. They taste most salty, and I like salty meat.'

'You ate my wife Netty. Was she unfaithful to me?' asked Jack.

'For certain. She was the saltiest of the lot,' said Cup o' Salt. 'Let me prove it to you, Jack.' The beast gave a roar and captured the attention of all the men in the tavern, and then he said this:

'Gentlemen of Skombley! Tomorrow you will all be sober and young Jack here, like the rest of you, will forget this conversation: raise your hand if you have bedded this poor cuckold's wife. Tell the truth, or I will slice you to pieces with my fine tusks!'

All of the men in the tavern raised their hands, but kept their heads downcast, for the shame of it all.

'There, do you see?' asked Cup o' Salt, 'Your wife was a henpecking truant.'

'She deserved being eaten, then,' said Jack, bitterly.

'Were you faithful to her, young Jack?' asked the elephant.

Jack did not answer, but took another swig of beer, before falling into a drunken stupor.

The other men in the tavern began cursing their wives who had been eaten by Cup o' Salt, realising that they too had been betrayed. The good landlord was the only man in the place whose wife was still alive; he walked over to her as she cleaned some jugs and kissed her.

Cup o' Salt sniffed the air, as if to make sure there were no more adulterous women lurking about, before announcing it was time to leave Skombley as he had feasted well enough.

After a short sleep, the elephant walked back down to his boat and passed Margaret Whelk on the way.

'I hear that you ate well of the strumpet women on Skombley,' said the woman.

'I did, madam. Be not afraid of me – I can smell that you are a loyal wife,' said Cup o' Salt as he fondled Margaret's neck with his searching trunk.

'I must leave now, for I see that you have another visitor coming ashore; good evening, madam,' said the elephant as he gathered up his oars and rode off into the brine.

Margaret nursed her aching back and put her basket of mussels down to greet the new arrival to Skombley.

'Hullo, there!' said Margaret as the boat drew up to her. A strange beast – like a toad with eight legs and a great black beak – hopped from the boat and crawled up to her.

'Good tidings, madam,' said the creature. 'I am Bedderkin and I come to your island seeking for food.'

Margaret wondered for a moment as Bedderkin began sniffing the air with his glistening ebony beak. She wondered about her husband and where he spent his days and why her bed was so lonely so often.

'What do you eat?' asked Margaret.

'I eat unfaithful men,' said Bedderkin, who was becoming more and more excited as he drew the island's air into his dark little nostrils.

'You are most welcome,' said Margaret. 'Why, if you follow that path up the cliffs, you'll soon be where you want to be.'

The old, overworked woman watched as Bedderkin ambled up the cliff towards the village. She emptied half of her basket of mussels back into the rushing seawater, as she reasoned that her household would not need so much for supper that night.

I lived for about three years on the Isle of Wight (for those of you unfamiliar with this place it is a medium-sized island, in the shape of a spoilt fried egg, just off England's south coast), and it is quite remarkable for having almost one hundred and twenty churches and a surprisingly low divorce rate. Unfortunately there are a number of islands in existence that are quite bereft of any places of worship, just like Skombley appears to have been. Inevitably, the people living on such islands tend to start revering and worshiping more carnal things, just as a way to pass the time when Sunday comes along. Rather ironically, my mother forced us to relocate to the mainland as my father was spending too much time engaged in brass rubbing in the many churches on the Isle of Wight. Mother was becoming incredibly jealous of all the pretty saints that father spent hours rubbing; she announced one day we would be moving to Shadwell, and that was that. I was going through some of Dad's paperwork a few years ago and discovered a whole batch of brass rubbings that he'd secreted away in a manila folder; I think I saw then what my mother had seen – there was an almost indecent vigour to his rubbings, and it was for the best that we left that lovely island and moved to the industrial murk and clamour of East London.

Miss Mummisfere's Curse

Witchcraft is very much alive and well, which may be a surprise to some of the more naïve amongst you. Gone are the days when the craft was practised solely by old women who lived on the edge of villages. Now there are child witches and even some prominent male rugby players dabble in the Dark Arts. A lot is said of black witches and white witches, but I fancy there are more grey witches around these days. It's a less thrilling prospect, but it's true. Our politicians are grey, our skies are grey, and so are our witches. Obviously, the following tale is going to feature a witch; this one is something of a caricature, what with her hobble and ugly features. Still, it harks back to a time when Evil was evil – I rather like that.

One hot summer afternoon, on the eve of her wedding, Maria Loomley was strolling down a wooded hill in the village of Alecaster carrying a small bundle of biscuits. This was the last practical thing she needed to do before she was married, so she was whistling a jolly tune to herself, accompanied by the pretty chorus of birdsong, as she wended her way home.

All of a sudden, she was disappointed to see a rather ungainly figure lower down the track, making its way toward her. There was something unlikeable about the awkward gait of the figure as it limped along; Maria felt sure the beggar was going to assail her in some way, so she crossed her fingers and made a wish that the loping vagabond would pass her in silence. To her dismay, when the vagrant was but twenty yards away, it began to wave arthritically at her, making a series of dislikeable slurping noises, as if in great excitement.

'Good day, madam,' said Maria cautiously, as the hobbling figure drew closer.

'Ah, that it be, that it be,' croaked the shambling old woman – if indeed it was a woman, for Maria could not be entirely sure.

Unfortunately for Maria, the old woman clapped her filthy paw on her shoulder and drew her grimy, puckered face close to hers.

'Aye. 'Appen it'd be a better day indeed were I t'have a few more pennies. I'm as skint as a flint. A lady like you in sooch a comely dress would surely 'ave a few coins for a poor old wretch like me – aye?' said the old woman.

'Come, lady; I am not in the habit of giving alms to a stranger,' said Maria crossly, for her day was quite spoiled now. 'What is your name?'

The old woman took this question as an encouraging sign of forthcoming charity, though Maria had not meant that at all.

'My name is Miss Mummisfere,' said the old beggar.

'Well, Miss Mummisfere, be gone and trouble someone else, I am far too busy and I have spent my last pennies on these biscuits,' said Maria.

'Just one biscuit then, kind lady. My belly is as empty as a pauper's purse,' moaned Miss Mummisfere.

'No,' said Maria rather sharply, 'these are for my wedding tomorrow.'

'Oh, aye, I 'eard about that wedding. You moost be Miss Loomley and you be marryin' Sir Matthew Puce to-morrow.'

Maria felt rather uncomfortable that this stranger knew so much about her and she was anxious to be away.

'Unhand me, madam, I must away to make preparations for my wedding,' said Maria.

'Well, I tell thee this: I have t'power t'make your marriage a good one, Miss Loomley,' said the old woman.

'Please, stand aside,' whined Maria.

'Or I can mek it a bad one.'

Miss Mummisfere's threat sent a shiver of apprehension down Maria's back, in spite of the warmth of the day.

'Madam, I am not in two-minds as to whether to give you alms. I have no money, and the food is for my guests. I repeat again: stand aside.'

'Very well, very well. But I curse thee. I shall put thee in two minds about thine marriage! Just you wait an' see!' cried Miss Mummisfere. Upon saying this, the old woman reached up to the branch of a beech tree that hung over them, plucked two leaves from it, put them in her mouth and chewed them, before spitting the green pulp onto the ground.

Maria hurried away down the path, but could not resist looking back over her shoulder to where the horrid meeting had just taken place. Miss Mummisfere was still there although she now seemed to be making a series of rapid, busy gestures with her hands. Though she could no longer see the old woman's eyes, she felt sure she was being stared at most balefully. Maria turned away and ran to her parents' house.

The next day all of Alecaster was out to celebrate the marriage of Maria Loomley to Sir Matthew Puce at St. Nonnus's church. The day was exceedingly merry, and the whole town seemed to rejoice in this blessed union of souls.

However, it was not long before queer things started to happen. After the wedding itself, there was a great party and Maria Puce was several times approached by guests who commented on Maria's sister and her strange conversation. Each time Maria, growing ever more puzzled, would say the same thing: 'I do not have a sister, nor even any female cousins – save for fat Bess who is thirty years my senior at least!'

'But my dear,' said one guest, 'she is the very image of you – a twin I shouldn't wonder – and she even introduced herself as 'Miss Loomley'! I would have said you were playing tricks on me if it wasn't for the fact that you and she were not standing but ten yards apart!'

And so the guests continued making such remarks all evening long. No matter how hard Maria looked, she did not see her double, and she half-suspected that it was a game they were playing with her. Before retiring to her new home that night, Maria confided in her mother about the strange declarations of her guests:

'Oh, I'm sure it is a joke, my darling,' said Mrs Loomley. 'Either that or it's the wine. Now, make haste to be off with your husband – he is waiting for you. You must away and consummate the marriage.' Maria's mother kissed her tenderly on the cheek and walked her over to Sir Matthew's side.

'Sweet Maria! Climb into the coach and let us ride to Rutchard Hall! I have such a tale to tell you!' said her husband.

Mrs Loomley had not even finished tearfully waving her daughter goodbye before Sir Matthew began to say this to his bride:

'Why, Maria you never said that you had a twin sister! You are the mirror image of her! I fancy, however, that I chose the better of the two! Your sister is a peculiar woman, if you'll pardon my frankness. She seemed to spend the whole time making jokes at my expense. I wonder not why she is the spinster and you are married.'

By now Maria was so distressed at yet another drear tale of her doppelganger, that she buried her head in Sir Matthew's lap and wept.

'What is this? Tears? Come, good lady, this is a happy day! Do not let your sister spoil it for both of us,' said he.

'Oh, Matthew! I do not have a sister!' cried Maria.

The rest of the twenty-minute ride to Rutchard Hall was spent with Maria telling the tale of the strange old witch Mrs Mummisfere and her curse. Her husband listened to this with great interest and concern and assured her that it was most likely a jape in bad taste. Before long, the newly married couple took to their bed, forgetting the weird Miss Loomley, and entertained themselves most energetically into the early hours of the next day.

Upon waking later that morning, Sir Matthew kissed his wife's head entreating her to wake from her slumber.

'Good morning, my love,' said Sir Matthew. 'I trust you are well-rested?'

'Somewhat, my love,' said Maria, as she lay softly amongst her pillows.

'I perceived you were rather restless in your sleep,' said her husband softly.

'Was I? I do not recall, dear,' replied Maria.

'You seemed rather determined to put that mirror upon the wall,' said Sir Richard, but he found himself pointing to a blank wall opposite the bed.

'That is most odd. I would swear that you'd hung a mirror there in the early hours. I must have dreamt it,' said Sir Matthew.

'Oh, mercy! It must have been my fetch! That awful woman must have been in our bedchamber in the night!' cried Maria, who once again wept with fear and frustration.

'Forget her. We have both been overexcited and fantastical these past few days. Come now, let us be dressed and enjoy our first married breakfast,' said Sir Matthew.

The meal was duly consumed and Maria seemed somewhat fortified by the repast and began to smile and laugh again. Afterward, the couple took a constitutional through the beautiful, fragrant gardens of Rutchard Hall, walking arm-in-arm and talking as lovers do. Eventually their stroll took them to the edge of the lawn where they sat on a bench that overlooked the hazy fields beyond. They had been in sweet conversation for some five minutes when a rustling, thumping noise began to distract them.

'What is that frightful sound?' asked Maria.

'Yes, it is rather odious. Some daft sheep must have stumbled into the ha-ha. Come, let us see.'

Sir Matthew took his wife over to the edge of the ha-ha and peered down to see the source of the commotion. To their horror they spied Maria's double thrashing about in the ditch.

'What manner of beast are you?' shouted Sir Matthew to the uncanny wretch below.

'I am Miss Loomley, of course,' said the woman.

'How come you to have my face and manners when I have no sister, madam?' said Maria angrily.

'Why, I am your maiden self. You were once Miss Loomley. Now you are Lady Puce. I am now Miss Loomley,' said the woman.

'You are the Devil, of that I am sure,' said Sir Matthew.

'Were you sent here by Miss Mummisfere?' asked Maria, full of dread.

'Maybe I was,' replied the woman with a sly grin. 'I am sore jealous of you and your handsome husband. He should be mine. And he shall be. When I replace you, your dear husband shall not know it has even happened!' said Miss Loomley before she began to squeak with unconcealed mirth.

Sir Matthew was an enlightened man and did not doubt the reality of witchcraft. Enraged at the mocking beast in the ha-ha, he took his wife by the arm and marched to the top of Alecaster Hill where he knew Miss Mummisfere to live. They soon found a small track that led off the main road and presently came upon a dismal little cottage. There, leaning out of the unglazed window was the witch they were after. Maria shuddered at the sight of the withered crone whose toothless mouth was smiling broadly at them, as if in a mockery of welcome.

'Welcome, Sir Matthew and Lady Maria!' said the old witch.

'Do not try my patience, hag. You have bewitched my bride. Her maiden self is running amok and causing intolerable mischief. What has my dear wife done to you to merit such ungodly persecutions?' asked Sir Matthew.

'She refused me alms. I am but a poor old lady living in this 'ere wreck. She denied me a biscuit,' said Miss Mummisfere.

'I should laugh at you for your vindictiveness, if I knew you not to be as dangerous as you are. I demand,' continued Sir Matthew, 'that you release us from these torments,' said he with great firmness and resolution.

'Oh, do thee now! Well, I first mek a demand on thee both. I will vanish Miss Loomley in return for som'it from thee,' said Miss Mummisfere.

'And what, pray, is that?' said Maria.

'Ye will commission the greatest architect in London town t'build me an 'ouse in your fine garden. It will 'ave twenty windows, two floors and covered all over in fine plasterwork. Ee, it'll be grander than your own 'ome! On the day the foundation stone is to be laid, the three of us will meet there one hour before sunset, and I shall undo me hex on thee.'

Maria was about to argue with the demanding old witch, but her husband knew better than to remonstrate.

'Hush,' whispered Sir Matthew, 'we must assent to her orders or there will be worse to come.'

'Do ye both agree to me terms?' asked Miss Mummisfere as she picked something wet and odious from the corner of her mouth.

'We do. I shall dispatch a servant to London tonight and in a week you will have your wishes,' said Sir Matthew.

With that, the witch drew back into the gloom of her filthy abode whereupon Sir Matthew and Lady Maria heard the unmistakable sound of a chicken being throttled from within.

A servant was sent off to London on Sir Matthew's finest horse and men from the village were readied for building the new house. Over the course of the next slow week, Miss Loomley continued to appear and wreak havoc wherever she went. The rest of the stables' horses were hag-ridden and too exhausted to be of any use. Blankets were pulled from Matthew and Maria's bed every night, paintings were torn from the walls and dashed onto the floor below. The last night before the architect arrived, Lady Maria's nightgown was set alight and Miss Loomley was seen bustling about the corridors of Rutchard Hall on various mysterious, yet doubtless malicious, errands.

Miss Loomley's diabolical naughtiness started to diminish the moment the architect was at the Hall, and it was not long before the bricks and timber had arrived for the Miss Mummisfere's house. The witch was duly called for, and she was most pleased with the plans for her new home.

'Now, Sir Matthew,' said the witch, where is t'foundation stone?'

'There,' said he, pointing at a block of pale white stone.

'Good. Now Lady Maria must stand next to it, where the stone is to be laid. Her shadow must fall upon the exact spot where the stone will be placed,' said the old woman.

Maria let go of her husband's hand and gingerly walked down into the foundation pit.

'Like this?' enquired the good lady.

'Yes, that be good. Ah, that's a fine shadow at this time a' day,' said Miss Mummisfere.

As soon as the witch had said this, Sir Matthew felt a cool hand clasp his own. To his disgust, he saw that it was the likeness of his dear wife, Miss Loomley. She was smiling at him quite sweetly, but he was just in time to notice that she carried in her free hand a great black rock that she appeared to be aiming at his wife's head.

'For God's sake, man,' shouted Sir Matthew at the workman below, who was lugging the foundation stone over to Maria's shadow, 'move that blasted stone now!'

With a great thump, the stone was moved in place and Miss Loomley disappeared from Sir Matthew's side. The stone the terrible double had been holding fell to the ground and bounced into the foundation trench, hitting Miss Mummisfere on the temple. The old witch fell to the ground with a moan, and Sir Matthew got to work.

It was once a custom to wall up a living being in the walls of every new house, to ensure its integrity for years to come. Sir Matthew knew that the witch was never going to cease her meddling, and made the decision to have her bricked up in the foundations of the house before she was roused from her faint. Of course, Sir Matthew knew that by burying his wife's shadow under the house, she would be freed from her frightful doppelganger, but would forever be vulnerable to Miss Mummisfere's wonder-working, for a person without a shadow was open to the wickedness of sorcery. The witch's house was built, but never a soul set foot in it after its completion. The curse lifted, Lady Maria, forever without a shadow, and Sir Matthew spent many happy years in Rutchard Hall, untroubled by the evil eye of Miss Mummisfere, and raised over sixty children in the blissful years that followed.

Meanness with one's biscuits is a trait peculiar to Britons, and Maria Loomley/Puce is a good example of this. All sorts of bother could've been prevented if only she'd been a little more generous of spirit with her comestibles. I always make strenuous efforts to ensure I stock a wide variety of teatime snacks, lest I unknowingly invite a warlock into my demesne and upset them with a deficit of crackers and whatnots. Doppelgangers are interesting things; I too have a doppelganger that appears to friends around the country when I am in trouble. These are sometimes known as 'crisis apparitions'. Unfortunately my own crisis apparitions seem to make themselves appear to friends when I'm encountering only mild difficulties; my double once appeared in front of my chum Sylvia who lives in Leeds. She raced down to Shadwell in her Fiat Uno only to find that I'd cut my finger when slicing a cucumber and couldn't find a plaster. This was very embarrassing as I was fine and had in fact made a perfectly serviceable bandage from three squares of kitchen roll tissue. That said it was good she came as I'd made far too much salad for one person to eat, and cucumber doesn't keep well in the fridge once it's been chopped. On another occasion, I'd had a really exhausting day spring-cleaning and I'd spent about forty-five minutes at the basin scrubbing pots, pans and utensils. I'd just finished washing what I thought was the last bit of cutlery when I saw a teaspoon appear amongst the draining suds in the sink. I couldn't believe there was yet another thing to clean, and I felt utterly desolate at the prospect of one more thing to wash and dry. Frustratingly, a crisis apparition of me appeared to my niece Veronica whilst she was watching Holby City *on BBC One. The medical nature of the programme must have fired her imagination and she managed to get a cheap flight from Glasgow airport and was with me in a few hours. It was awkward to say the least when she did arrive, hammering at my door at about two in the morning. However, I had a nice clean spoon to make her a cup of tea with and we had a pleasant chat, enjoying a broad selection of biscuits. I actually think she is a witch, so it all worked out for the best and I seemed to dodge any curse she may otherwise have laid upon me.*

Chukwuma's Bag

Just like the character in the story below, I too am telling you old stories that my ancestors have passed down to me. The key difference between the storyteller in this narrative and me is that I am not Nigerian. I would very much like to be Nigerian, but I cannot lever up the plastic and microchipped laminate on my passport to effect this deceit. Instead, I have had to settle with simply telling people I am African, and so far this has worked very well and has initiated some quite interesting conversations at the Post Office.

One day a stranger called Chukwuma Obiajulu visited the busy little valley village of Clough Hulme. He was a member of the noble Igbo people from the far off country of Nigeria. Unlike a lot of rural villages in the seventeenth century, Clough Hulme was full of friendly and pleasant folk, and strangers were always given a warm welcome.

Chukwuma was a storyteller by trade, depending entirely upon the coins that might come his way after relating his fabulous tales. He had been in Clough Hulme for a week by now, and each night he had spent in the Gangley Inn his audience had grown and grown.

Chukwuma knew well the importance of theatre in making his stories come alive, and each night he would take out finely carved wooden puppets and fabrics woven with incredible African scenes to enrich his wonderful narratives. He always opened up a beautiful gilt-edged book, as big as a church bible and bound in soft Oryx hide, asked the crowd what kind of tale they would like to hear, before thumbing through the pages. However, like all really gifted storytellers, he had no real need of the book, as his heart knew them better.

That night Chukwuma told the tale of the leopard, the tortoise and the bush rat which drew great cheers, and he finished with the story of the Odudu bird and the 'Nsasak bird, which earned him a hatful of coins for his work. Here is a shortened version of the story:

The king wanted to know if there was a bird in his realm that could survive great hunger, so he put two birds to the test. The first was the 'Nsasak bird, colourful and small; the second was the Odudu bird, dull and large. Each was commanded to build a house and remain there for a month. The birds built their houses, but the 'Nsasak bird, being a wily thing, built his with a tiny hole in it, large enough to escape from to find food in the night, but too small for the king to see. After a month, the Odudu bird was dead, but the 'Nsasak bird was in fine health, so the king made him the chief of all birds.

Not only was the 'Nsasak bird the most beautiful in all the world, but Chukwuma's puppet was so well crafted it was impossible to tell if it was a marionette or the real thing. After his storytelling, Chukwuma let the bright little bird fly around the inn, though it was always attached to his hand by a string.

Whilst the crowd in the Gangley Inn enjoyed this entertainment hugely, one young man watched on with great jealousy – his name was Silas Kelp, and he had decided to steal Chukwuma's bag of tricks and make himself some money in villages far from Clough Hulme.

That night, when the village had gone to sleep, Silas crept into Chukwuma's room and stole the traveller's bag. This dishonest boy had learnt the art of stealth after years of pinching chickens and rabbits; it was not long before Silas had fled into the night with his stolen goods.

When the Gangley Inn's landlady, Sally Muzzleclasp, woke Chukwuma in the morning, she asked him where his famous bag was, as it was nowhere to be seen in the small room.

'Mr Obiajulu!' cried the woman, 'Your bag is gone!'

'So it would seem, dear lady,' said Chukwuma.

'Who could have done this? And all of your money as well! How shall we ever find it?' asked Sally.

'Have no fear,' said Chukwuma, and then he held up his hand, from which trailed a fine length of thread. 'We shall soon find my bag again,' said the storyteller.

He gave the string a tug.

Far over the hills in the town of Pollard Dramley, Silas Kelp was sitting by a stream, rifling Chukwuma's bag. He'd just counted the money and was planning what he would do with the cash when he spotted the storyteller's book inside, which was perhaps more useful than the money, as contained within were all of Chukwuma's incredible tales. He licked his lips, opened the book and promptly let out a cry of horror. He dared to turn another page, then another and another; his anguish only increased.

At that very moment, the bag seemed to leap from his trembling lap and started bumping over the hillock behind him. Silas slammed the great book shut and ran off in pursuit of the bag.

However, the bag was always too quick for the young thief, and before long Chukwuma, who was still lying comfortably in his bed, had wound up the last of the string around his hand, and his beloved bag jostled over the windowsill and was back in its master's arms once more. Chukwuma and the astonished Sally Muzzleclasp then got up to peer out of the window. There, collapsed outside from exhaustion, was Silas Kelp, still clutching Chukwuma's book.

'I think,' said Mr Obiajulu, 'we have found our robber.'

The pair went downstairs and Chukwuma picked up his book and kissed it gently before squatting next to the red-faced Silas and asked him this:

'Why did you take my bag, young man? It was not yours to take.'

'Please, sir,' gasped Silas, 'I only wanted to be as famous and as magical as you.'

'So, you thought fit to steal my stories?' asked Chukwuma. 'That is no good; you must find your own tales to tell.'

'But, sir! Your book is blank! All the pages in it are empty!' cried the boy.

'Ha ha! Yes my book is blank. That is because all the stories are in here,' said Chukwuma, patting his heart.

'How did you make your bag run back to you?' asked Silas, relieved that Chukwuma was being so kind.

'Why, that's my little 'Nsasak bird – he's attached to an everlasting thread. One is wound around his leg,' said Chukwuma as he lifted the colourful little bird from the bag, 'and the other is tied around my thumb – do you see?' said the storyteller, showing Silas his hand.

'I am sorry, sir,' said Silas.

'My name is Chukwuma Obiajulu, not 'sir'. I am sure you have tales of your own to tell. What is your name, boy?'

'Silas,' replied the thief.

'Come inside, Silas. Let me tell you how to tell stories. Maybe one day you will travel to Nigeria and tell my people of life in England! Would that not be an adventure?'

With that, Chukwuma helped the young man up and led him back into the inn. He unwound the 'Nsasak bird's thread from his thumb and handed it to Silas.

'Here, take this bird and this cord and twine it about your own thumb. I have no need of it, for I have so many other stories to tell. This can be your first story to tell – the bag, the bird and the boy!'

Chukwuma and the boy talked long into the night; after a week both had left Clough Hulme forever - one went north, the other went south and they told tales wherever they went, for the rest of their lives.

This is one of those stories within a story that makes my head ache a bit when I think of the complexity of it all, especially as Grandma Berrial told it to me and her grandmother told it to her – I don't know where it starts or ends. If you find the unending story (and indeed, the unending string) concept quite frightening, perhaps you will take some comfort in the depressing finality of the fact that no such thing as a 'Nsasak or Odudu bird has ever existed in the annals of ornithology. Perhaps they did once, and leopards ate them all up before David Attenborough got there to catalogue them. Returning to the story again, I have to say how much I admire Chukwuma Obiajulu for moving on to a new town before he'd started recycling his stories and becoming boring to the folk of Clough Hulme. Now that you've come to the end of this book, I would kindly ask you to destroy it, as I do not want to be accused of hypocrisy. Or you could do even better than that and give it to a charity shop. Why not save the time of the shop workers by fetching a pencil now and writing '20p' on the flyleaf?

Afterword

I first met Derek, my late husband, when I was still but a slip of a girl and he had only very recently acquired his first suit. I remember the suit very well since it had belonged to his uncle Charlie, and I had been present when he had died. There had been some discussion, I understand, as to whether Charlie should be buried in his tweed suit or whether Derek should have it. In the end it was decided that Uncle Charlie would be buried in his pyjamas. It was not to be an open casket you see on account of how Uncle Charlie had met his demise campaigning for universal suffrage by getting himself trampled underfoot during the running of the Derby. It was not a pretty sight and to this day I cannot hear the sound of horse's hooves without coming over all queer. In the end I think it was the best decision since Derek got far more wear out of it than Uncle Charlie would have done, being as how he was dead and Derek was not. We all had to be more practical in those days you see, as those were the times. It's ironic now to think on it really, since Derek is now dead. We cremated him so his burial clothes were something of a moot point.

Anyhoo dears, this should be about Kitty's book after all. I grew up in a household where books were objects to be treated with great care. It's different now of course. I suspect that some of you might even be reading this on a Kindle or other type of device from the future, in which case you could spread jam all over it, give it a quick clean with a jiffy cloth, and it'd be as right as rain.

Margaret Stamen

Appendix I

My very good friend Margaret Stamen has kindly allowed me to reproduce one of her own folk tales here. I haven't read it, so I've absolutely no idea whether it's any good or not. On the strength of the title alone I think it's worth a whistle. I've tried getting Margaret to write her own volume of folk stories but all I hear from her are excuses; she's not a lazy woman but she's very disordered. If you ever meet her, never lend her anything – she means to give it back, but you'll never see it again. I suppose the following narrative is her way of saying sorry to me for this and very many other things.

— *K.B.*

The White Glove

Every year, during those years I was a girl, there used to be a fair held on the last Tuesday in July in the village of Netherfold. I cannot say for how many years the fair had been held there prior to my being aware of it, since these were the days long before technology, when knowledge of these traditions was therefore passed on in the oral fashion. As you know, dears, anything passed on orally is bound to be rebarbative when it comes to being historical. Nevertheless the tale you are about to read has stood the test of time and is passed on to you in as true a form as it was passed on to me all those years ago.

It is a tale of death, and as death comes to us all in the end, I do think it wise to understand something of its ways before we must ourselves take him by his hand and travel to what Hamlet called, 'that undiscovered country.' Personally I think it stands to reason that death must be actually quite a discovered country, since it must have been discovered by very many, if not all, of those who have, well, died, but I shall not argue with the wisdom of Shakespeare on such matters. Apart from anything else, he is dead after all.

Growing up in the village of Netherfold at this time were two girls by the name of Meg and Mara. Meg was the daughter of the local squire and widower, Sir Henry Marchmare. And she was as fair and gay a child as her father was foul tempered and mean. Meg's mother had died following the complications of childbirth, which many took to be the reason for Sir Henry's subsequent cruelty towards her and anyone else that crossed his path. Mara's origin was the subject of much local gossip and speculation. Some had it that she was the daughter of a gypsy fortune-teller that Sir Henry had beaten to death with a riding whip.

The truth of it is that she had been found by him under an elm tree, clearly left there by the fairy folk. And so Marchmare had, one afternoon appeared at the nursery door and thrust a swaddled and mewling baby into the arms of Meg's wet nurse, Anabentine Kind, saying, 'Here's another bitch for your milk. You are to call her Mara.'

'But, she's injured; her hand is bleeding,' replied Anabentine, looking down at Mara's crudely bandaged left hand.

'Never you mind about that; you just see to her,' shouted Sir Henry, turning on his heels and crashing away down the stairs to his own room.

Later that night Anabentine could have sworn she heard the sounds of crying from behind Sir Henry's locked doors. But she never repeated this to anyone, save for her fiancé, Obidiah Wenscott, who was later killed in a threshing accident.

From that very first moment of their encounter, the two girls were inseparable, and not only whilst feeding. Mara seemed to have the ability to ease Meg and calm her troubled mind. Many's the time the nurse would rise sleepily in the night upon hearing the sound of a fretful Meg, only to find that by the time she arrived at the nursery, Mara had cooed her back to sleep or had laid her bandaged left hand across Meg's forehead like a soothing vinegar rag.

As the years passed the girls grew to be as physically alike as two cox in a coxcomb and Marchmare himself nary knew which one was which. The villagers too would have had a difficult time of it telling them apart save for the fact that Mara was never seen without her left hand covered by a delicate white glove. The glove had taken the place of the bandage and covered a wound that had never seemed to quite heal, despite the passage of time and the continuing attentions of Anabentine, who begged Mara repeatedly to have it tended to by a doctor.

'Our Lord and Saviour carried his wounds for all to see. I am only happy to resemble Him in my own small way,' was always Mara's response to the nurse's imprecations. Until, that is, one day when the nurse mysteriously and suddenly disappeared from Marchmare Manor only to be found, several days later, dead at the bottom of a disused well, her entire body covered in what those who saw her rotting corpse described as 'the bite marks of Satan'.

For many years after the event villagers would tell the tale of how the large granite boulder (put there to block the entrance to the well) had inexplicably seemed to roll away uphill, leaving the gaping maw wide enough to doom the unsuspecting nurse.

The girls had now grown to be very comely young women and, as was the custom of these times, they had begun to attract the attentions of men. Truth be told it was Mara that proved to be the more popular of the two in the area of courtship, and her social calendar was as full as her dance card.

Now Meg loved Mara as if she were her own sister but as is often the way with affairs of the heart she began to grow jealous of Mara's ability to charm all and any of the gentlemen that came within her sweep. This jealousy took the name of action one evening as the young women were preparing to attend the spring ball of one Sir Thomas Cranthorne.

Meg had fallen in love with Sir Thomas whilst he only had eyes for Mara. In an attempt to sabotage any chance of the friendship becoming a romantic one, Meg did something that precipitated a series of tragic events that would also include her own death. At this time Mara had come to be known as 'the lady with the white glove' and Meg's jealous mind attributed her social successes to that mysterious item of clothing and so she had begun to fixate her attentions on how she could remove the glove from Meg and, taking advantage of their physical similarity, wear it, passing herself off as Mara. She knew that the one opportunity she would have to steal the glove would be when Mara was at her toilet; for Mara always removed the glove during her ablutions lest it be stained.

So this night Meg lay in wait in an adjoining room and hearing the familiar sounds of a lady at her toilet, she stole into the room, whereupon she saw the white glove lying on the Escoffier and, quick as a flash, removed it. Oh but the screams and cries of anguish that ensued when an abluted Mara discovered the white glove was missing. She flew to Meg in such a state that Meg almost relented of her plan. (Would that she had).

'Oh Meg! Know you of what has become of my white glove? Dearest sister, I fear my doom if it is not recovered. Please tell me you have taken it for a lark and will now return it to me?'

'Dearest sister of mine,' Meg replied, 'do not fret. Come, you can spare one evening without it, and tomorrow we shall find it together.'

'Tomorrow will be too late. I fear it is already too late.' And with that she let out a wail such as would render ewes sterile, and then she flew from the house.

That was the last that anyone saw Mara alive. She was discovered two days later, by some local village boys, lying by the same elm tree where she had been found all those years before by Sir Henry Marchmere. When the villagers came to remove the body of their beloved Mara, they found her left hand was inexplicably inside the elm itself. Try as they might, they could not remove her hand from the tree's grasp and so neither could a grief and guilt-stricken Meg ever replace the glove she had so foolhardedly stolen. Instead Meg placed the glove atop the tomb where they laid Mara's armless body. To this day it is there, guiding her owner as once it did in life, as fair, white and delicate as ever it was and all know never to remove it. As for the elm tree, well it brings forth white flowers every year upon the anniversary of that fateful ball which Mara never attended.

I do not know whether an elm tree sprouting white flowers is in and of itself, a supernatural occurrence, but I think it at least gives the tale an opportunity at verisimilitude. As for who precisely Mara was, well it is a lesser-known fact about witches that upon their bodies one will often find particular marks garnered by their association with demon kind. Many such witches will attempt to cover up these markings and walk amongst us as if they were just like us and had not been foully mutilated by Satan. Or Lucifer. Whether Mara was such a being we shall never know, but I do think it is important not to be fooled by a pretty face.

THANKS

The compilation of this volume of tales would not have been possible without the love and tireless devotion of Rose Stewart. Her joy and happiness shone like an endless candle in all that she did.

Robin Sachs's inventiveness and humour outlive him in a way he could never have known.

My thanks extend to Leopold Sachs – a man whose warmth and love reach out to the stars; his memory is beloved of all those who knew him – and even those who didn't.

They are deeply missed and forever loved.

Printed in Great Britain
by Amazon